I0630605

DUST
AND
DESTINY

Book Three of THE DUST TRILOGY

HEATHER HAYES

This book is a work of fiction. Any references to historical events, real people, or real places are used fictitiously. Other names, places, and events are a product of the author's imagination, and any resemblance to actual events, places, or persons, living or dead, is entirely coincidental.

First soft back edition December 2024

© 2024 Heather Hayes. All rights reserved.

No part of this book may be reproduced, stored in a retrieval system, or transmitted by any means without the written permission of the author.

Published by AH Digital FX Studios, INC 12/09/2024
AH Digital FX Studios, INC
10551 E. Ririe Hwy.
Idaho Falls, ID 83401
www.ahfx.net

ISBN: 978-1-945597-11-4

Library of Congress Control Number: 2024951724

Cover by Adam Hayes
Book Layout, Design & Editing by Adam Hayes

The views expressed in this work are solely those of the author and do not necessarily reflect the views of the publisher, and the publisher hereby disclaims any responsibility for them.

Paperback printed in San Bernadino, United States of America

For my amazing students

Thanks for reading and writing with me
and making my life exciting.

Chapter 1

THE WIND HOWLS RELENTLESSLY as paper, plastic bags, wrappers, and other litter hit the window of my cell in a rhythmic way. I try to ignore the incessant noise as I roll over on my narrow mattress. My head is kinked from sleeping without a pillow and positioning myself to avoid the biggest stains on the mattress. My blanket is barely more than a sheet and doesn't quite cover me from chin to toes. If I keep myself balled up, I stay the warmest. This is not the coziest way to pass the winter.

Tap, tap. "Dandra?" Mom calls from the cell to my left. "Do you have an extra jumpsuit?" I stand up and slide the privacy blind up so I can look through the bars of the window between our cells. My sister's chin jitters as my mom wraps her in her arms. Mom continues, "I want to double Everley's layers, so she doesn't get sick." My sister coughs and moans into her own thin blanket, which of course breaks my heart.

"I don't have one, but she can have my blanket." I grab my pathetic blanket and try to fit it through the bars of the window. The bars are grimy and too close together for my plan to work well.

A deep male voice from the other side of Mom's cell says, "I have an extra jumpsuit she can have." The privacy blind of the window on the opposite wall rolls halfway up.

Mom raises her eyebrows at me in surprise as a freshly-laundered yellow jumpsuit appears. She rushes to the other side of her cell and takes the jumpsuit before it falls to the dirty floor. Mom stammers, "Thank you. I appreciate this so much. What is your name?"

The man's face is hard to see, and he closes the privacy blind without a word before we can examine him closer.

Mom shrugs at me and says to the closed blind, "Thank you again, sir." Mom takes the jumpsuit and helps my weeping little sister into it. It's way too big, but the extra layers will keep her warm. I will never tell Everley this, but I'm jealous that she gets to share a cell with Mom. I wish I had someone to hold me and keep me warm right now. I guess that's what you get when you're considered a dangerous criminal mastermind instead of the young child of a...criminal accomplice?

My sister isn't the only person weeping in this cold heartless detainment center. Marcella's quiet crying in the cell to my right makes her sound like a lost child. At least Gordon is on the other side of her, so they can hold fingertips through the bars of the little window. My heart feels for her, but not as much as it should. She and Gordon had the chance to get away from Patrolman Darius, but they didn't take it. Not all of us Layland refugees had the chance to get away yesterday.

I keep second guessing every move we made yesterday on the academic assembly stage, but what's done is done. All nine of us gave ourselves up despite Conrad and Baldwin's attempt to take the fall and save us. I guess I'm not so different from Marcella after all.

The helicopter ride to Layland was short, but the night in this cell was long.

When we were mercilessly marched into the detainment center, I tried to convince the softest, least-intimidating patrolman to put Conrad in a cell next to me, but he refused. He said my boyfriend would probably be moved to a different floor in the detainment center soon. That and *Bubba's Pastry* flavor of the day are the most information we've gotten from the patrolmen so far. Their tight lips are slightly unnerving. I always thought the patrolmen of Tifton were pathetic; that's why we were able to dig a tunnel under the border wall and get out of the country in the first place. Patrolman Darius' influence must be spreading.

My calls to Conrad throughout the night were a waste of breath. It was impossible to hear his answers because everyone was talking, and we are six cells apart. All nine of us were extremely vocal with frustration at Mrs. Abbot and full of theories about what will happen to us, especially my politically active ex-boyfriend Baldwin, but today, the silence is deafening.

My body is already protesting from the pancake-thin mattress and the filthy narrow walls that feel like they are closing in around me. Will we be here for a month? A year? Many years? Dreading my fate, I drift off to sleep yet again.

Creak, BANG. The sound of a cell door opening and closing nearby startles me awake. My dark window and my growling stomach tell me I've slept the day away. I watch from my uncomfortable bed until I see an unfamiliar patrolman with Conrad in handcuffs about to march him out of sight.

Conrad's eyes never leave mine as he approaches my cell; he calls out, "Dandra, don't worry about me. Just take care of your mom and Everley."

"No, Conrad!" I jump to my feet and question the patrolman, "Where are you taking him?"

The patrolman barks, "He is being moved upstairs to a more private cell for questioning."

Conrad's eyes reach out to me. "Dandra, I'm sure this has

4

something to do with my dad. Don't worry about me. I'll see you as soon as I can."

"No!" Banging on the bars of my cell does nothing. I slump down onto the floor next to my cold dinner tray and watch my boyfriend disappear. If his dad has any power here, I won't see him again. The reality of my situation hits me like a ton of bricks.

Tears run down my cheeks. My sobs are interrupted by Baldwin, who says from a few cells down, "Don't cry for him, Dandra. Cry for yourself. He's probably being moved to his dad's cozy cell with nice furniture and five-star food."

From the floor, the grimy corners of my cell glare at me. "Baldwin, is his dad here?"

"Yep. Not even unlimited money could get Zane Chesterton off for murder. You should pay attention to the news, Dandra."

I don't let his jab affect me. "Why should I do that when I have you?"

Baldwin scoffs, "You won't always have me."

My sobs turn into full-on crying as my ex-boyfriend's cold tone pierces me. I deserve this. He's right of course. I broke his heart when I chose Conrad over him.

My tears are interrupted again by the same patrolman coming back and unlocking Adamar's cell. The patrolman's echoey voice says, "Someone is here to see you. You have 10 minutes."

5

Surely Adamar has been waiting on the edge of his bunk for this moment. His voice rings out, "Charlisa! It's Charlisa! I know it!"

I watch longingly as Adamar hurries out of our private corridor to see his girlfriend who didn't escape with us months ago. Mom taps on the window bars between our cells. "You should eat something, Dandra. Answers are coming. Keep your strength up so you can act when they do."

I lift the spoon on my tray and watch the gray mystery goop plop out. "I'm only eating this for you, Mom."

I hear my mom sniff as I gag at the first bite.

The last cold bite of what tastes like flavorless oatmeal slumps down my throat when a patrolman comes to collect our empty trays. I shove the tray through the slot at the bottom of my barred door. A man in uniform picks it up.

"Thank you, young lady." There is something familiar about that voice, but my foggy brain can't place why. I stand up, stretch, and peek through the barred window at my sister huddled on her bunk and notice that my mom is kneeling by the door to her cell holding a folded up note in her hands.

I whisper as loudly as I can, "Mom, where did you get that?"

She whispers back, "Patrolman Mark just slipped it to me when he took my tray."

No wonder that patrolman seemed familiar. I didn't recognize him with a beard. Patrolman Mark's crush on my mom used to make me cringe, but I'm suddenly glad we have someone on our side.

Mom and I lean into our shared window so we can both see the writing on the paper. I call out, "Marcella, listen up, we have news!" She presses her ear against the barred window on the other side of my cell, so she won't miss a single word.

Mom clears her throat and reads aloud:

Dearest Laurel,

I don't know how much you know about the situation you left and where things are now, but I thought I would fill you in. The tunnel you escaped from was filled to the top with concrete, and your whole property has been taped off as a crime scene. I know it has been months since that happened, but the tape is still up, and no one has been allowed in or out of there by order of the Tifton Patrolchief.

Zane Chesterton was arrested for the murder of your husband. He has been bribing patrolmen and one of the judges involved in his case. Thanks to the evidence Hector provided about being bribed to plant evidence and the recording of Conrad's confession, he was found guilty just two days ago, which means 20 years in the detainment center. He was outraged by his lack of political and civil influence. It took everything I could do to bring this conviction about. Unfortunately, he has bribed his way into an agreement with the judge that if he shows good behavior in the detainment center for a year, he will be given work release for four days a week for the rest of his 19-year sentence. This means he is still the richest and most powerful man in Tifton.

Zane Chesterton has also made a strong case to the judge that your group kidnapped his son and started a rebellion and illegal mass exodus from the country. I don't know how eight youth and three adults is considered a mass exodus, but you will probably have an angry judge to deal with at your trial tomorrow. I am trying to get a change of judge. Prepare yourself. Write down your case for leaving the country with the piece of paper and pencil I have enclosed with this letter. Tell them about the harassment you received at Zane Chesterton's hand, and since he killed your husband, declare that self-defense and preserving the life of your family were your reasons for leaving the country. I hope all goes well, and you are allowed back to your home. I will be there to speak in your defense tomorrow.

Until tomorrow, you will be in my every thought,

Mark

Mom's voice cracks when she reads those last few words. I thought she had forgotten Patrolman Mark once we were in the United Cities, but the tear rolling down her cheek proves me wrong. He certainly didn't forget about her if he was brave enough to go after the richest man in town for my dad's murder, even after we were long gone.

Marcella leaves the shared window of our cells and passes

the information from Mark's letter on to Gordon, who is on her other side, and he passes it on to Ed, and so on until everyone in every cell knows.

Something about the letter confuses me. I ask my mom, "Why did he say three adults left when you were the only one?"

Mom rereads that sentence in the letter and mutters, "I don't know. Maybe he lost count."

I'm so glad we finally have some news. I grin and say as enthusiastically as I can, "We get to plead our case tomorrow, and Zane Chesterton won't be there since he's locked up. That's a good sign; isn't it, Mom?"

Baldwin's voice calls out from a few cells down, "Don't get your hopes up. They might let Zane be there since he's here somewhere in the detainment center, and our case includes his son, but even if he's not there, you know who he will send in his place."

Chapter 2

THE BRIGHT SUN MAKES ME SQUINT as I'm shoved out the detainment center side door. I'm sure we are a sight to see in our yellow jumpsuits all handcuffed and walking through ankle-deep litter across the parking lot with armed patrolmen to the City of Tifton building next door.

I wonder if the litter smacking into the mayor's office window bothers him as much as it bothers me in my cell. I see him look up from his desk as we pass his window. He looks just as grouchy as he did when he banished me from working at the library. I scowl at the mayor as I remember Zane Chesterton admitting to me before we escaped that he was working with the mayor to shut the library down.

Baldwin purposely steps on the back of my shoe. I stumble forward and snap, "Hey, knock it off!"

Baldwin nods toward the building we are about to enter. "The mayor's office is in the same city building as the Tifton judge's chambers." Baldwin continues, "There are three judges for the City of Tifton, and I hope that we get Judge Brend or Judge Lemons because Judge Hoage is on Zane Chesterton's payroll." How does he know everything about everything?

I absolutely despise the smug look on Patrolman Darius' face when the eight of us are marched into the judge's chamber.

It's nice to have the bright sun out of our eyes as we are seated on a long bench in front of the judge's enormous desk. There are two smaller desks on either side of the huge one. Patrolman Mark waves at Mom from the small desk closest to us, and Patrolman Darius scowls at us from the small desk farthest away.

Mom almost sits on me on one side, and Baldwin gives me a wide berth on the other side. Though I don't love his stand-offishness, I'm thankful for this arrangement since Baldwin can answer my questions.

The giant door at the back of the chamber creaks open again and lets in someone I am over-the-moon happy to see. My heart leaps in my chest when Conrad starts walking toward me. I reach out with my cuffed hands, hoping for even a second of physical contact. Unfortunately, he doesn't come close enough for me to get it.

His hair is gelled and spiked just like he used to do it, and he has dark circles under his eyes, but those eyes latch onto mine as soon as they see me. My lifted heart drops again when I see his father come in right behind him. They are both in yellow jumpsuits and handcuffs and take a sharp turn to sit on the bench nearest to Patrolman Darius. Conrad gives me a sad smile. Baldwin leans over and says in my ear, "What do you want to bet that Zane Chesterton has been filling his son's head with lies about us all night?" My smile at seeing Conrad disappears.

The head patrolman who led us here from our cells this morning suddenly stands and says, "All rise for the enforcer of Layland justice, the honorable Judge Hoage." My heart sinks all the way to the bottom of my feet. Will we ever get to work with someone who isn't in league with Zane Chesterton?

We all stand as a surprisingly young-looking judge wearing a deep red robe comes in whipping his long, black hair around his head with a flourish and sits at the imposing desk before us. He picks a single strand of dark hair out of his eyes and winks at Conrad's dad.

Patrolman Mark immediately stands up and says, "There has been a terrible mistake. Judge Lemons is supposed to be working this case today."

Judge Hoage laughs humorlessly and says, "I'm afraid my

dear colleague finds himself unwell this morning, so I will be filling in for him since I have equal knowledge of this case."

Patrolman Mark looks at Judge Hoage's smiling face and then looks at the equally happy faces of Patrolman Darius and Zane Chesterton. "This trial will wait until he is well then."

Patrolman Darius stands up and says, "We have been working on this case for months. I will not wait a single day longer for the trial."

Patrolman Mark erupts, "Patrolman Darius, we were both here with Judge Lemons yesterday. He was perfectly healthy then. Unless someone has been…interfering with him, he should be ready to go today."

Patrolman Darius snarls, "How dare you accuse me of tampering with a judge!"

Patrolman Mark shrugs. "Did I do that?"

The head patrolman who led us from our cells this morning suddenly stands up again and declares, "All rise for the enforcer of Layland justice, the honorable Judge Lemons."

We all stand up for a second time as a middle-aged judge wearing a slightly disheveled red robe comes in and stands by the imposing desk Judge Hoage is sitting at. His hair is as yellow as his name and melts over his head like a lemony glaze over a pound cake.

He looks through his glasses at Judge Hoage and says, "Sorry I'm late. Thank you for covering for me, Judge Hoage. Someone accidentally put something in my coffee this morning that I am severely allergic to. Luckily, someone suggested that I keep an allergy remedy on hand at all times, so I am all better now."

Judge Hoage's eyes dart to Zane Chesterton before saying, "How fortunate. I'm glad you're well. I was more than happy to cover for you, and to be honest, we've already started, so why don't you go home and rest."

Judge Lemons shakes his head. "No, thank you. I am ready and anxious to work. I'll see you later."

Judge Hoage looks like he just swallowed detainment center oatmeal. He looks at Zane Chesterton and Patrolman Darius' unhappy faces before standing up and trudging slowly to the door.

Judge Lemons sits down in the vacated seat and waits patiently as his colleague takes his time leaving the room.

Once the door clicks behind Judge Hoage, Judge Lemons looks at the papers on his desk. He scrutinizes them for an uncomfortably long time before saying, "Please be seated." We all sit down, grateful for something to do. Judge Lemons continues to examine the papers on his desk and lines them up into a row as he matches our paperwork to our faces sitting on the bench.

Judge Lemons finally looks up at us and says, "This is a case I have been involved with for over two months. Your faces are not new to me, though mine may be new to you. I heard testimony from both Patrolman Darius and Patrolman Mark all day yesterday and the day before that, and today is the day that we decide what your punishment will be for knowingly digging an illegal tunnel out of the country and leaving with Zane Chesterton's son, who was allegedly taken by force."

A familiar male voice interrupts, "Judge Lemons, I object to this accusation. I was not taken by force." Conrad is on his feet speaking with authority just like he did at the academic assembly a few days ago. His dad shakes his head at him and pulls his sleeve as he continues, "I was under house arrest by order of my father, and I left his house of my own will and had to knock him out in the doorway of our house in order to do so. I'm sure the doctor's notes from when this case started can prove that what I am saying is correct. My father will not remember because he was extremely drunk at the time. Dandra Metty did not force me to leave and is too physically small to force me or my father to do anything. I forced my way out of my father's house as an act of self-defense." Zane Chesterton growls and folds his arms aggressively as his son sits down.

Judge Lemons nods and picks up two pieces of paper from off his desk. "This is a picture of Zane Chesterton the day of your escape, and a medical examination record. Your story checks out, Conrad Chesterton." The judge sets those papers down and picks up another one. "Conrad, you just made half my job today extremely easy." He writes something on the paper and says, "In the matter of the kidnap of Conrad Chesterton, I find the Metty family and Baldwin Kole not guilty."

Mom sighs with relief next to me. I didn't think Zane could prove that anyway; my boyfriend has proven more than once that he can withstand the pressure of his father and tell the truth. It's the rest of this trial that I am worried about.

Judge Lemons clears his throat and declares, "Now for the second accusation. A tunnel was created in the Metty backyard that went under the border wall of the country into the United Cities. I have seen pictures and heard witness to this. Nine people illegally left our country through said tunnel."

"Objection, Judge Lemons. Eleven people were involved with the mass exodus from our country, and they were all led by Dandra Metty and Baldwin Kole," says Patrolman Darius vehemently.

The judge turns to him and says, "I assume you are talking about Jim and Susan Yesterly who are on trial for trying to leave the country as well."

"I am, Judge Lemons."

The judge shakes his head dismissively. "That is a completely different trial for two individuals who may or may not have tried to leave by a completely different route, unsuccessfully, I might add. The evidence that connects these two groups is insubstantial and hardly warrants the claim that this was a mass exodus."

Patrolman Darius fumes, "This was not an accident, this was not an underground mushroom garden. This tunnel was started years ago for the purpose of escaping."

Patrolman Mark stands up and looks from my mom to the judge. "That is an excellent point. This tunnel was started by Gifford Metty who died at the hand of Zane Chesterton. His family didn't want the same fate and therefore left out of fear for their own lives, which is very different than trying to start a mass exodus."

Patrolman Darius brandishes a finger at the anti-gamers. "That excuse might work for the Metty family, but what about the rest of them? Baldwin Kole and his friends had no reason to fear for their lives. They wanted to leave. This was a purposeful departure." Gordon, Ed, and Adamar look at the judge and start complaining.

Judge Lemons holds up a hand for silence. "We have not had anyone purposefully and illegally leave the country of Layland in 100 years. I've heard Patrolman Darius and Patrolman Mark's philosophies on why the escapees left, but I'd like to hear from the escapees themselves." Judge Lemons looks Baldwin in the eye and asks, "Why did you leave?"

Chapter 3

BALDWIN DOESN'T FLINCH at the judge and stands up to speak. "Judge Lemons, as a person who values education, community progress, and personal freedom, I was also harassed by Zane Chesterton. The educational amendment that passed last year and the invasion of privacy that the GameComs have brought to this country have made this a very undesirable place to live. I gathered up everyone I hold dear, and I left because I wanted to be free of Zane Chesterton and his spying devices, and I wanted a chance to learn and become someone great despite my poverty."

The judge looks at the other anti-gamers. "What about the rest of you?"

Adamar stands up. "We consider Baldwin Kole our friend, our leader, and ultimately our family. Wherever he goes, we follow."

Judge Lemons frowns at Gordon and Marcella. "Is this true for all of you?"

Gordon, Ed, and Marcella nod their heads and mutter, "Yes."

Judge Lemons looks at my mom and asks, "Do you have anything you would like to say in your defense before I make my decision?"

Mom stands up and asks Patrolman Mark to take a piece of paper out of her pocket and hand it to the judge. When Judge Lemons has the paper, she says, "I feel like my motivations have been expressed by Patrolman Mark already, but I would like you to read my personal testimony of what my family has endured at the hand of Zane Chesterton and know that I would never have left the country if I had felt like my family had any other option to live without fear for our lives." Mom slowly sinks back down into her seat and looks at me nervously.

Judge Lemons takes his time reading Mom's testimony and finally says, "I have heard testimony and read reports about this case for multiple months, and now that I have heard from the actual people involved, I have reached a decision." Mom sits up taller in her seat. I lean forward so I don't miss a single word.

The judge clears his throat. "Since the motive for leaving the country was self-defense, I will not sentence the nine of you for inciting a mass exodus."

Mom and Baldwin sigh with relief on either side of me. I feel my body relax into the bench. We're going to be okay.

Judge Lemons continues, "However, you did break the law in pursuit of your own safety, so you will be sentenced to 1,000 hours of community service and fined 10,000 coins..."

Mom gasps in shock.

Baldwin elbows me. "That's not bad."

"Each," Judge Lemons finishes.

Mom folds in half and covers her mouth with her handcuffed hands.

Patrolman Mark stands up and says, "Judge Lemons, I understand the 9,000 hours of community service, but 90,000 coins is an outrageous fine when you consider the poverty that eight out of nine of these people live in."

Judge Lemons holds up a hand for silence. "I consider this a fair punishment for a crime that has not been committed since the completion of the border wall which has been in place for over 100 years. However, only half of the fine is required in order to be released from the detention center, and the remainder of the fine must be paid back by monthly installments over the next five years."

Baldwin speaks up, "Judge Lemons, what if we don't have

5,000 coins and have no friends or family who can loan us the money at the present time?"

Judge Lemons starts gathering the papers on his desk. "You are not the first convicts to find themselves in these circumstances. You will stay in the detainment center, sewing flags and jumpsuits or fixing city furniture in the basement by day until you have paid off your 5,000 coins. The Work-Detail Patrolchief will arrange your community service and your work options. You are dismissed."

I can't tell if Mom has passed out or is in shock as we are commanded to rise as the judge leaves the chamber. I pull Mom to her feet and hold her up. She lays her head on my shoulder and mutters, "He may as well have sentenced us to several years in the detainment center. It will take that long to pay off half our fine."

Once the judge leaves, the room erupts into chatter.

Patrolman Mark walks up to us and grins, "That went as well as we could have hoped."

I nudge my mom so she'll lift her head. She's definitely in shock. I smile and say, "Thank you, Patrolman Mark. I know it has taken you months of hard work to do this."

Patrolman Mark looks at Mom with concern. "I would have done more if I needed to." He puts a hand on Mom's arm and says, "Are you okay, Laurel?"

Mom moans, "15,000 coins is so much money."

Patrolman Mark tilts his head to the side. "Judge Hoage

would have given you double that. You'll just have to take out a loan."

Mom sobs, "No one will loan us money; we're international criminals."

Mark's face softens as he says, "It's that or work in the detainment center basement, unfortunately."

The patrolman who led us here makes us wait as Zane and Conrad are taken out before us. Conrad mouths the words, "It'll be okay," to me as he walks past me.

I wish I could believe him, but he has 5,000, maybe even all 10,000 coins for his fine. I don't.

Chapter 4

I AM NOT SURPRISED when Conrad and Zane are taken upstairs instead of to our cells on the main floor of the detainment center. Conrad's eyes look apologetic as he disappears up the stairs, but Zane looks as proud and condescending as ever.

I enter our block of cells realizing that this is probably going to be home for quite some time. The loud *clunk* of the barred door locking behind me seems to cement my fate into place. Why did I come back to this miserable country?

Patrolman Mark helps the other patrolmen get us out of

our handcuffs and into our cells quickly. I hear crying coming from both of my neighboring cells. Mark clears his throat and says to all of us detainees, "I know your sentence seems harsh, but considering what would have happened if Judge Hoage had stayed, I'm counting this as a victory."

Ed says what we're all thinking. "Thank you for your help, Patrolman Mark, but none of us has a single coin to our names. We'll be in here for years until we can pay our 5,000 coins."

Patrolman Mark sounds optimistic, "Not necessarily. I would consider staying here a temporary thing. You can get your sentence reduced for good behavior, and you may be able to get a loan."

Baldwin scoffs, "If we were ridiculously lucky, we might find someone who could loan us enough money for one or two of us, but we're basically a family, so we won't leave any of the eight of us behind. We may as well get used to this."

Patrolman Mark responds, "Don't lose hope. I'll do what I can from my side, and you all behave like angels from yours."

Mom presses herself into the bars on her door. "Mark, do they have any mercy for children?"

Mark approaches Mom's cell and looks at Everley. "They usually do. I will see if they will make a special exception on the amount needed to leave the detainment center for Everley's sake. As for the rest of you, you'll be taken to the Work-Detail Patrolchief today to arrange your community service and work opportunities until other arrangements can be made. Things will get better, so keep your chins up."

I try to keep my chin up, but I feel more and more hopeless as everyone else gets taken out before me. My stomach keeps growling, and Mom keeps crying. When it's finally my turn, Adamar gets to leave with me because he has a visitor again. I'm only a lot jealous when I watch a patrolman lead him to a giant window with a metal grate in it to talk to Charlisa.

My red-headed friend looks good. She's healthy and happy and just as fiery as ever. Just like the days at the Tifton Library, she slips a note to Adamar through the metal grate. He is happier than I've ever seen him. I wonder if she's willing to come here every day for years to see him until he can earn 5,000 coins for his release. At least she's willing now, and he's smiling again.

The Work-Detail Patrolchief is actually a patrolwoman. The name block on her desk says, "Work-Detail Patrolchief Reba." She looks at me above her black-rimmed glasses and asks, "Are you in the same boat as the rest of your escapee friends?"

I force my eyes up from my lap and ask, "What do you mean by that?"

Patrolchief Reba fans her hands out to show me all the

piles of paperwork on her desk. "You have no money to pay for half your fine, so you're going to have to work and do community service from here for as long as it takes?"

I sigh, "Yes."

Reba nods and starts filling out a form on her desk. "Don't cry about it; you'll be all right, sweetheart."

I swallow and push my short hair behind my ears. "I know. What do I need to do?"

Patrolchief Reba yawns like I have made this the longest day of her life. "You have a few options. Would you rather sew or fix furniture?"

I twist my hands together. "I've never done either."

"It's not that hard. I'd recommend sewing since the furniture spots are filling up fast. You get paid by the quality and quantity of completed products you make in a day. You'll get faster and earn more money as you go. You have to work a minimum of six hours a day and a maximum of ten."

I guess it could be worse. I try to see what is written on the piles of forms sitting on her desk, so I can match schedules if possible. "What about my community service?"

Patrolchief Reba taps my form with her pen. "You'll have to do a minimum of five hours a week while you're in here."

I give up on reading backwards. "Can I do an hour a day?"

My interviewer nods. "Sure thing, sweetheart. You can start with that right after breakfast, and then you'll go straight to the sewing room in the basement after that."

I look around Patrolchief Reba's office, hoping to find something positive to cling to. She has a daughter who looks a few years older than me. I look at this less-than-motherly looking person and ask, "What will I be doing for my community service?"

She places my paperwork in a folder and says, "Either cleaning city-owned buildings or picking up trash around town."

I smile inside. I can do that with my eyes closed.

Chapter 5

I TRY TO DECIDE if I feel more embarrassed or intrigued as I walk toward the Tifton Library with my yellow jumpsuit and yellow bag for trash. It looks closed, but is it? I wonder if the two patrolmen who are guarding Baldwin, Ed, Adamar, and me notice that we picked up trash twice as fast coming down the road as we are now that we're at the library. I practically move in slow motion as I pick up wrappers and empty disposable cups in a path that leads me to the front door.

The bigger, meaner patrolman barks, "Hey, get away from there. You can't go inside."

I give him an innocent look and say, "I'm not going inside; I just want to get these old fliers off the door."

He grunts, "Be quick about it then."

I slowly peel all the trash off the door as I read the signs announcing the modified hours of operation on it. The sign says:

Library Hours of Operation

Sunday — Closed

Monday — Closed

Tuesday — Closed

Wednesday — 10:00-6:00

Thursday — 10:00-6:00

Friday — 10:00-6:00

Saturday — 10:00-6:00

That is not many hours for two librarians to share. Mayor Monroe and Zane Chesterton's plan to shut down the library seems to be working. I wonder who will quit first, Agatha or Zelma.

I'm not the only one snooping for information around here. Baldwin, Ed, and Adamar are picking up trash awfully close to the window they formerly used as a door into the library basement. They call it "the crypt." Baldwin mouths the words, "Keep them busy," as he tugs on the latch to the window.

My garbage bag is practically full, so I drop it at the feet of our patrolman guards and say, "My bag is full. What should I do now?"

The skinnier, kinder patrolman pulls a new bag out of his backpack and says, "Tie this full one up, set it on the side of the road, and fill up another one, just like you did on the last block."

I nod like this is a revelation to me. "How long will it take before we have to pick up trash on this stretch again?"

The grouchy patrolman scoffs, "It'll be full of trash tomorrow."

I put my hands on my hips and act unbelieving. "Are you sure? I bet we could go a week at least."

The patrolman flexes his bicep and snorts, "I'm sure kid. You've been gone too long. Welcome back to Layland, United Nine."

My eyebrows scrunch together as I ask, "What's United Nine?"

The skinny patrolman says, "That's what everyone in Layland calls the nine of you that escaped into the United Cities."

Huh, I kind of like that. I inquire further, "Have our faces been on the news much?"

The big patrolman scoffs, "Uh, yeah, blondie. But even more than that, your names and stories were broadcast on the GameComs at least 10 times a day. It was so annoying."

I chuckle at the thought of my story annoying all the gamers. I force down my smile and say, "You should have seen the streets of the United Cities. They were so clean. I rarely saw trash in any public area."

The skinny patrolman picks at a zit on his chin and says, "Well, sorry to disappoint you, but those days are over."

I look at Baldwin out of the corner of my eye. He is climbing out of the window. I look the patrolmen in the eyes and ask, "If all of us 'United Nine' pick up trash every day for an hour, it'll get significantly better, don't you think?"

The mean patrolman barks, "No, I don't think so. Look around you. You're not even putting a dent in it. This isn't meant to change anything, it's just meant to punish you, so get back to work." He turns toward Baldwin and says, "Don't get so close to the building, curly. It's time to pick up the pace."

I obediently move my full bag of trash to the curb and start filling my next one as Baldwin joins me. I give him a sideways glance. "Any luck?"

Baldwin leans in close. "Yeah. The window is still unlocked; there is heat down there, but most of the furniture is gone. The flag is still hanging on the wall, so I bet our stuff is still safely locked in the little room behind it. The crypt is just waiting for us to come back."

I'm glad to have some good news for a change. The skinny patrolman whistles as a sign to cross the road and head back the way we came. Another community service group, probably my mom and the girls, will pick up our filled bags later today. It's not quite gamer's morning as we get back to the detainment center, but I am shocked to see that every person on the street except the patrolmen on duty and ourselves has a GameCom around their wrist.

Chapter 6

I KIND OF WISH I HAD ASKED for an hour or two in my cell before starting work in the basement, but it's too late for a break now. I wipe my sweaty forehead with my sleeve as I enter the huge sewing room with twenty sewing machines in four rows of five. I wash my dirty hands in a large sink and stare at the shelves of raw fabric completely covering two walls. One wall has ten enormous rolling bins of finished flags and jumpsuits lined up against it.

Mom and Marcella are already sitting at sewing machines with a stocky lady in a yellow jumpsuit, who looks vaguely familiar, sitting between them giving them instructions as she watches them sew. Everley is jumping from one sewing station to the next collecting finished items and cutting the extra thread that is left behind before storing them in their appropriate bin.

I'm not sure if I should be happy or sad at this sight. It's good to see Mom and Marcella actively learning and working instead of crying, but it's sad that Everley is working just as hard as everyone else when she should be in school right now.

The lady who is helping Mom and Marcella moves to my side to help me once I sit down to a sewing machine.

She leans toward me. "Hello, Dandra. Do you remember me?"

I look at her face carefully, but I can't remember where I've seen her before. "I'm sorry, but I can't quite place your face."

"I'm Susan Yesterly. We have bought dirt from your family for years."

I grin. "Oh! Of course! It's nice to see you again, but not here. Why are you here?"

The friendly woman threads the needle of my sewing machine as she responds, "Well, it's a long story, but the short version is that once you guys left, the City of Tifton got real bad for a while. There were angry patrolmen everywhere. Our homes and businesses were searched, and what do you think they found when they searched our backyard?"

I cringe. "The stairway you were building to the top of the border wall."

Susan nods. "Yep."

My eyebrows come together. "You hadn't even tried to leave yet?"

Susan shakes her head. "Nope, but it was pretty obvious that leaving was our intention, so here we are."

I feel so bad, but I'm also full of questions. "How much longer do you have here? What was your fine?"

Susan frowns. "Oh, we got six months in the detainment center and a fine of 1,000 coins each."

I slap the table in front of me. "That's terrible!"

Susan sighs, "I know, but our sentence was cut in half for good behavior, so we'll be out of here soon."

Guilt runs through me. "I'm so sorry. It's our fault you were searched."

Susan's lips tighten. "Yeah, it is, but don't beat yourself up about it. It's our government's fault more than anything, and we're almost done with our sentence and our fine. Let me help you do the same thing. It's probably easiest to start with flags. Jumpsuits are tricky."

Mrs. Yesterly is so impressive. Even though she should be furious at us for being the cause of the search that landed her here, she gives up precious time to help us.

Sewing is hard work. It gets easier the more you do it, but my hands get dry from the fabric, and my back aches after only an hour at the sewing machine. My half hour lunch break is not long enough, and the cold oatmeal does not fill me up, but at least it's a break.

When the patrolman counts the finished flags in my bin, only wincing at the quality of the first three, he says, "I'm subtracting 20 coins off your fine."

I flop into the nearest chair and cover my face with my hands. How am I ever going to earn 5,000 coins?

"Dandra, how much did you earn toward your fine?" Baldwin's voice calls out to me as we all lay exhausted in our bunks.

I sigh, "20 coins."

Baldwin scrapes the oatmeal off his tray loudly. "Hmm. I earned 22 fixing furniture today, so I was considering switching to sewing, but maybe not."

I glare at the gray glob of oatmeal waiting for me on the floor. "I'm not very fast, so maybe sewing is better."

"It's not," says the unknown man located on the other side of Mom's cell.

I still wonder who he is, so I clear my throat and ask, "How long have you been here, sir?"

His hoarse voice is not very loud. "I've been here over four months, and sewing always pays out a coin or two less than furniture fixing."

I press my face to the bars of my door. "What's your name again?"

The hoarse voice is barely discernible. "Don't worry about my name."

Chapter 7

THE OATMEAL IS LESS GRAY TODAY; it's almost pink. Maybe they put some strawberries in it. I take a bite hopefully.

Nope.

"Dandra Metty, you have a visitor," a loud male voice calls out.

Who in the world would visit me? The only friends I have are in cells with me. Well, I guess there's always Agatha or Zelma from the library or Charlisa or my homebound grandmother. I stand up and stretch. "Thank you. I am ready when you are, patrolman."

I wait impatiently as the patrolman opens my cell, handcuffs me, and takes me out of our corridor and right past the visitor windows. I'm shocked when we don't stop. What is going on? We march up the stairs, past quite a few offices and interrogation rooms. Am I about to be interrogated? My sentencing is complete. I don't have to answer any more questions. This is not right.

The room I'm ushered into is labeled "Large Interrogation Room."

My eyebrows knit themselves together as I cautiously walk inside, but this room doesn't look like an interrogation room. It looks almost like a house. It is divided into four different areas by bookshelves and cabinets. The left front partition has a thick fluffy rug with couches and chairs and a coffee table in the middle; a desk and bookshelves are to the right, like an office. The back area is divided in two with a table and chairs on the right side and two king-sized beds on the left.

"Welcome, Dandra," Zane Chesterton says as he walks toward me with a bottle of my favorite cherry soda in each of his free hands.

I immediately freeze and grab the wrist of the patrolman who brought me here before he leaves. "I do not wish to be here. Please take me back to my cell."

"Dandra, no! Please don't go!" Conrad jumps over the

couch from the bedroom area into the living room area and pulls me into a hug.

I feel myself melt. I could cry his arms feel so good around me. I just wish my arms were free to wrap around him as well. I speak into his shoulder, "Conrad, what is this place?"

He licks his lips nervously. "It's my parents' cell."

Conrad's dad slams the two sodas on the coffee table next to a bowl of fresh fruit and gives me an annoyed look as he walks back to the bedroom area where his wife is barely noticeable, tucked into one of the king-sized beds.

Conrad's eyes follow his dad and then snap back to me. "My mom isn't feeling well. That's why she didn't come to our trial. My dad will tend to her as we talk. He promised to give us some privacy."

I'm shocked at what I'm seeing. "Are you staying in this fancy cell too?"

My boyfriend looks uncomfortable as he says, "Well, I was. Sit down and have a drink."

I obediently move to one of the couches and gesture to the patrolman that he can leave me here.

Conrad pops the top off both sodas and takes a drink from one of the bottles. He offers me the other one, but I hesitate to take it. I blush as I ask, "Would you mind taking a sip of mine, too?"

Conrad looks hurt, but he nods and takes a sip of mine as well. I can't be too careful with my dad's murderer in the room.

The cherry flavor of the soda is delicious to my deprived palate. I savor it before saying, "You said you *were* staying here. Where are you staying now?" I take another sip greedily.

Conrad gives me a guilty look. "Uh, at home. My parents paid my fine and have put me in charge of everything that they can't do while they're here for the next year."

I close my eyes and nod. Of course they did. He's free. He's the only one of us United Nine who can afford to be free. I find a smile despite my jealousy. "Congratulations! I'm so glad you're free, but..." I lean close and whisper, "Why are you working for the guy who put you on house arrest?"

Conrad takes a sip of his soda and says, "I know what you're feeling, and I understand it, but this is my best option right now." He leans closer and whispers, "This is the only way I can do what I want to do."

My eyebrows come together. "What do you want to do, Conrad? I'm completely out of the loop."

Conrad looks slightly hurt. "I want to change Layland. Just like we said we wanted to on our Christmas walk in the United Cities. Remember?"

I look at him sideways. "How will working in the gaming district do that?"

Conrad takes my hand. "I'm not just working in the gaming district; I'm making big decisions about where the future of the gaming industry is going and where to spend the money coming in. I can do so much good!"

I see so much excitement and purpose in Conrad's eyes that I hope he's right. I hope he can make a difference, but I'm also a realist who knows what his father is like. I lower my voice and ask, "How are things between you and your dad? He must have forgiven you to give you so much responsibility."

Conrad looks over his shoulder before saying, "We're... okay. It's not fixed yet, but it's headed in the right direction. I told them I would come here to see them every day, and once the year is up, I'll visit every day that they don't have work release."

My eyebrows come together. "Why did they put you in charge instead of Milo? He's older than you."

Conrad grins. "Well, Milo was in charge once Dad was arrested, but he wasn't being very responsible and lost quite a bit of money. Dad decided to hand over the responsibility to me instead."

I sit back on the couch. "Is Milo mad?"

Conrad shrugs. "No. He seems relieved. Desk work isn't really his thing."

I look around the room at the plush furnishings and whisper, "Do your parents spend all day in here?"

Conrad lowers his voice, too. "Yep. My mom is not handling it well. She misses her house and her privacy."

I roll my eyes. "Well, she should feel lucky that she has this 'cell' instead of mine." I say while making quotation marks with my fingers.

47

Conrad's guilty look comes back. "I know, Dandra. It's not fair, but their money did give them some perks, and they are being punished, so I try not to make her feel worse."

I take another long drink of cherry soda. "Where do the sodas and fresh fruit come from?"

Conrad picks up his bottle. "Milo has been bringing it. I can help bring them groceries now, too."

I take a tiny sip. "Does your mom have to stay as long as your dad does?"

Conrad pushes a loose strand of my hair behind my ear. "No, she has a lesser sentence than Dad because she was an accomplice, not the mastermind of the...you know."

I choke as I say, "Yeah, I know."

Conrad holds me again, for a long time as I close my eyes and shake as I keep my sobs in. I don't want his dad to see me cry. Conrad kisses my forehead. "What can I do to make things better, Dandra?"

I glower, "Do you have 15,000 coins in your back pocket?"

Conrad looks behind us at his dad and then gives me a sad smile. "No, not yet, but I will. I promise I'll get you and your family out. You took care of me, and now I will take care of you."

That statement is like a magic ointment that relieves the tension in my mind and body. I have someone who wants to help me after all. I give him a genuine smile. "You have no idea how much that means to me, Conrad. It feels hopeless when you're in the basement sewing flags."

He kisses my forehead again. "I can't even imagine. I thought cleaning Casswell's storeroom was hard."

My nose wrinkles. "Sewing is fine, but boring."

Conrad sees me pulling on my jumpsuit leg. He takes a closer look at my cement-burned flesh. "You need something to soak your legs in each day. I can at least do that."

I fidget with my handcuffs. "I doubt they will allow me to keep vinegar water and aloe vera in my cell, Conrad."

He tilts his head to the side and says, "I'll talk to Dad. He said he'd do something for me if I did something for him."

I squint at him. "What did you do for him?"

He sits back and repeats, "I'm doing his job while he's in here."

I look at him sideways. "You sound like you don't want it."

Conrad pinches the bridge of his nose and sighs, "I do, but I don't. It's so much responsibility."

Seeing Conrad with fancy clothes and hair makes me feel like we have nothing in common again. I try to push my negative feelings away. "Tell me about your new job."

Conrad finds his smile and takes a drink of soda. "Today was my second day. Almost everyone is very nice. I'm mostly being trained on how to run the business as it is right now, but I get to start making new decisions in a couple of weeks. I have my own office!"

I raise one eyebrow. "Who isn't nice to you?"

Conrad sighs. "My dad's business partner Felix didn't like Milo taking over my dad's responsibilities, and he is already acting like I'm no better."

I roll my eyes. "Why doesn't Felix do the work himself then?"

Conrad looks back at his dad, who is preoccupied, before responding, "He is the half of the partnership that supplied the money to start the Gaming District, and my dad was the half of the partnership that ran the business. Felix doesn't want to hire, fire, pay bills, and make day-to-day decisions. He just wants to make investing decisions."

I take a grape out of the fruit bowl and say, "Well, if he doesn't want to help, he has no right to complain."

Conrad chuckles, "That's right."

I pop the grape in my mouth and smile at my boyfriend. "How often do you get paid?"

Conrad glances behind us at his dad before whispering as quietly as possible, "I get paid every other week, so it'll take me a few months to pay your fine. My dad says that not a coin of his money is to pay for your fine, so let's keep this plan between us."

My heart sinks a bit. "Oh, I see." I can tell that Conrad is walking a fine line between keeping his parents happy and keeping his conscience happy. I reach for his hand through my handcuffs and whisper, "Mom is worried that it will take us multiple years at the rate we're sewing flags. I think your job pays more than mine does."

Conrad chuckles and leans in for a kiss. "Yeah, I think so."

Once the warmth of Conrad's kiss leaves my lips, my insecurities surface again. I look down at my cuffed hands. "Is our relationship going to last, Conrad? You're free. I'm locked up. You have an important job and influence in the community. I'll be locked up for months, maybe even years."

Conrad stretches his back. "So?"

My cheeks suddenly feel hot. "Will you still have time for me?"

Conrad's eyes melt. "I've always made time for you, and I always will, Dandra."

I want to protest, but he stops my lips with a kiss.

I wish I could stay here and kiss him forever, but from behind us, Zane Chesterton clears his throat loudly, and not long after that my patrolman guard enters the room to tell me it's time to go.

Chapter 8

THE BUBBLES CASCADING DOWN my body feel so good. My short hair, which I used to spike out to disguise myself in the United Cities, needs a shampoo. It looks more brown than blonde these days. Shower day only happens twice a week, so I savor every moment.

Mom frowns when she looks at my inflamed, cement-burned legs. They've been neglected since we were captured.

This shower feels great, but non-convicts would hate it. The shower heads are all in one big shower room with no privacy curtains, so I'm completely exposed to all the female convicts in this facility. Luckily, that's only Mom, Everley, Marcella, Susan Yesterly, and two women picked up for theft last night. We all agree to keep our eyes to the wall, so I guess it could be worse.

Once I'm clean, I look forward to community service because I get to see the city I've kind of missed, even if it looks like a trash-filled ghost town at 9:00 in the morning.

Baldwin stays awfully close to me as we pick up garbage. "I hear your visit was with Conrad the other day, and that's why you have a leg bath in your cell now." Baldwin looks at me pointedly. "Has he paid his way out?"

I speak loud enough for him to hear, but not loud enough for our patrolmen guards to overhear. "Yes."

Baldwin nods like he isn't surprised. "Is he going to pay your way out?"

I mutter, "Yes, but he can only use his own money and has to wait until he gets paid."

My ex-boyfriend looks at me intently. "Is he going to get your family out?"

"Yes."

He scratches his fake-blonde, curly head and asks, "Who all does he consider your family?"

I frown. "I don't know."

Baldwin swallows and looks me in the eye. "Do you consider me your family?"

54

All the memories I have of us together, bad, good, and amazing, flood over me. I look into his worried eyes and mumble, "Well, yes."

"Make sure he knows you feel that way." Baldwin holds my eyes for a moment before he walks off to pick up trash with Adamar.

Someday he'll get over my choosing Conrad over him. But, in typical Baldwin style, he is looking out for the good of the group over personal feelings. I want to help him. I want to help all of us. I just don't know how much Conrad can do, and he's the only person we know with any money.

I keep thinking about what Baldwin said as I sew flags. I am getting faster. I sew 26 coins worth today. Every little bit helps, right? I bet Conrad is making 40 coins every hour.

I'll get out. It may take a while, but I'll do it. Conrad said it would take him a few months to save enough. I can last three months.

My thoughts are interrupted by a wail from my mom. Everley drops what she is doing and runs to Mom. I stop midline on a flag and run to her as well. "What's the matter, Mom?"

She starts crying, "The needle is jammed."

I pat her knee. "That's okay. We can fix that."

Mom flings her hands in the air. "I know, but by the time we fix it, we'll lose two flags. We'll never get out of here! Everley will never go back to school or have a normal childhood!" Mom covers her mouth with her hands and breaks down into sobs.

"Calm down, Mom," I whisper as I notice that the other women sewing in here are frowning at us. Mrs. Yesterly leaves her sewing machine to help Mom fix the jammed needle.

"Don't lose hope, Laurel," she says. "I will be done with my three months and 1,000 coin fine this week. This experience will come to an end, believe it or not. Just keep your chin up."

Mom wipes the tears off her cheeks, takes a deep breath, and rethreads the fixed needle on her sewing machine. "Thank you, everyone. It won't happen again."

Mrs. Yesterly squeezes Mom's shoulder and says, "I would request a meeting with the Patrolchief to see if they will do something for Everley. Maybe they'll let her live with a relative or let you three out before you've paid off half your fine. It's worth a try."

Mom rewipes her tears with the back of her hand and nods. "I will do that. Patrolman Mark said he would try to get an adjustment for Everley's sake, but obviously he's busy."

I squeeze Mom's hand. "Mom, you don't know that he hasn't done anything. We know almost nothing in here. Your worrying about Everley is getting the best of you. Go ask the patrolman over there if they can get you an appointment with the Patrolchief."

A single tear trickles out of Mom's left eye. "Okay." She stands up and pulls back her shoulders.

Chapter 9

I WAKE UP TO THE SOUND of Mom and Everley leaving their cell. The patrolman who handcuffs them says, "Laurel and Everley Metty, you have been summoned for a meeting with the Patrolchief."

Mom gives me a hopeful look as she leaves with my little sister. My mind races as I soak my cement-burned legs in vinegar water. Surely this meeting can only help us, right? It can't get any worse than it already is.

They aren't back before I leave for community service. I try to update Baldwin on my mom's mental state as we clean litter out of the park playground equipment, but he has a newspaper in one hand that he is reading while his other hand absentmindedly picks up trash, stuffing it in my bag. "Baldwin, are you even listening to me? My Mom might have another mental breakdown if Everley has to spend the rest of her childhood behind bars."

Baldwin nods, "Yeah, yeah."

I growl, "You're not listening."

His eyes stay on the paper. "Yes, I am."

"What did I just say then?" I demand.

"Your mom might have another mental breakdown if her meeting with the Patrolchief doesn't go well."

I frown at how accurately he absorbed what I was saying even though he cares more about the story in the newspaper. I clear my throat, "What are you reading?"

He finally lowers the paper and looks at me. "Brock Hamble is proposing a change to the border wall law in the United Cities."

I light up. "Really? So soon? Do you think people will vote for it?"

Baldwin wrinkles his nose. "Not the way he has it written up now. He wants the whole wall brought to the ground immediately. I don't think the citizens of either country are ready for that much change."

I look at him sideways. "Is there another option?"

Baldwin pockets the paper. "Of course there is. He needs

to open the border with as little disruption as possible to both countries. I think people would vote for that."

I shove a disgusting bottle of mystery liquid into my garbage bag. "You mean try to get only one or two entry points in the wall?"

"Yep." He makes sure the newspaper isn't showing in his pocket and starts picking up trash with both hands. "Have you talked to Conrad about getting all of us out yet?"

My face falls. "No. I haven't seen him in a few days."

Baldwin's eyes linger on mine for a second. "I bet he comes to see you today. Tell him to call in all favors to anyone he knows with money to get us out."

I scowl, "I can't just boss him around. Especially when it's going to cost tens of thousands of coins!"

Baldwin's bossiness drops and he leans closer. "Please, Dandra? We all need this. Your mom isn't the only one on the edge of a mental breakdown. You are the only one who has a good relationship with someone with money."

I grab Baldwin's arm and look him in the eye. "Conrad is walking a fine line with his dad right now. His dad told him not to pay my fine with his money. If Conrad angers him, he'll get cut off."

Baldwin meets my stare and doesn't blink. "He would do anything for you. Even get cut off from his father."

I practically run to the sewing room in the basement to find out how Mom's meeting went.

She is sewing like a madwoman, so I'm guessing it didn't go well.

I slow my pace down as I approach her sewing machine. "How did it go, Mom?"

She doesn't stop sewing. "It went pretty well. The Patrolchief said that I was right in not wanting Everley to spend the rest of her childhood in the detainment center. He said that Patrolman Mark had already asked for an accommodation for Everley, so he called Grandma to see if she could take her until we get out."

I bounce up and down with this good news. "That's great! When will they take her to Grandma's?"

Mom frowns and keeps sewing. "Grandma is apparently not doing very well, health-wise. She said she couldn't take her."

My face falls. "When did they talk to Grandma?"

"Yesterday."

I feel the wheels turning in my head. "So, was the Patrolchief willing to give a different accommodation?"

Mom throws a finished flag at Everley and grabs a new one. "He decided to call Judge Lemons and ask if Everley and I could be released now and have more time to pay the rest of our fines through monthly installments."

I raise my eyebrows. "What did Judge Lemons say?"

Mom sews the edge of the new flag in three seconds flat as she responds, "He said he would allow Everley and I to leave once we had paid 1,000 coins each. The remaining 9,000 coins each could be paid through monthly installments."

I feel a grin coming on. "Is that why you are sewing like your life depends on it?"

Mom responds through gritted teeth. "Yes."

I sit down at the closest available sewing machine and start my first flag of the day. I turn to Mom and ask, "Did they say anything about me?"

Mom's determined face cracks, and she stops sewing. She stands up and wraps her arms around me. "They aren't going to accommodate you, Dandra. Patrolman Darius did a good job convincing Judge Lemons that you are the dangerous one in the family." She squeezes me tighter. "I'm so sorry, sweetie."

I swallow the lump in my throat and squeeze my eyes tight enough to stop any tears from coming out. "It's, it's...okay, Mom. We need to think of Everley."

Mom catches her breath and pulls back to look me in the eye. "Are you willing to donate your sewing money to Everley's cause?"

I feel my already sad heart sink, but I don't wallow for very long as I look into Mom's desperate eyes. "Yes. Absolutely." Mom squeezes my shoulder one more time and kisses my forehead. I force a smile and say, "I love you, Mom. I better get to work, so we can get you out of here. I'll sign the paperwork giving my wages to you after my shift."

I am numb as I sew. I've gone on autopilot like this before. I cleaned the Tifton Library after my dad's death like this. It's easier to just get lost in the motion of your work and refuse to feel anything.

Chapter 10

I SHUT BOTH BLINDS when I get back to my cell, curl up in a ball on my pathetic mattress, and finally let myself feel the pain that I've been holding inside. I have no regrets about donating my sewing money to Mom and Everley's cause, but that means I'll be in here without them, and for who knows how long. Conrad said he'd have enough to get me out in a few months. I can last that long in here, without my family, right?

I muffle my mouth with my blanket and cry myself to sleep.

I wake to the sound of my cell door creaking open. "Dandra Metty, you have someone here to see you."

I'm careful as I get to my feet to avoid stepping in my tray of cold oatmeal. Once I'm handcuffed, I'm taken to Zane and Jerika Chesterton's cell upstairs.

Conrad greets me at the door this time. His hug makes me start to cry again. He smells so clean, and his black spikey hair looks so nice with his new glasses. He acts like I look and smell just as pleasant even though I don't. "Dandra, why are you crying?" I just shake my head and hug him tighter. He guides me to the couch. "Sit down and tell me everything."

I do as he says, noticing that his dad and mom are giving me the side eye as they eat some delicious-looking sandwiches at their kitchen table in the back. My stomach growls without my permission. Conrad stops me and asks, "Are you hungry? What would you like to eat?"

I shrug and say, "I'm okay. I forgot to eat my oatmeal before I left my cell."

Conrad wrinkles his nose. "Oatmeal for dinner?"

I shrug. "That's all we get here."

Conrad glances at the sandwiches his parents are eating and frowns. "I should have bought more sandwiches...Well, I just brought some fruit, cookies, and sodas. I'll grab you some."

I try to keep my composure as I eat in front of him. It's so good to eat and drink something with flavor. He keeps looking at me with pity as I stuff my face. "So, why are you so upset? Is it the food here?"

I swallow a bite of juicy pear and say, "No, the food is what it is." I look down at my shoes. "I just want to get Mom and Everley out of here. They got permission to go back home once they have 1,000 coins each since it's cruel and unusual for a 10-year-old to live in the detainment center." I sigh, "But I did not get the same accommodation."

Conrad shakes his head sympathetically. "That's not fair."

I wipe pear juice off my chin and sigh. "We're pooling our sewing money." I set the remains of my pear down on my plate and try to hide my shaking hands. "I realized when I signed the paperwork how lonely I'll feel once they get out, and I'm still here."

Conrad wipes a tear off my cheek. "I'll get you out as soon as I can, Dandra." He looks at a calendar hanging on the wall. "I get paid next week, but it won't be enough."

Baldwin's request creeps into my mind. "Do you have any relatives or friends who might lend you some money? I will pay them back as soon as I can."

Conrad opens a cherry soda, takes a sip and hands it to me. He leans closer and says, "I could ask my Uncle Ty or my brother, Milo. Uncle Ty thinks the United Nine are celebrities, and Milo likes you way more than my dad does, but they don't seem like the type of guys who save their money."

I sigh with relief. "Thank you for asking. Like I say, we

will pay them back. We just don't have many connections with money."

Conrad looks at me sideways. "When you say 'we,' are you talking about your immediate family or all of the United Nine?" My boyfriend's face is unreadable to me.

I start to sweat a bit. "Well, aren't the United Nine one big family?"

Conrad leans back and looks at me as he thinks. "You want me to pay for Baldwin, who hates me, to get released."

I set the cookie I was about to eat down on the plate again. "Do you still hate each other? I thought you were somewhat okay with each other now." Conrad raises his eyebrows, but I don't give him the chance to speak. "I know it's so much money, but I don't know if I could live with myself leaving someone or several someones behind." I sigh and concede, "If you can't or won't find a way to pay for all of us, I understand. Our detainment center jobs will eventually earn us enough to get out."

Conrad sighs, "I know how you feel about all of them, Dandra, but they haven't exactly been buddy-buddy with me." I sink into my seat realizing how true this is. Conrad looks at me and then backward at his dad. He covers his mouth as he thinks. "I'll talk to my brother and uncle, Dandra. You know how my father feels about this, so I can't promise more than my own wages."

I put a hand on his knee and say, "That's all I ask. Just try your best, and whatever that ends up being, we'll make it work."

Conrad takes my two cuffed hands in one of his. "Do you miss me ever?"

I feel my eyes well up. "Yes, I miss you! I miss working with you at Casswell's, I miss our stolen moments, I miss freedom to see you whenever I want. I think about you all the time."

He pulls me in and holds me for a while. He whispers into my hair, "I'm sorry I haven't visited you much. I'm so busy trying to figure out how to run a business and a big house and going to skin therapy that I don't get here until almost lights out." He entwines his fingers with mine. "Last night I demanded Milo start alternating visit days with me just so I can catch up."

I don't know if I should be happy or sad about this news. I squeeze his hand encouragingly and say, "I hope you figure out your job soon, so you can visit more." I look down at his legs. "What is your skin therapy like?"

Conrad looks guilty. "Dad sent me to a specialist because my legs were looking pretty bad again. I go every day after work. They stick me in a therapy pool and then do laser and light therapy on me."

I tap his knee with my fingertips. "Can I see them?"

Conrad lifts up his pant legs, and I gasp. His legs look so healthy. There is no red or black flesh. Both legs are pink and

69

almost completely healed. "They look amazing, Conrad." I pull my jumpsuit legs down as far as they can go over my patchy flesh.

He smiles at my approval. "I know, right? I only have a week left of therapy, and then I'm as good as new!"

I love seeing him take care of himself. "You seem good, now. You really do. I'm so proud of you!" I squeeze his hand through my handcuffs.

He blushes. "Well, it's a tough job keeping up with you."

I'm about to disagree with him but he silences my lips with a kiss.

Chapter 11

I AVOID BALDWIN as we pick up trash in vacant city lots along the city border wall. It seems like ages ago that we were digging with all our strength to get under it, and not just it but the country border wall 15 feet beyond this one. As I watch Baldwin eye the border wall, I think about what he said about not taking the whole wall down but cutting out entry holes in it. That seems so doable to me. Especially since there are so many vacant lots next to the wall on this side of town.

Adamar helps me heft my unusually heavy bag of trash to

the curb. He is as upbeat and energetic as ever. I have to ask, "How is Charlisa doing?"

He is all grins. "She's doing pretty well. She has a job now. She wants to help me get out faster."

I nod. "I'm surprised her mom is letting her help you."

Adamar smirks, "Her mom doesn't know that the money is going to help me. She is just glad her daughter is taking on more responsibility and not visiting me as much."

I know what it's like to have disapproving parents involved in your relationship.

When we get back to the detainment center, I find myself all alone in the sewing room, which is a bit unnerving. I turn to the patrolman guarding the door and ask, "Where is everyone?"

He shrugs and says, "Everyone else paid their fines today and were discharged."

My jaw drops. "Did my mom use my sewing money?"

The patrolman scratches his back against the door frame. "If you signed the paperwork to give it to her, then yes."

I frown. "She only had a quarter of the money she needed yesterday, where did the rest come from?"

The patrolman looks at me sideways. "From what I heard—I believe it was an anonymous donor."

A smile erupts on my face. Conrad must have talked to his brother and uncle and got enough money to release them! I hope he has enough for me soon.

Since I have no one to talk to, I sew faster than I ever have.

I decide that if Conrad is working hard out there, I should work just as hard in here.

I felt so good about my talk with Conrad and about my work ethic today, but when I'm led past Mom and Everley's empty cell, I choke up. My tears are partly happy that they are back home, but also sad because I'm still here without them.

Once my sobs stop, Baldwin calls over, "Dandra, did your talk with Conrad work? Did he pay their fines?"

I wipe my eyes. "I—I guess so."

His voice is insistent. "Is he going to pay for the rest of us?"

I sigh, "He's doing the best he can. It might take a while."

Baldwin's voice gets louder. "I assume you gave up your spot for them, but you'll be next?"

I close my eyes. "I don't know, Baldwin. I'm as surprised as you are to see them out this soon. I didn't even get to say goodbye."

Baldwin scoffs, "Don't cry about it. They'll come back to visit you."

I roll my eyes and growl, "Thanks, Baldwin."

A deep voice clears its throat. "It could have been someone else who paid their fine, you know," says the man on the other side of Mom's vacant cell.

I sometimes forget that guy is there. He's so quiet, I've never seen him leave his cell, and he keeps his privacy blinds shut. I answer him, "Maybe, but I don't think our other friends and relatives have enough to help us, sir. What is your name again?"

"It doesn't matter."

The creaking of my cell door wakes me up. "Dandra Metty, please come with me."

I jump up faster than a streak of lightning and comb my hair down with my fingers the best I can. Is it Conrad? Maybe it's my mom!

I practically skip out of our corridor of cells to the glass window visitor stations. It is Mom and Everley! But the patrolman doesn't let me stop at the window. "Uh, sir. Those are my visitors."

The patrolman points down the hall. "Well, you can visit them on the outside because someone is here to pay your fine."

I stop so fast, I almost trip. "What?"

I am taken to a small office that has a gold plaque on the door that says, "Fines." When I walk in, Conrad is sitting there with his brother, Milo. I could hug and kiss them both, but my hands are cuffed, so that will have to wait.

The patrolwoman behind the desk says, "Please take a seat, Dandra Metty."

I take the last open seat and smile like it's Christmas morning. Milo looks at me and says, "I was wondering what I

74

should spend my birthday money on, and you seem like as good a gift as any!"

I try to hug him, but a cuffed hand squeeze is the best I can do. "Thank you, Milo! Thank you so much! I owe you homemade cookies for life! Oh, and I'll pay you back every coin of course!"

Milo smiles at me and signs the piece of paper the patrolwoman hands to him. She turns to me and says, "Do you agree to make monthly payments of the listed amount until the remaining 5,000 coins of your fine is paid?"

I practically shout, "Yes!"

"Then please fill out your contact information and sign on this line."

As soon as I sign, the patrolwoman motions for the guard to take off my handcuffs. The guard doesn't let go of my left wrist and immediately puts a snug yellow bracelet on my wrist instead.

When the patrolwoman sees my confused look, she says, "Thank you for your cooperation in the laws of the land. This bracelet can only be removed here at this facility with a special release mechanism. When you have paid the remaining 5,000 coins of your fine, come back to have the bracelet removed. Your first monthly installment is due the first of next month." She hands me a piece of paper and says, "Here is your community service schedule. If you miss a payment or a community service shift, this bracelet will send an unpleasant electrical shock into your body every half hour until the payment or service shift is made up. If you still haven't paid in a week, you will be brought back and locked in a cell again." The patrolwoman slides a mesh bag with the clothes I was wearing when they arrested us at the Educational Assembly towards me. "As soon as you change back into your own clothes, you are free to go."

My hands want to flail around in the air. I am amazed that I am free this quick and easy. I turn to Conrad and ask, "But what about everyone else?"

He looks at Milo and then at me and says, "Uncle Ty has 5,000 coins to lend, and Milo has 5,000 more in savings, but that won't pay for everyone. What do you want to do?"

I think about it for a minute, then I look at the patrolwoman at the desk. "How much do my five friends have left to pay on their release fines?"

She goes through her files, adds numbers, and says, "They've each earned about 500 coins so far, so it would take 22,500 coins to release them all.

We don't even have half of that. I look at Conrad and say, "Well, I guess I better pick two."

Milo squirms in his seat and pulls a stack of $100 bills out of his back pocket. "Dad gave me this to get my car painted this morning. I'm fine with the color it is. Go ahead and pick three people to release."

My free hands immediately hug Milo and kiss him on the cheek.

Conrad looks shocked, but Milo laughs. "I can see why you like her now, brother."

Conrad shakes his head and asks me, "Which three do you choose?"

It's a hard decision, but it's not at the same time. "I want to pay for Adamar, Gordon, and Marcella. I think Baldwin and Ed will understand." Conrad looks relieved.

The patrolwoman asks, "Do you want to be here when we release them? It will take a couple of hours to transfer the money and fill out the paperwork and bring them out."

I notice Conrad looking at what looks like a big, fancy watch, but I wouldn't be surprised if it's a new kind of GameCom. He's probably late for work, and I don't want Milo to see where the antigamers live. "No, that's okay. I'm sure they can take care of themselves, and I have two people waiting for me in the visitor's lobby right now. I don't want to keep them waiting."

Chapter 12

CONRAD AND MILO WALK ME OUT to my mom and sister, and we all hug like we've lived a lifetime apart. Everley glues herself to Conrad's side and keeps thanking him. I give Mom a quick update on what just happened. Mom claps her hands excitedly when she hears that Adamar, Gordon, and Marcella will be out today, too.

Conrad looks at his watch again. "I wish I could stay and help you get settled, but Milo and I are late for work, so I'm afraid our reunion will have to wait until after work and skin therapy. I promise to bring Tifton's best beefy patties as a housewarming dinner tonight though!"

I am so happy to be out that I'm not disappointed that Conrad has to leave again. "That sounds perfect! Please bring a list of who we need to pay back and how much when you come."

Conrad shrugs. "Okay. See you tonight!"

His kiss keeps me warm as we go our separate ways.

I link arms with Mom and Everley as we walk home. The air smells surprisingly clean compared to the detainment center. Not even the litter sticking to my legs can make me frown today. I'm free!

As we walk home, I drink in the smile on my sister's face. "How does the house look, sis?"

Everley gives me a thumbs down sign, and Mom shrugs. "It's kind of a mess, but a solid day or two of work can fix that."

I let that sink in as I wonder about the timing of our releases. "I wonder why Conrad came on two separate occasions to release us."

Mom turns to me and announces, "Conrad didn't pay for my fine."

My eyebrows crease together. "How do you know that?"

Mom slows down her pace and says, "We walked to his

house yesterday night to thank him, and he said he didn't do it. He was still gathering money as we spoke."

I stop walking. "Who do you think paid the remaining 1,000 coins then?"

Mom shakes her head. "I have no idea. I'm guessing it was Mark though. He brought flowers to the house this morning."

Everley says, "I think it was the nice old man in the cell next to ours."

I am completely confused and ask my sister, "Why do you think that?"

Everley shrugs and says, "He was always nice to me, and he said I deserved to be outside running and playing with other kids."

Mom shakes her head. "That is sweet of him to say, but I'm sure he is trying to pay off his own fine."

Everley stops to pick some shredded newspaper off her leg. "Maybe, but he told me that he was old and didn't have much to live for anymore."

My legs keep moving me toward our house, but my mind is back at the detainment center needing to know more about the mysterious man.

Chapter 13

A SPIDERWEB FULL OF FLIES. That's what our house reminds me of at first glance. The yellow caution tape is the web. The litter stuck in it are the flies. Mom looks at me with apologetic eyes. "I didn't have time to work on the outside when they released us yesterday. It took all day to clean up the inside."

I feel my determination wilt a bit when I see how much work is ahead of us. I never realized how much the litter and filthiness of my surroundings drained me before spending time in the United Cities. I want the confidence and the energy I felt there to come back to me. So, I lift my shoulders and say to my mom, "We did so much the last few months. We can make this house a home again. Is the inside this bad?"

Mom shrugs. "There was tape around many things inside too, but I threw it all away and just started attacking the dust."

I sigh as I pick a piece of litter out of the front gate. "Dust. It's everywhere we go, isn't it, Mom?"

Mom reaches out and squeezes my hand. "Well, it's an unfortunate thing that doesn't stop, but it's also a fortunate thing that proves what is so big and important today will someday decompose and become the dust of tomorrow."

Everley frowns. "What is fortunate about that?"

Mom picks out another piece of litter from the gate and says, "I'm glad the little mental breakdown I had a few days ago in the detainment center sewing room is now dust, now past. I can just wipe that dust away and move forward."

Everley looks at Mom crosswise and says, "I still don't get it, but I will help you dust the house, Mom."

Mom chuckles. "Thank you, Everley. If you do that, and Dandra starts picking up tape and litter out front, and I start doing the same in the back, we'll be done and looking somewhat respectable by the time Conrad gets here with dinner."

Everley looks from me to Mom and nods. "You've got a deal."

I am a bundle of mixed emotions as I stuff garbage bags with yellow caution tape and litter from all over our neglected property. I'm glad Mom assigned me the front. I'm not ready to face the shed in the back yet. My cement burns throb just thinking about the day we escaped. My community service has helped ease the shock of how much litter there is in this country, at least. I've filled five bags already, and I need more, but we're out of them. The melting snow has made all the litter heavier than it would be otherwise.

The fifth bag barely makes it into the back of the truck before I let myself collapse against the side of it. The hubcaps still have dirt caked on them from the last load of dirt we pulled out of the tunnel and sold to the Yesterlys. I kick the dirt off the hubcaps, hoping that the Yesterlys are out of the detainment center, too.

There could be empty leaf bags in the shed... I just need a few more, so I can finish de-littering the front yard... Some unknown force pulls me to the shed even though my mind tells me not to go in there.

Mom calls out, "Dandra, I'm going to get us both a drink. I'll be right back."

"Okay, Mom," I mutter as my arm reaches out without my permission and opens the shed door. What I see leaves me gasping for air.

The tools and nicknacks on the shelves and in the corners are still the same as they've always been, but the floor of the shed used to be a hole that started a tunnel that led out of the city and out of the country. This is where we escaped this miserable place. Now, the hole is gone.

In its place is a rough, three-foot mound of concrete. Patrolman Darius didn't try to skimp on filling in the hole. He filled it to overflowing. I was kind of hoping there would be a gap at the top, so I could see the wooden braces my dad built to keep the tunnel from caving in. After he died, this is where I would go to feel close to him.

Not anymore. The only person I sense in this shed is Patrolman Darius. The three-foot mound of concrete in the middle makes this shed unusable.

I have had enough. I slam the door shut and lock it. I don't want to go in that useless building ever again.

Chapter 14

"ARE YOU OKAY, DANDRA? You've barely touched your beefy patty," Conrad says as we sit quietly at the kitchen table.

I snap out of my trance. "I'm fine. I just—went into the shed today."

He eyes me warily. "How was that?"

I shudder. "Haunting."

Conrad swallows. "Oh. I bet."

I stand up and start cleaning up the table. "I don't want to talk about it. Did you bring the list of people we owe money to?"

Conrad wipes his mouth with a napkin and nods at me cautiously. "I did bring it. Don't get obsessed with this list though, Dandra. You still have monthly installments to make, and I know for a fact that Milo is fine with waiting for you to get back on your feet before you pay him back."

I nod as I read the list. "We still need to get Baldwin and Ed out. I need a job."

Mom clears her throat, "And you and your sister need to get back to school."

Conrad looks away from my mom. I narrow my eyes at him. "Are you going back to school?"

He twists the fancy watch on his arm nervously. "I don't know. I hear it isn't very rigorous anymore, and I'm needed more than ever at work."

I was afraid he'd say that. I reach out and take his hand. "I need a job, too, but I don't know how I'll handle school without you there."

My boyfriend looks truly troubled. "I—I'll talk to my dad about it. I may be able to take a couple important classes at the beginning of the day before I go to work."

Mom clears her throat and stands up. "Thank you for dinner and the bag of groceries, Conrad. Everley, why don't we finish cleaning your room together?"

My sister moans, "But Mom, it's already pretty much—"

Mom is insistent. "Let's get it done now."

"Oh, okay," my sister grumbles as Mom pulls her from the kitchen table.

I am grateful for the privacy as I feel tears filling my eyes, but I blink to keep them from falling. I whisper, "Remember when we were preparing our speeches in the United Cities, and we talked about changing things here. Are you still going to do that? Or are you going to do what the rest of Layland does and drop out of school?"

Conrad fills with indignity. "I don't want to drop out! I am trying to keep so many people happy right now! Can't you see that? School is important, but so are the other things I'm trying to do! Starting with earning enough money to get your ex-boyfriend, who hates me, out of the detainment center."

The tears can't be held back any longer, and they fall on my beefy patty. "I know you are. You are doing a great job. I'm sorry. I'm just missing you already."

Conrad touches my yellow bracelet. "Do you need help finding a job? You know there are always jobs at..."

I pull my arm away. "No! I will not work at the Gaming District. That place started all of my problems." I wipe my tears away. "I can find a job on my own."

Conrad reaches for my hand. "I'm sure you can. I just want to help, and I want to see you as much as possible."

The realization of how little I will see him until our fines are paid slaps me in the face. He is right that I would see him more if I worked at the Gaming District. I have too much pride in my cause to do that though.

I squeeze his hand. "Thank you. Thank you for dinner and the groceries. We truly appreciate it." I stop him from interrupting me. "We will be out job hunting and signing up for school tomorrow. We will start over like we did in the United Cities, and hopefully we come out on top."

Conrad smiles at me but then looks at his fancy watch and says, "I'm sure you will. You always come out on top. You're smart and you're a fighter."

Curiosity gets the best of me. "Is that watch a GameCom?"

Conrad looks at me warily. "Uh, in a way, yes. It's called a GroCom, and it's much smaller than a GameCom, but it's more of a communication device than a gaming system. I'm trying to steer the company's money in this direction. I think more communication and less gaming would do this country good." I nod in agreement. He steals a kiss and says, "I wish I could stay longer, but I still need to visit my parents tonight. Can I bring dinner again tomorrow? I asked if I could get my paycheck a few days early, and my dad's accountant said he's have it ready for me tomorrow after work."

I look at the empty cupboards and fridge surrounding us and say, "Yes. Of course you can." He follows my gaze and tries to hide his concern. I hug him tightly before he leaves because it feels like I'm losing him even though he says he'll be back tomorrow.

I notice after he leaves that he has added his name to the fine pay back list with tomorrow's date and the amount of 8,500 coins. He is giving all he has to release Baldwin and Ed tomorrow.

Chapter 15

"DANDRA! MOM IS SIGNING US UP for school today! Wake up! Wake up!" Ugh. How can Everley be a human hurricane after I've only been back to our house one night?

I pull the covers up to my chin. "I know. I'll get up in five minutes."

"No! Get up now! I've already picked an outfit for you. Let's go!" Everley throws my blankets to the ground and squirts some cold aloe vera on my right leg.

The icy cold texture sends a jolt through my body. "Ahh!

No! I have to soak my legs in vinegar water first, Everley! Get out and let me do this myself!"

Everley puts her hands on her hips. "You have 15 minutes and then Mom and I are leaving without you!"

I give her a fake salute. "Yes, ma'am."

It takes me 30 minutes instead of 15, much to my sister's disapproval, but I am medicated, dressed, and fed in time to leave with Mom and Everley. The walk to Everley's school is longer than I remember, or maybe I am just walking slower to take in the change of our surroundings. I swear there is more litter than there used to be. I used to pick a piece of blowing litter off my legs a couple of times on the way to the school, but I've been covered in it the whole time this morning.

Signing Everley up for school is quick. I don't appreciate the way the school secretary stares at our yellow bracelets though. She is cold but cordial enough. Everley doesn't seem to notice the staring and waltzes into class without a backward glance.

As Mom and I leave the lower level school, I ask, "Do you think kids will be mean to her with that bracelet on?"

Mom shakes her head and says, "I don't think the kids will know what it signifies, but the adults will."

I shift my coat sleeve down so it covers my bracelet. "We can focus on jobs today and my school tomorrow if you want."

Mom cocks her head sideways. "I bet we can do both today. I want to see if the bank will take me back."

"Let's do that first."

"Okay."

Unfortunately, the bank manager is more discriminating than the school, and after a single glance at her yellow detainment center bracelet sends us away. "Laurel Metty, you were a good employee when you worked here before, but you have proven your disloyalty to the entire country, so we cannot risk taking you back." Mom shakes slightly as we leave the building.

I am not completely surprised, but disappointed. It would have been great to get that income back. We stop at five other businesses but get the same reaction to our yellow bracelets and well-known faces on the news.

I can't help but feel discouraged. "What can we do, Mom? If we can't make our first payment to the detainment center, they'll zap us every half hour and maybe even lock us back up."

Mom sighs. "I know. Surely someone will take us." She looks down litter-covered Main Street and then the Gaming District lights start flashing in the distance. "If we get desperate enough, I'm sure Conrad could get us a job at..."

I hold up a hand. "No, Mom. Absolutely not. I will clean the mayor's toilet with a toothbrush before I work at the Gaming District."

Mom tries to hide her grin, but I see it. She shrugs and says, "Well, we may as well sign you up for school. We should get something good accomplished today."

"Okay."

As we walk down Main Street, we pause when we get to the library. "Mom, can we just stop in and say, hi?"

Mom shrugs. "Why not?"

The door feels like it needs more grease on the hinges as I pull it open. I'm thrilled to see Agatha sitting behind the circular desk in the atrium. A quick glance up reveals that four more rooms have been boarded up since I left. There is a fresh, light coat of dust on everything, but it still looks so much better than it did before I deep cleaned this place months ago.

Agatha straightens up in her chair as soon as she sees me. "Dandra! You're back!"

I smile and inquire, "Did you miss me?"

Agatha grabs my hand. "Yes, and I have been worried sick about you! What was it like in the United Cities on the run?"

I smile at her reaction. "It wasn't that bad. It's a beautiful, clean place with lots of schools and jobs. I liked it there."

Agatha lets go of my hand and straightens out her skirt. "I guess it's a disappointment to be back, huh?"

I pause, unsure of how much to reveal. "Well, we did not get a warm welcome back. We've been job hunting all day, and no one wants us."

Agatha frowns. "I would take you back if I could, but I'm only working two days a week myself, and the mayor keeps hinting that the library will be closing this fall. He says the city can't afford to heat a building that isn't being used anymore."

Mom shakes her head. "When is the mayor up for re-election?"

"This year."

Mom sniffs. "I hope he gets voted out. He is easily bribed and cares nothing for Tifton's future."

Agatha nods and says, "I agree with you, but he might go uncontested. I don't know of a single soul willing to stand up against him. No one likes the state of the city, but no one is motivated enough to do anything about it either."

Mom shakes her head. "That's too bad. You don't know of any available jobs, do you?"

"I know the hardware store hires a few people in the spring, but they lay them off again when the work tapers off."

Mom nods. "Well, that's better than nothing. We'll stop in there on our way out."

Agatha looks sad to see us go. "Do you want to get a book or two to pass your evenings? If we only have a few months left, you might want to take advantage of it."

I grin. "Actually, yes. I want to get a couple of Steadman mysteries before we go. Is that okay, Mom?"

"Sure, go ahead. I need a book on trimming trees. I got scratched to death yesterday."

I run up the stairs two at a time and barge into the mysteries and detective stories room. It takes me just a second to remove the Steadman novels from their shelf and take off the piece of wood paneling blocking the secret note hole to the basement. I rip a blank page out of one of the books, hoping Agatha will forgive me, and scribble a note to Gordon, Adamar, and Marcella letting them know that Baldwin and Ed will be released today, and that the library will be permanently closed before winter. I get a strange thrill using the library's secret tunnels like my friends used to do when I was just an innocent and easily-startled custodian here. I move everything back into place as quickly as I can and grab a couple of books to check out.

My thrill-seeking heart finally slows down once Mom and I check out our books and head to the hardware store. I hope we have better luck there.

The store looks the same as it used to, with misspelled signs and all. The lady behind the desk looks more annoyed than happy to see us. I hope this isn't the way she greets customers. She scratches her curly head with a pen and demands, "What can I do for you ladies?"

Mom clears her throat and says, "We are looking for work, and we hear you usually hire in the spring."

The thin woman looks at Mom's yellow bracelet before Mom can cover it with her sleeve. "What did you do to deserve that?" she asks with a frown.

"Mom, you know what they did. You've seen these two on the news. They are part of the United Nine," a deep voice says.

I turn to see the owner of the deep voice coming from the back of the store. It's the strong young man who brought the ladder to the library so I could clean the chandelier. I'm pretty sure his name is Jed. Zelma tried to set us up on a date.

I'm not sure if Jed approves of us or disapproves of us from the tone of his voice. His mom turns to him and asks, "What did they do again?"

Jed places a box of hammers on the counter like it's a box of feathers and says, "They dug a tunnel into the United Cities and escaped for a few months. But they were caught and brought back."

Jed's mom frowns at us and mutters to her son, "We probably shouldn't hire criminals."

Jed's eyes look us over and settle on Mom's look of despair. "We've hired people with yellow bracelets before. Sometimes they work the hardest because they are so motivated to get the bracelets off."

His mom nods and whispers loudly, "That is true, but most of our work is manual labor. I'm not sure delicate females can handle it."

I look at Jed's mom's name tag and say, "Sharry, we aren't delicate females. We are used to manual labor. You can ask Agatha at the library or the Community Service Patrolchief. We promise to work just as hard as any other employee." I hold up my hands to show her my calluses.

Sharry looks at Jed and gives him a noncommittal shrug. I feel my heart drop into my feet. We are never going to get a job. I put a hand on Mom's shoulder to move her toward the door when Jed asks, "Why did you dig the tunnel and leave the country?"

Mom looks at me and gives my hand a squeeze. I take it as a signal to answer. I look Jed in the eye and say, "We think gaming has ruined this country. My dad was killed for speaking out against it, and once the educational reform bill was passed, my classes emptied out. We want to live in a clean place where we can feel safe to learn and grow and be around other people who feel the same way."

He holds my eyes for a second and then looks at his mom. "I don't think these are hardened criminals. I think they want safety and will do whatever it takes to get that, even if it takes years of digging. That's the kind of work ethic we need in our employees." His eyes find mine, and he says, "I say we give them a chance."

Mom's head visibly lifts. I look at Jed's mom and hope she feels the same way. She looks at a stack of papers on her desk and declares, "We just got a work order from the city to clean and paint around all major landmarks and city buildings before the big international convention happens here in a month. I need workers, and I need them now, so I'm willing to give you a job on a trial basis." Mom and I sigh with relief. Sharry continues, "If you do anything that I don't like, you're gone. Am I understood?"

Mom nods enthusiastically. "You are understood. You won't be disappointed. When can we start?"

"We only have a month, so can you start tomorrow?"

Mom bounces on the balls of her feet. "Yes! Absolutely! I can start tomorrow morning right after I get my younger daughter off to school. Dandra here can work as soon as she gets out of school."

Sharry asks, "Can you work weekends, too?"

I answer enthusiastically, "Yes, we can."

Sharry looks at Jed one last time and says, "Okay, you have a job. We will see you both tomorrow."

Chapter 16

MOM PRACTICALLY DANCES to the mid level school. "It's going to be all right! We won't be sent back to the detainment center!" I laugh and hope she keeps her enthusiasm as we spend our days bent over a paint can or a garbage bag.

It doesn't take long to sign me up for classes, and the school counselor says I can start tomorrow. She says she can't print me a schedule today because my grade-level classes are being shuffled at the current moment and starting tomorrow will be different based on requests from people in power.

"Conrad's dad," I mutter to my mom as we leave.

Mom shrugs. "I assume that means Conrad will stay in school. That should make you happy." Mom pauses by the front door. "Look at the time. It's almost time to pick up Everley."

I look down the road in the opposite direction Mom is pulling me. "Um, I kind of want to go to the detainment center to be there when Baldwin and Ed get out. Is that okay?"

Mom nods. "Sure. I'll see you at dinnertime."

I can tell which roads were cleaned by detainees this morning as I walk to the detainment center. They have significantly less trash on them than the other roads. When I walk into the detainment center, a sudden feeling of dread comes over me. What if they don't let me leave? What if there was a glitch with the money or the paperwork? I lean against the doorway, take a deep breath, and push my anxiety away. I have every right to be here as a free woman.

I stand as straight as I can and approach the visitation desk. My voice wobbles for only a second when I say, "Excuse me, I am Dandra Metty, and I was released yesterday. I was wondering if I could talk to the man who was two cells away from me in cell C1."

I should ask to see Baldwin first, but there is plenty of time for that, and I kind of want to talk to the man who might have paid to get Mom and Everley released.

The patrolman behind the desk is unfamiliar to me, and he seems suspicious of my motives. "Why do you want to see him?

Do you have a grudge against him for something he did to you in here?"

I frown at the negative turn our conversation is taking. "No! I think he gave some of his work credit to release my mom and sister, and I want to thank him."

The patrolman's creased eyebrows relax. "Oh. Do you know his name? That would speed this along considerably."

I feel awkward answering his question, but the man refused to give me his name every time I asked. "No. I don't know his name."

"Hmm. C1, you say? I will look into it and bring him out. Go ahead and seat yourself at visitation window six."

A full 20 minutes pass before the patrolman meets me at the window and says, "I'm sorry, but the man was released this morning."

I frown in disappointment. "What is his name? I still want to thank him."

The patrolman sighs, "I looked into it, and apparently, he did donate some of his money to release Laurel and Everley Metty."

I slap the counter in front of me. "I knew it. So, what is his name?"

The patrolman smirks, "He left strict instructions with the Fines Patrolchief not to release his name to anyone, especially your family."

My eyebrows come together. "What? Why? I just want to thank him."

The patrolman raises his eyebrows. "Apparently he worked off his release amount a long time ago and was even pardoned for his fine over a week ago, but he was insistent that he would not be released before the Mettys, and he was equally insistent that the Mettys not know who he is."

I am flabbergasted. Who would do this for us? Why did he care that we got out before him? I want to thank him even more now, but this patrolman is not going to help me out at all.

I sigh, "Well, if that is the case, I hope I bump into him again on the outside."

The patrolman shrugs. "Good luck with that. Is there anything else I can help you with?"

I nod. "Is Baldwin Kole about to be released? I would like to greet him when he comes out that door."

The patrolman frowns. "Not that I know of. Sorry, miss."

I am not deterred. "Thank you. I know he will be released today. I'll just wait in the waiting room until his benefactor arrives."

"Suit yourself, miss."

I wait for 30 minutes on the waiting room bench completely lost in my thoughts. Is Conrad coming? He said he was, but if I'm honest, he probably wouldn't mind keeping Baldwin behind bars for a while longer.

My thoughts shift to the mysterious man in cell C1. I'm

sure the man was not Mr. Yesterly. He is the only prisoner I can think of who would want to help us. Maybe the man was a friend of my dad's. I try to think of all the people I know who have gone to the detainment center when Conrad shows up. "Sorry I'm late. I had a meeting that ran over by an hour."

I jump up and give my boyfriend a kiss he won't forget too soon. "I'm so happy to see you! I was starting to worry that you wouldn't come."

Conrad hugs me back. "I promised I would. Don't you trust me?"

I let go and look at him. "Yes, I trust you. I just know the Gaming District isn't crazy about anti-gamers."

Conrad shrugs. "Well, I'm not the Gaming District. Let's go free our friends."

I stop in my tracks. "OUR friends?"

Conrad nods. "Yes. OUR friends." That statement deserves another kiss.

Baldwin's jaw drops when he and Ed enter the fines office and see who is bailing them out. It takes him a minute to find his words. "Conrad, I can't thank you enough. I will pay you back every coin. This means the world to me."

Ed's head bobbles up and down. "Me, too."

Conrad stuffs his empty wallet back in his pocket. "Ed, I know you will, and Baldwin, I know you are someone who will help me turn things around in this country. If there is anything I can do to help you, just let me know."

107

Baldwin's eyebrows come together. "Do you really want to change things? Big things? Things your dad has done?"

Conrad stands straighter. "Yes. I do. Even if my dad doesn't like it."

Baldwin tilts his head. "Well, I do need a job."

"Anything except that."

Baldwin laughs, "Oh. Yeah. My name is probably on the Gaming District blacklist, huh?"

Conrad forces the corners of his mouth up. "Yep, and on Dandra's boyfriend's blacklist."

Baldwin's eyebrows come together. "So, how can we make changes in this country if you won't work with me?"

Conrad adjusts the fancy watch on his arm and says, "We will find ways, but they won't take place at the Gaming District."

Baldwin eyes the watch distrustfully. "Fair enough."

Baldwin and Ed go into a nearby lavatory and change into their own clothes. Baldwin examines his new yellow bracelet and asks me, "Do you think the library will notice we're back?"

I think about my visit there this morning and respond, "Probably not, and according to Mayor Monroe, it will close before winter, so you better start looking for a better place to live."

Baldwin huffs, "The mayor is the worst. He will not get my vote at the next election."

I chuckle, "If you were old enough to vote, you might have to. Agatha says he's running uncontested."

Baldwin looks deep in thought. "Hmm. That needs to change."

Chapter 17

I CAN'T BELIEVE THIS is considered an appropriate school for my age. The United Cities spoiled me. It's painful to sit in classes with 10 students and a teacher who knows they are not respected or wanted and try to have a meaningful learning experience. At least our teachers are all smiles when we walk into their classrooms. The United Nine more than double their class sizes. Our former classmates are less enthusiastic. I keep hearing the word "yellow" muttered under their breaths.

I just have to tell myself that a yellow bracelet is less noticeable than a Patrolman-Darius-style chaperone. I sit by

Conrad for first hour math and again during second hour
English, wishing that I could feel even a little bit intellectually
stimulated. When the bell rings at the end of English, Conrad
puts his coat on like he's going outside.

"Where do you think you're going?" I demand.

"To work," he responds.

I frown. "But there are five more class periods."

Conrad shrugs. "My dad says I don't need anything else but
math and English to run the family business."

My eyebrows come together. "That's ridiculous. No new
knowledge is ever a waste."

Conrad gives me a look as he zips up his coat. "Did you
learn anything new today?"

"Uh..."

Conrad gives me a knowing look. "We need to ask
for more challenging material, but for now, this is the best
compromise I could get out of Dad. I'll see you tonight!" He
hugs me quickly and is off to the Gaming District.

I tell myself two classes are better than none, but it's so
much quieter after he leaves. Particularly at lunch. Especially
with Charlisa and Adamar all over each other. I try to keep my
eyes on my sandwich. I notice that Baldwin keeps giving me
sideways glances. I want to talk to him, but I don't want to lead
him on, either.

When the bell rings at the end of lunch, I follow the
lovebirds to science class. They are holding hands and kissing

at regular intervals. They kept their relationship a secret before we left the country, but not anymore.

It's kind of freeing to be back at this school with my friends, not keeping secrets from anyone. Everyone knows who we are and what we did, and they either like us or hate us, and there is nothing we can do about it. We still try not to talk too close to anyone's GameCom though. It's not hard to avoid them in a school this empty.

In my last class at school, History, I receive a note from the office. My heart starts pumping out my chest as the teacher hands it to me. Baldwin gives me a worried look. I sigh with relief when I realize it's from Mom, letting me know that Everley will be walking home with a neighbor girl from now on, so I should go straight to work after school.

Baldwin swipes my note as the bell rings. "You have a job? Where at?"

"Tifton Hardware Store on Main Street."

Baldwin's bag keeps bumping into me as we walk toward the front doors. "Are they hiring?"

I shrug. "I believe so. I don't know how many workers they need, but the city has hired them to clean and paint landmarks and city buildings before a big international conference in a month."

Baldwin's face lights up. "This is great news. I knew Brock Hamble would come over here to talk about taking down the border wall."

I raise an eyebrow. "Are you sure that's what the conference is about?"

Baldwin smirks. "I'm sure."

My face twists with skepticism. "So, do you want the job, or not?"

Baldwin shrugs. "I'm sure some of us will, but I kind of want to be inside the city building for my job. I need to know what is going on in there."

I avoid eye contact as I zip up my coat. "Suit yourself."

I walk with Baldwin, Adamar, Gordon, Marcella, and Ed down Main Street towards the library since the hardware store is on the way. I hope Marcella is okay being the only girl in the library basement again. I sidle up to her and ask, "So, how does it feel to be back at the crypt?"

Marcella shrugs. "It's not as comfortable as before since they got rid of most of the furniture, but it's nice to be back with the guys."

I give her a nudge. "You know you can always move in with us if you want to."

Marcella is not enthusiastic about my offer. "Thanks, but I'm happy where I am."

I shrug. "Okay."

I'm about to wave goodbye as I approach the hardware store, but Gordon opens the door for me, and Adamar walks in right behind me. Confused, I ask, "Are you all going to apply here?"

Baldwin shakes his head. "Ed thinks he can get the two of us jobs at the city building as janitors, and Marcella got her bakery job back, so just Adamar and Gordon are going to apply here."

"Oh."

Baldwin squeezes my shoulder. "Good luck and see you at school tomorrow."

I give him a small smile and say, "Thanks, and good luck to you, too."

Chapter 18

MOM MUST HAVE MADE A GOOD IMPRESSION on our new boss today because Gordon and Adamar have no problems getting hired on the spot. They hired another guy named Neil today, too.

Jed loads us all up in a giant work truck and takes us to the city park. It's not quite knee-deep in litter. The United Nine are no strangers to picking up trash, so we all grab a garbage bag and get to work. Neil has to take a break to wipe the sweat off his face an hour in, but the rest of us just keep going until Jed calls us over to the truck for a water break two and a half hours later.

Mom takes a long drink and sighs, "It has been a long day."

I ask, "What did you do while I was at school?"

She scrunches up her lips. "Neil, Jed, and I picked up all the litter in the cemetery and painted the gardener's shed."

I watch our squishy coworker collapse on a nearby bench. "Has Neil been taking breaks every hour?"

"Yep."

I look at the supplies in the back of the truck. "Do you think they'll make us paint anything tonight?"

Mom blows on her cupped hands to warm them. "Yep. Since it's over 40 degrees today, Jed loaded white paint for all the benches."

I look at the peeling and mostly brown bench next to us. "These benches are white?"

Mom smirks, "They're supposed to be."

I look around the now litter-free park and remark, "There are only twelve benches; if we each paint two, we'll be done in a jiffy."

Mom rolls her eyes. "I'm sure 10 benches will be done in a jiffy."

I'm confused about what my mom means until it's completely dark, and Neil hasn't even finished half of one bench. I want to go home and get some dinner, so I walk my paint can over to his bench and help him finish it up. Jed and my mom do the same with Neil's second untouched bench.

Adamar and Gordon take our paint cans and wash out our paint brushes and rollers while the rest of us wash our hands at the community lavatory and get a drink. I gulp the water so fast that it dribbles down my chin. *Brr.* It's definitely cold once the sun goes down. The snow is melting, but it isn't all the way gone. I will need more layers tomorrow.

My stomach growls as I climb into the truck. Jed looks at me out of the corner of his eye and asks, "Are you hungry?"

I fold my arms across my stomach to quiet it, embarrassed that it is so loud. "Well, sort of. Lunch feels like a long time ago."

He reaches his muscly arm over the front seat and points under my seat. "There is a box of crackers under there. Pull them out and help yourself and share with everyone else, too."

I pull the box out gratefully. "Thanks!"

The ride back to the hardware store is kind of cramped on the back seat of the truck with Neil taking half my seat and taking half the box of crackers. Jed frowns when Neil throws the empty box into the front seat and asks if there is anything else to eat. I wish our new boss could just drop us off at home since the hardware store is farther from our house than the park, but Gordon, Adamar, Neil, and probably Jed live closer to the hardware store. I don't worry about it and just sit back and let my muscles relax, thankful to have a job.

Chapter 19

"DON'T YOU DARE walk into my freshly cleaned house with those dirty shoes," Mom chimes as we approach the front door. I look down at my shoes and immediately agree with her. They are caked in mud and need to be left on the front porch to dry out tonight.

The clock in the living room chimes eight times as I hang up my coat. A heavenly aroma leads us into the kitchen where Conrad is making Metty soup with Everley at the stove. I run up to them, give each of them a squeeze, and ask, "How long have you been waiting for us?"

Conrad sets his stirring spoon down and says, "Oh, just an hour."

I grab a clean spoon and sample the soup. The blend of meat, vegetables, and spices is perfect. I ask my boyfriend, "How do you know this recipe? It's supposed to be a family secret."

Everley gives me a dirty look and says, "He is family."

Conrad winks at Everley, samples the soup, and declares, "Everley found it in your recipe book."

I look around at our mostly empty kitchen and inquire, "How did you find the ingredients?"

Conrad starts pulling out bowls and cups from the cupboard. "I brought them from home. I spent all my money on something else today," he says with a wink.

My heart fills with joy as I reflect on how unselfish Conrad has become. He has never looked more attractive to me. I wrap him in my arms and kiss him until Mom clears her throat. She says, "Uh, let's sit down and eat. We're all hungry." She eyes Conrad's hands around my waist and mutters, "Or, at least we were..."

After dinner Conrad tells me about his new GroCom watch and how excited he is to have it hit the market next week. I try to be excited for him, but I don't know what he is talking about half the time.

"Dandra, Dandra! Did you hear what I said? You're falling asleep."

I force my eyes open and apologize to Conrad. "I'm so

sorry. I'm so tired. Is it okay if we call it a night? We can talk about this again tomorrow."

He looks a bit disappointed, but he looks at his watch and nods. "Okay." He gives me a soft kiss and says, "I'll see you at school in the morning, good night."

The next day at school, Conrad is anxious to retell me about the new watches coming out. I stay awake this time, but I still can't show the enthusiasm he expects from me. I know he means well, but gaming devices are still gaming devices in my book.

During lunch, Baldwin tells me that he got the job at City Hall as a janitor, and he found out that there has been a vacant council seat for the City of Tifton for several months.

I raise an eyebrow at Baldwin's sudden interest. "So? Who cares about that? It's not surprising that no one wants to get off their couch and fill the position, is it?"

Baldwin finishes the last bite of the stale roll he brought for lunch. "It's not surprising, but since it has been vacant for three months, the law states that any citizen of Tifton who is age 17 or older can take the seat until the next voting cycle without a campaign or vote."

I frown. "Do you know someone 17 or older who would do it? Mr. Yesterly, maybe?"

"Me, of course."

I scoff, "You're not 17."

Baldwin sweeps his crumbs off the table. "I will be next week."

I shake my head. "So, you are going to mop city hall as a 16-year-old on Saturday and then claim a Tifton counsel seat on Monday as a 17-year-old."

Baldwin smiles. "Yep."

I point at his wrist. "Won't they throw a fit because of your yellow bracelet?"

Baldwin shakes his head. "Nope. I read the law in full last night. They can't deny me the spot based on criminal history or debt to the city."

That fact saddens me a bit and makes me wonder at the respectability of the rest of the city council. I lean in closer and ask, "Do you have to have physical proof that you live in the city of Tifton?"

Baldwin looks unsure for the first time during this conversation. "Heh, heh, yeah. That could be a problem. The law states that I do need to have a legitimate address in the city limits."

I look my ex-boyfriend in the eye and guess what is coming next. "You want to move in with me, don't you?"

Baldwin grins but then gets serious. "Well, kind of, but not really. I just need to claim your house as my permanent residence."

I lower my voice. "You know as well as I do that Zane Chesterton and Patrolman Darius will throw a fit when they find out what you are doing. Patrolman Darius will watch you day and night to prove you are a liar and get you kicked out."

Baldwin shrugs. "Then I may have to spend the night once in a while."

I shake my head and feel a slight blush on my cheeks. "You know how well my mom liked us all staying together in Herrington. She'll never agree to this."

"Can I at least come over tonight and ask? I'm not just doing this for me. It's for all of us and every citizen of Tifton. This is the first step in changing things in our country. Remember our speeches at the Educational Assembly? Were those just words to you? They weren't to me. I don't want to just sit back and ignore the problems. I want to fix them." Baldwin sighs and sounds unusually uncomfortable when he says, "I want to fix things, but I am—homeless. You're not. You have the permanent address I need. Will you please help me with this one thing?"

His eyes are so sincere, and even his peeling fake tattoo seems to soften as he pleads with me. I know Mom won't like it, but how can I not help someone who is trying so hard to do the right thing in a city filled with so much wrong? "I—I guess you can come over tonight at 8:00 to ask her."

He takes my hand and kisses it. "Thank you, Dandra." Then he gets up and walks away.

Chapter 20

THE SEVEN PONDS of the city-owned golf course should be empty on the second week of March, but they are full, full of pond scum, dead fish, litter, and by the smell, I'm guessing urine. My shoes will have to dry on the front porch again tonight.

Mom's balance is not suited for this job, and she keeps slipping. I think Jed feels sorry for her because he decides that she alone will pick up trash on the golf course while the rest of us clean out the ponds. I have four giant buckets filled with slimy debris, but I take a minute to warm my hands in my armpits before I haul them out when Jed comes to check on my progress.

Jed takes a quick scan of the pond. "Nice work, Dandra." I hurriedly grab two buckets and start walking up the slanted side of the pond when he jumps over the edge and takes them from me. "Your hands are cold, aren't they?"

"I look at my cold, red hands and say, "Yeah. I should have brought some gloves."

He climbs out of the slippery pond with a heavy bucket in each hand like he's just strolling through with a couple of snow cones on a summer day. He's back in a minute with newly emptied buckets and a pair of padded leather work gloves. He hands the gloves to me and says, "These aren't waterproof, but they should help. I'll make sure I pack better equipment in the future."

I hug the gloves. "Thank you. These will help a lot."

Jed pinches the shoulder of my pathetic coat. "Do you have a thicker coat than this?"

I think of the beautiful velvety coat Conrad bought me at Casswell's for Christmas. Even if I had been allowed to gather my possessions when we were arrested, I still wouldn't wear that coat to work in the mud. "No. I'm afraid not."

Jed thinks as he chucks some mucky branches out of my pond. "I'll see what I can do about getting warmer work clothes."

It's refreshing to have someone notice my needs and do something about it. "Thank you, Jed."

He twitches slightly when I say his name. He grabs the last couple branches in my pond and climbs out. He flings them into the pile he's made and says, "I don't want any of my employees getting sick from the cold," and walks off.

When we're loading up into the truck after the golf course is clean, Jed corners my mom and asks, "Are you doing okay?"

She reassures him, "I'm fine. I'm just a little cold."

He nods. "I'll provide work coats tomorrow, so you're not so cold."

Mom smiles and says, "That will help so much. I think the coldest part of the job is the walk home from the hardware store, honestly."

Jed frowns and says, "You don't live too far from here. I will drop you off at your house, so you don't have to walk home from the hardware store."

Mom beams, "Thank you! I'm not sure I agree with your distance assessment though. Are you sure you know where we live?"

Jed raises an eyebrow. "I read the newspaper; I know."

I feel my cheeks turn red with embarrassment as we drive

toward our very newsworthy house. It's a miracle we even got this job.

When we get to our house, Mom thanks Jed as I make a beeline for the front door. I stop only to wrestle out of my muddy shoes and leave them on the porch before I slam the door.

Chapter 21

EVERLEY MEETS ME IN THE ENTRYWAY with a big frown on her face. "Why did you invite Baldwin to dinner?"

I answer through gritted teeth. "I didn't. He just came to ask Mom something."

Everley stomps her foot and pulls me into the living room where Baldwin is sitting on the couch. He jumps to his feet as soon as he sees us and says, "I hope this isn't a bad time. I just wanted to talk to you about something, Mrs. Metty."

Mom sighs as she hangs her coat in the closet. "It's not a great time, but no time is a great time these days."

Baldwin rolls up his sleeves. "What can I do to help?"

Mom looks at the door to the kitchen. "Are you willing to peel potatoes?"

"Yes. Absolutely. Just point the way."

I don't think he's ever peeled a potato before, judging by how many times he peels his own fingers, but with everyone pitching in, we all sit down to mashed potatoes and canned gravy in no time.

After a quiet dinner where Everley glares at Baldwin the whole time, I offer to help Everley wash the dishes, so Baldwin can ask Mom his question without my little sister's interference.

Baldwin sounds less confident than he usually does when he scoots his chair closer to the table and admits, "Mrs. Everley, I have come to ask a favor."

Mom sighs and asks, "What can I help you with, Baldwin?"

Baldwin sounds a bit more confident as he tells Mom about his new job and opportunity to take a vacant city council seat when he turns 17 next week. Mom doesn't interrupt him until he says that he needs a permanent physical address in the city. She leans closer to him and asks, "Where are you living now?"

Baldwin looks at me. I nod at him encouragingly, so he says, "In the basement of the library."

Mom sounds surprised when she says, "That doesn't sound very comfortable or...legal." Her voice raises when she asks, "Are you asking to move in with us?"

Baldwin backpedals, "No. No, I just want to claim your address."

Mom scoffs, "What if they start spying on you? That tends to happen to people like us."

Baldwin holds up a hand to calm the coming storm. "If, and only if that happens, then I would request the option to rent a sleeping space once in a while..."

Mom doesn't answer for a minute. Everley and I finish the dishes and join them at the table. Mom looks at Everley and then at me. "What do you girls think? We've lived in the same place as Baldwin before. I'm just not sure it was a good thing in the past."

Everley shakes her head vehemently. "No. It was bad then, and it would be bad now."

Mom looks at me and asks, "What do you think, Dandra?"

I can see beads of sweat forming on Baldwin's forehead as I think about it. He hasn't been particularly warm or kind to me since our breakup.

I speak slowly and carefully, "I think Conrad won't like it if my ex-boyfriend ends up spending the night here." Baldwin's shoulders drop as my sister nods enthusiastically. I continue, "However, I think that if there is anyone who can turn this city around, it's Baldwin." My ex-boyfriend raises his head. I continue, "I think we should do what we can to give him this chance to change things around here. If that means he has to spend the night in Dad's old office on a cot once in a while, so be it."

Mom searches my eyes for a moment and then nods. "Now that you say that, I think you're right, Dandra." She turns to our nervous guest. "Baldwin, I wasn't your biggest fan when we were sharing a roof while you were Dandra's boyfriend, but when I think of you as a person, you remind me of my husband in many ways. You are smart and resourceful, and you are a doer. We don't have many people like that in Layland." Baldwin visibly exhales. Mom goes on, "Our address and the cot in the office are yours whenever you need them."

"Thank you so much, Mrs. Metty."

Mom holds up a hand to stop him from going on. "Please do your best to make our city a better place, and please be careful. You know how things ended for my husband."

Baldwin jumps to his feet, and we follow suit. He shakes my mom's hand enthusiastically and promises, "I will do my absolute best to make you proud, Mrs. Metty. Thank you so much for giving me this opportunity and thank you for taking care of me and my friends while we were in the United Cities. I will always regard you as the mother I never had."

Mom looks shocked as Baldwin hugs her and then hugs me and tries to get a hug out of Everley, but he only gets an awkward one-arm squeeze. Mom chuckles and says, "You better get out of here before Conrad gets here. Good luck, Baldwin."

He grins as he zips up his thin coat. "Thank you, Mrs. Metty. Good night!"

"Goodnight!" Mom says as she opens the front door.

Baldwin almost walks into Conrad as he's coming up the steps. Baldwin stops and grabs Conrad's arm. "Thank you for paying for my release. It means more to me than you'll ever know. I will start paying you back when I get my first paycheck. I look forward to working with you, Conrad."

Conrad looks at Baldwin curiously. "I look forward to working with you, too. See you around."

We all watch Baldwin practically dance down the street. He almost bumps into a black car parked across the street that I haven't seen before. His joy brings me joy. Conrad hands a plate of homemade cookies to me and asks suspiciously, "Why is he so happy?"

I smile and give him a quick peck on the lips. "He is going to be on the city council next week. This is his first chance to lead more than antigamers."

Conrad looks shocked. "Really?" He shakes his head in a dazed way and asks, "Why didn't I think of filling the city council seat?"

I take a bite of cookie and say, "You've been busy getting us out of the detainment center and making changes at the gaming district. Both jobs are important."

Conrad takes a cookie off the plate and stares at it. "Yeah, yeah, if you say so."

Mom puts a hand on Conrad's arm and says, "I just gave Baldwin permission to use our address on his city council application. I hope you understand why I would do that."

Conrad looks slightly confused but answers, "Yeah, I understand. Baldwin is homeless, but he wants to start doing respectable things. I get it."

I exhale slowly. "He does plenty of respectable things. You heard him at the academic assembly. He is a leader, and he needs a permanent address to get a leadership role at city hall."

Conrad glowers. "Okay, okay, I get it. Let's stop talking about him and have some dessert."

I give him a kiss and let Everley pull us into the kitchen.

Chapter 22

"DANDRA, DANDRA, WAKE UP! You forgot to set your alarm! We're going to be late for school!" My sister shakes my legs hard enough that I have to kick her away to protect my tender flesh.

"Get out! I'm changing!"

I jump up and change clothes at the speed of light and call through the door, "I'm sorry, Everley! Make me some toast to go. I'm almost ready!"

I cringe as I remember how muddy my shoes are on the front porch. It is going to take me several minutes to smack the mud off of them. Everley pulls me out the door so roughly that I almost step on my shoes. My shoes that are already clean and have a single pink flower laying across them.

I just stare at them for a second. Who did this? It reminds me of when Baldwin used to leave purple wild asters in a cup on the porch for me before we escaped the country. Did he do this? Yet this is a bigger, prettier flower that I don't recognize. It must have been Conrad. He is the sweetest!

Everley pulls on my coat. "I'll go put the flower in water. Grab your shoes; let's go, Dandra!"

I fling her hand off me and say, "Okay, okay. Hold your horses."

When I get to school, I almost make it to my first class before the bell rings. My math teacher shakes his head at me as he marks the role.

Conrad asks out the side of his mouth, "Why are you late?"

I pull my notebook out of my bag and answer, "I forgot to set my alarm. I slept in."

Conrad wrinkles his nose. "Oops."

"Yeah." I look at him curiously. Did he clean my shoes and leave the flower? I whisper so only he can hear, "Thank you for the gift you left last night."

"You're welcome." He reaches over and gives my hand a squeeze.

Mystery solved. I am so touched that I keep trying to steal glances with him in first and second hour, but he seems too preoccupied about getting to work to notice. He gives me a quick peck and leaves for work as soon as English is over.

I plop down in a desk next to Baldwin third hour. He is still on cloud nine about having a permanent address. We get our science experiment done quickly, so he leans over and inquires, "What's up?"

I shrug and say, "I don't know. So many mysterious things I wish I had the answers to."

Baldwin raises his eyebrows. "What mysterious things?"

I don't think he is the right person to spill my soul to right now, but I answer, "Things like who was in Cell C1, who cleaned my shoes, how am I going to pay all my loans off, stuff like that."

Baldwin looks at me sideways and says, "I don't have the answers to all your questions, but everyone knows who was in Cell C1. Do you really not know?"

The bell blares loudly, and Baldwin jumps up and grabs his stuff. "I'll tell you another time. I have to go. I have an important meeting right now. See you later."

"Just tell me!" I call, but Baldwin doesn't turn around.

I don't see him later; he doesn't even come to class. I wish he was here though. He knows who donated money for my mom and Everley's release. I have to know who the man in cell C1 is.

Chapter 23

"THIS IS SO NICE AND WARM, Jed. Thank you!"
I say as I pull on my new leather work coat. When I stick my
hands in the pockets, I find thick leather gloves in them. The
hardware store logo on the back makes us all look like official
employees. I am actually looking forward to cleaning and
painting at the Tifton City Monument today.

As we pile into the work truck, Jed stops Neil from sitting
next to me. "Neil, you sit in the front with me. I don't want you
squishing anyone in the back."

"Uh, okay, you're the boss," Neil says as he plops into the front seat.

The space to breathe and stretch is greatly appreciated as we head to our work site for the day.

I haven't been here much, but the Tifton City Monument is kind of a mini park with a giant stone in the middle displaying all the previous mayors' names on one side and a list of city awards given to citizens on the other side. I take a quick glance at the list as I wash the bird poop off the stone. One name jumps out at me. It's the second to last name on the list: "Gifford Metty—Community Service Organizer of the Year."

I wave my rag in the air to get my mom's attention. "Mom, look at this!" Mom walks over and reads the plaque.

Her face softens when she reads it. "I remember the day your dad received this. It was for organizing and teaching free night classes at the high level school in the evenings. I was pregnant with Everley."

It's been 10 years since someone has done something worth awarding in this city. So sad.

Gordon wanders over and says, "I can't believe they gave Zane Chesterton an award for opening the gaming district."

I look at the all too familiar last name on the list. Mom's eyes darken. "That was a monumental year. Everyone left the night classes and started gaming."

Jed interrupts our conversation. "Okay, I want Neil, Laurel, and Adamar to pick up trash. Here are your bags. Gordon,

Dandra, and I will paint the benches around the monument. Painting supplies are in the truck. Let's do this."

I'm glad Neil isn't painting, since he's so slow, but I kind of wish I could pick up trash. I don't want to get paint on my new work clothes.

I grab a paintbrush and join Gordon at the nearest bench. "How long do you think this cleanup is going to last?"

He picks crumpled paper out of the bench he's about to paint. "Days if we're lucky."

I slam my paint can down on the bench. "Then why are we bothering with this?"

Gordon frowns at me. "I don't care how long it lasts. A job is a job." He pauses and looks toward city hall. "Do you want Brock Hamble to sit on a shabby bench when he comes to talk with our country's leaders?"

I shrug. "How do you know it's Brock Hamble that we are prepping the city for?"

Gordon stands up taller. "Ed heard it from the mayor's lips himself."

"Really?"

"Yep." Gordon looks at the ground around us. "Honestly, I think the streets are staying clean longer the more days we do this."

I scoff, "It should be when you consider how much trash we pick up for this job plus our community service."

Gordon wrinkles his nose. "Yeah. Gotta love working without pay every Saturday morning."

I stop paying attention when I move to the next bench and accidentally drip paint on my shoes. "Oh no!"

Jed looks over at me. "What's the matter? Are you okay?"

I drop to the ground. "Yeah, I'm fine. I just dripped paint on my shoes."

My boss waves me off. "They're work shoes. It won't hurt them."

I frown as I try my best to remove the drip without smearing it bigger. "I—don't have any—actually, you're right. It won't hurt them."

It just doesn't feel right to tell your boss that you only have one pair of shoes.

Gordon, Jed, and I get the painting done before the trash collectors get the park clean. Jed hands the two of us water bottles from the back of the truck, and we relax for a few minutes. I drink mine so fast I spill on my shirt.

A tall, broad, official-looking man shows up in a silver car and approaches us as we enjoy our water break. "Excuse me, but I was told I could find Laurel Metty here."

Jed gets awfully close to the man and says, "What do you want with her? She is on the clock and doing a great service for the city at the moment."

The man holds up his hands and says, "I am on the city

council, and I just need to ask her a few questions about a person who wants to join the city council."

Jed looks at him for a second and then says, "Okay, you have five minutes."

My eyes don't leave Mom and the man for even a second. Their conversation is calm and relatively short. The man nods to us as he leaves. When he climbs into his car, an empty sandwich wrapper flies out onto our newly cleaned area. Gordon nudges Jed with his elbow and asks, "Do you think we'll have the whole city clean before the international meeting happens?"

Jed winces. "I hope so. That's what we've been hired to do."

Gordon grimaces as the sandwich wrapper flies into his chest. He crumples it up and says, "We may not have it ready. Why don't you hire more workers?

Jed throws his hands in the air. "We've tried. I've put advertisements up everywhere. I've personally gone to the gaming district and the mid level school to recruit. I've interviewed ten people, but none of them accepted the job once they knew what I expected. No one wants to do manual labor."

Gordon folds his arms in front of himself. "Oh."

Jed lowers his voice. "That's why I don't get rid of Neil. He isn't much, but he's better than nothing." He pulls something out of the truck. "Thanks for working so hard. Here's your pay for the day, you two."

I slip the stack of coins into my pocket, but Gordon counts

his and puts half of his coins in one pocket, and the other half of the coins in the other.

When we load into the truck, I ask Mom if everything is okay. She smiles and says, "Everything is fine." I notice that the back seat has a big box of crackers under the seat, and the front seat has a little box. A smile comes to my lips when I see evidence of how Jed feels about Neil.

Jed stops the truck in front of our house, so we don't have to walk as far, which I'm grateful for. I just hope Everley started some kind of dinner while we were gone.

We walk into a house full of giggles. Everley is playing a board game with Conrad at the table. My boyfriend looks up and says, "Hey, how was work?"

Mom takes my coins and disappears into her room to ration them for our various debt payments.

I stand a little straighter. "Good. I got a new work coat and gloves!"

Conrad looks confused at my excitement for a masculine leather coat, but then grins. "Nice."

I give a quick twirl, and then take my new coat off. "How was your day at work?"

Conrad lights up like a Christmas tree. "The mayor ordered 100 GroComs from us today!"

I put my coat away and ask, "What are GroComs?"

Conrad frowns and points to his wrist. "This is a GroCom. I've told you all about them more than once."

I feel my cheeks turn red. I kind of zone out every time Conrad talks about gaming devices. "Oh, right. What is the mayor going to do with them?"

Conrad takes out one of Everley's pieces on their gameboard. "If this first trial goes well, he's giving them to all city employees."

I wrinkle my nose. "I can't believe he wants to distract all of his employees with gaming devices."

Conrad looks at me incredulously. "They aren't gaming devices. Well, not really. There are only two boring games on them. They are communication devices. You can talk and send messages to anyone else who has a device. It's better than being tied down to a wired telephone."

"Oh, I see." I watch Conrad send a message on the tiny watch screen and insist, "I still think they will be distracting."

Conrad shrugs. "They could be, but it's worth a bit of distraction to know where your employees are with a quick call or message. It's the smartest move I've seen Mayor Monroe make to update our city."

I smirk as I think of how "modern" we are here compared to the United Cities, but even that country doesn't have GroComs. "Okay, okay. I kind of see what you mean." I smile as I think about someone in particular who will get a GroCom from the mayor.

Conrad raises an eyebrow. "What are you smiling about?"

I look at my fingernails. "Oh, I just know someone who

will be surprised to have to wear one of these as he mops the mayor's hallways."

Conrad's eyebrows come together. "Who?"

"Baldwin."

Chapter 24

THERE'S NOTHING LIKE WAKING UP early to do community service. I am thankful that my muscles are used to the labor, but I wish I could get a stack of coins to put in my pocket at the end of these shifts. This shift of community service is a bit more creative than it usually is. The mayor wants us to paint a mural of him over one of the most eyesore walls in the city—the side of the detainment center.

When I ask why a professional artist isn't doing this, the patrolman in charge says, "The only artist we could find said he would need a year to do it, and we don't have that kind of time.

The mayor said he'd settle for whatever cartoony version you guys can come up with, and if he doesn't like it, he's going to claim it's the President of Layland."

The anti-gamers and I literally bite our lips together to keep from laughing. There is no way this is going to look good, and considering who it's supposed to be, we aren't going to try very hard.

I volunteer to paint the background a sky-blue color, but Adamar wants the privilege of painting the man himself. I hold in a laugh when I see a few bulges strategically placed on our favorite man's frame.

Adamar takes longer than I think he should painting the mayor's pants black, but the closer I get to him, I realize he has painted the word "Fraud" into the black pants. You have to be standing at a certain angle and know it's there to see it.

Baldwin seems to be adding his own little message to the cuff of the mayor's black jacket, but I can't tell what it says before we're told we're done with the project.

As we clean up our painting supplies, I ask the patrolman in charge of us, "Do you think the mayor will claim this masterpiece as himself?"

The patrolman scrunches up his nose and says, "I doubt it." He looks at our sniggering faces, and says, "Load up your supplies and head to the city hall lavatories. You'll be cleaning those next."

We all groan, but reluctantly follow him inside to the lavatories.

I trade my paintbrush for a toilet scrub brush when I see that Baldwin has one and follow him into the men's lavatory. Everyone but Ed, Baldwin, and I go into the women's lavatory. As I scrub a particularly stinky toilet, I finally have a chance to talk to Baldwin about the mysterious cell C1 stranger. I lean around the stall and ask, "How did your meeting go?"

Baldwin pulls his shoulders back. "Great."

I flush the toilet to assess how much more scrubbing is needed and ask under the stall gap, "Are you ready to tell me who was in cell C1 now?"

Baldwin grabs a plunger and says, "Um, I'm not sure I am right now."

"Baldwin!" I grumble. "I convinced my mom to let you use our address."

Keeping me in suspense must be too much fun for him. "You're right. You know what, I will do one better than give you his name."

I narrow my eyes. "Okay...What does that mean?"

He stops plunging and leans around the stall. "I will arrange a face-to-face meeting with him."

I'm still annoyed that he won't just tell me the guy's name. "When?"

Baldwin slides his yellow bracelet down an inch to unstick it from his arm. "At my birthday party on Monday night."

"I have to work every day after school," I exclaim.

Baldwin flushes the toilet he's working on. "I know, but you're done and home by 8:00 pm usually."

I hold back my gag reflex as I wipe around the porcelain of my toilet. "That's a pretty late time to start a birthday party."

Baldwin passes me some cleaning wipes under the stall wall. "Not for working people like us. My party will start at 8:00 pm in the city council room at city hall."

"What?"

Baldwin lowers his voice. "Where were you expecting it to be? The locked basement of the library?"

I whisper back, "How did you arrange such an important meeting place?"

Baldwin gathers up his cleaning supplies and stands at the door of my stall. "I am going to be sworn in as a city council member at my party, so change out of your work clothes before you come."

My eyes pop. "You are?"

Baldwin puffs out his chest. "Yep."

I smirk, "Convenient timing."

Baldwin wipes the handle of my stall. "I'm nothing if I'm not efficient."

I look down at my current work clothes and cringe. I will have to dig to find something nice. "You are sure you can get cell C1 man to show up?" I stand up and stretch.

Baldwin squeezes my shoulder. "Yes. I am 100% positive."

I swerve away. "Watch it! You're covered in germs!"

He looks ashamed. "Oops, sorry."

I roll my eyes. "It's fine. Okay, I will be there. Happy almost birthday to you."

Baldwin squares his shoulders and gins. "This will be my most memorable birthday ever."

I should go straight to work after finishing my community service, but the library is so close by that I can't help but stop in for a new book before starting my second shift, my shift for pay this time. Zelma practically jumps out of her chair when she sees me come through the door. "Dandra! I was wondering when you would pay me a visit."

I feel so bad. "Sorry, I've been so busy going to school and trying to pay off my fines."

Zelma pats my hand. "That's quite all right. Did you find a job?"

I look around the atrium for anything interesting as I say, "Yes, I'm working at the hardware store."

Zelma giggles like a schoolgirl, "Oh! You sly girl, you! You are going after Jed, aren't you?"

I stare at my elderly friend in disbelief. "No, Zelma. I have a boyfriend."

The smile slides off her face. "Oh. Who is it?"

"Conrad Chesterton."

Zelma's eyebrows come together. "Oh, him. His dad and the mayor are going to shut this place down and put me out of a job by the end of the year. Did you know that?"

I wince at her sentiment. "I have heard rumors that go something like that."

"Dump him."

I glower at her, "I'm not just going to dump him for who his father is."

My librarian friend sneers, "He's no good for you or anyone else."

I retort, "Zelma, he's not like his dad. He's trying to fix some of the damage his dad has caused."

She folds her arms tightly in front of her. "Well, I hope he stops the library from closing. I feel like my days are numbered."

I reassure her, "I will talk to him about that."

Zelma offers me a mint from a small dish on her desk. "Do you want to know another thing?"

I take a mint. "Yes. What?"

She whispers, "When you fled the country, the weird noises in the library stopped."

I try to repress my grin. "Really?"

Zelma goes on, "Yep, and now that you're back, the weird noises are back, too."

I pop the mint into my mouth. "I can't believe it. You don't think I was the one causing the noises, do you?"

She eyes me curiously. "I'm starting to wonder."

I chuckle, "I can't promise you everything, but I can promise you that I was not the one making the mysterious noises in here."

Zelma pats my hand again. "I don't even mind because it's so great to have you back!"

I am tempted to tell Jed about Zelma's teasing, but his mom leads our shift today. Mom, Adamar, Neil, and I pick up litter and paint walls at a city equipment building near our house. Charlisa shows up to help just to be nice, which puts Adamar into a sunny mood. I am in a good mood too because a detective book from the library is waiting for me in my backpack when I'm done. As mom and I walk home, I see some kind of package sitting on the porch. I pick up my pace a bit and pick my jaw up off the ground when I find another mystery flower sitting on top of a pair of red dress shoes.

Chapter 25

MY HISTORY BOOK LESSON has a picture of the former President of Layland and his wife who is wearing yellow high heel shoes. Mondays at school are usually the worst, but this one is impossible to bear. All I can think about are my fancy new shoes. They remind me of the red dress shoes Conrad and I examined in a shoe store while we were in the United Cities. To this day, thinking about that moment, the moment Conrad kissed me to save me from being captured by Patrolman Darius' goons, gives me goosebumps.

The weird thing is that Conrad spent all his money getting

Baldwin and Adamar out of the detainment center. I wonder where he got those fancy shoes. Probably his mom's closet. I am okay with that. Last night he promised I could borrow some clothes to go to Baldwin's birthday party and swearing in. I wish Conrad would take me to the party in one of his dad's cars, but he can't go because his dad is demanding a meeting with him tonight. He didn't forget about me though; Milo dropped off some clothes and shoes for me this morning.

School and work are a blur because I can't think of anything but Baldwin's fancy party.

When Jed drops us employees off at the hardware store at 7:45 pm on Monday night, I rush into the lavatory to change into my dressy clothes. It's a relief to know I don't have to wear anything out of my own closet tonight. I slip on a ruffly red shirt Conrad gave me from his mom's closet and a black skirt to go with it. My new shoes look perfect with my outfit. I quickly twist my hair into a bun and wipe off the makeup smears from under my eyes.

Mom smiles at me and helps me secure my bun with hair pins. I give her a curious look. "Mom, why aren't you changing?"

"Um, I think I better go home to Everley. Is that okay? I hate how much time she spends home alone."

I'm slightly disappointed, but I don't let it show. "Yeah, that's fine." I give her my coins and a hug and watch her walk towards our house.

Gordon and Adamar clean up surprisingly well with their limited resources, and I'm grateful for their company as we walk to Baldwin's birthday party.

I can't help but look at my friends as we walk together. "Who cut your hair, Gordon?"

He shakes his now cornrow-free hair. "Marcella. She cut everyone's hair last night. B said we were all looking scruffy."

I grin at his use of Baldwin's old code name. "Well, you look nice, and so do you, Adamar."

They both mutter, "Thanks."

I look at the new and improved Adamar and ask, "Will Charlisa be joining us?"

He grins. "You bet she is. She says she's been waiting a long time for something like this to happen in this city."

My eyebrows come together. "I'm honestly amazed that the mayor didn't put a stop to it. He has no idea how much Baldwin will stir things up."

Gordon scoffs, "Oh, he tried to, but B knows the City Charter Rule Book better than Mayor Monroe and Zane Chesterton put together."

I grin. "I believe it."

The walk to city hall is quick yet chilly, but I feel important for the first time in a long time. Being invited to such a formal meeting when I see the mayor and the rest of the city council walk into the building before me makes me stand a little straighter and tuck my yellow bracelet under my sleeve. The mayor looks like he would much rather be home having a cold drink, but the rest of the city council look pleasant and content.

Baldwin is the perfect host as he greets everyone at the door, shaking hands and calling everyone by name. He looks nice with the beginnings of a goatee growing in and the remains of his blonde hair dye cut off and the fake tattoo removed from his neck. His navy-blue suit and black tie look relatively new. They probably came from a frugality store. His Christmas dress shoes go well with his suit. Other than the slight graying of his white shirt, he looks like he belongs with the rest of the city council. Why does he look older than his barely 17-years of age tonight? It's got to be the suit...

Charlisa meets us inside and latches on to Adamar's arm instantly. "I was worried you might not make it." She looks me up and down and says, "You look nice tonight, Dandra. I'm glad I'll have someone to sit by."

I nod as I look around the room. "I'm glad to have someone to sit by as well. I feel like a fish out of water." Charlisa weaves her fingers through Adamar's. It's too bad my boyfriend couldn't make it.

Gordon makes a beeline for Marcella and Ed, who both look great with new haircuts and dressy clothes on. I follow them while scoping out the room. Cell C1 man has to be around here somewhere. There are a couple of older, shabbier-dressed men in the room, and I'm pretty sure one of them is my guy.

A middle-aged city worker with stiff blonde curls and a

purple dress suit raps a mallet on the podium in the middle of the room. "Can I have your attention, please?" When the room quiets down, she says, "Would the mayor and the city council members please seat yourselves on the stand? Everyone else, please find a seat so we can begin."

Mayor Monroe looks like he would rather clean up dog poop in the city park, but he does follow the rest of the city council to the stand. The secretary waits for everyone to sit down before she continues, "The City of Tifton has been short one city council member for over six months. A candidate has come forward with a desire to fill the seat, and as per the City Charter Rule Book, we will fill that seat at last, tonight."

My friends and I clap enthusiastically. The mayor and one of the city council members barely put their hands together before they stop clapping. Mrs. Purple Dress says, "Would Baldwin Kole please come forward."

The door suddenly slams behind us, and before I can turn around, my least favorite person in the world marches to the front of the room to address Mrs. Purple Dress.

"Excuse me, Secretary Hansley, this swearing-in cannot take place because Baldwin Kole is a homeless teenager."

A few people in the audience gasp, but those who know Baldwin are not surprised to hear this accusation. Mrs. Purple Dress doesn't bat an eye. "Patrolman Darius, the city council has read and reread the city charter rule book, and it has been confirmed that anyone age 17 or older can take a seat that has been vacated for over 3 months."

Patrolman Darius bellows, "But that same rule in that same rulebook states that the person in question must have a permanent address. I know for a fact that Baldwin Kole is a squatter with no permanent address."

Mayor Monroe looks smug as more people gasp. Secretary Hansley holds up a hand to quiet everyone down. "Believe it or not, Patrolman Darius, but Mayor Monroe has voiced this same concern, and since Mr. Kole's application has a valid Tifton address, the owner of that house has been interviewed, and it has been confirmed that he lives there."

Patrolman Darius hisses, "He's friends with and a criminal accomplice to the Metty family; of course they'll lie for him!"

The big, tough-looking city council member stands up and points a finger at Patrolman Darius. "I interviewed Laurel Metty, the owner of the address in question, myself. Are you calling me incompetent?"

Patrolman Darius cowers slightly but doesn't back down. "I have spent years of my life tailing the Mettys and Baldwin Kole. I know their secrets better than anyone else on the planet. Did you know that Baldwin was found camping out in the basement of the library a few years ago?" A woman behind me gasps. Patrolman Darius smiles viciously and continues, "This swearing-in is a sham and cannot take place."

The city council member doesn't back down either. "We

have spent a solid week doing our due diligence to investigate, interview, and review the rules of the city charter. We have confirmed his permanent residence. Our findings are that no rules have been broken. If you don't like the rules, propose an amendment to the city council. Otherwise, sit down or get out."

Patrolman Darius stands in silence for a minute, but after a pointed look from the mayor sits down.

Secretary Hansley finds her composure again and picks up where she left off. "Would Baldwin Kole please come forward?"

Gordon, Ed, and I exhale as Baldwin stands up and walks to the stand obediently. She continues, "Place your left hand on the Layland City Charter Rule Book. Baldwin's hand is steady as he places it on the leatherbound book. "Raise your right hand and repeat after me. I, Baldwin Kole do promise to exercise the duties of the Tifton City Council honestly and faithfully. I will preserve, protect, and defend the Tifton City Charter and the citizens of Tifton and do so fairly, impartially, and to the best of my abilities...." Baldwin repeats everything the woman says, and then Secretary Hansley proclaims, "May I present to you the newest member of the Tifton City Council, Councilman Baldwin Kole!"

Everyone claps with varying levels of enthusiasm, except the mayor and Patrolman Darius. When the clatter quiets down, the secretary goes on to say, "We have chocolate cake in the back for refreshments. Please help yourselves to a piece while you mingle and express your congratulations to Mr.

Kole." Mayor Monroe and Patrolman Darius immediately stand up and leave without a backward glance.

I am starving, so I don't need telling twice. Ed and I grab the two biggest pieces of cake and retreat to a quiet corner to enjoy them. The chocolate frosting is rich and decadent. I don't think Baldwin provided this. It must have come from the city budget. Baldwin is good at saving a coin every chance he gets. I am awkwardly licking the last of the frosting from my fork when Baldwin takes my arm. "How do you think that went?"

I smirk, "Uh, honestly, pretty typical. Whenever you appear on a stage, Patrolman Darius is right there, too."

Baldwin laughs and looks around the room. "So true. I'm just glad it's over and official. It's been a long week." He waves to someone as they walk by.

I narrow my eyes. "How do you know everyone here?"

He grins and shakes his head. "I've had a personal interview with almost every person who works at city hall. Like I said, it's been a long week."

I nudge him with my elbow. "Good job, and happy birthday."

"Thank you." Baldwin looks around the room again and then leans forward, "So, I have a gift for you. I want to introduce you to someone."

I grin. "I was hoping you would say that." I place my fork and plate in a black bin and follow Baldwin willingly. I can't believe I'm finally going to find out who cell C1 is.

Baldwin takes me to the front of the room where an older man is eating a piece of cake with his back to us. He is one of the two men I was eyeing earlier. He looks as shabby as the rest of us yellow-bracelet wearers feel. Baldwin clears his throat and says, "Dandra, I would like to introduce you to Vern Craigstaff."

"What?" My strength leaves me, and I almost fall to the ground. Baldwin grabs my elbow and pulls me up.

The Vern Craigstaff I remember from before and even right after my dad's murder was 40 pounds heavier and didn't have a long gray beard like this man. This can't be the Vern Craigstaff who was always friendly—and drunk—the man who apologized profusely after almost bumping into me with his truck. As I scrutinize his face, I suddenly see the kindness I remember staring back at me through sad, wrinkled eyes. The detainment center was not good to him, and no wonder. He didn't murder my dad. He was innocent.

Chapter 26

I HIDE MY SHAKING HANDS behind my back. "Vern? Is that you?"

Vern's wrinkles pull upward into a smile. "Yes, little lady. It is."

Now that I'm listening closely, I can hear him behind the beard and the raspiness in this voice. "Why didn't you tell me it was you when we were locked up together?"

Vern looks down at his scruffy shoes and shakes his head. "You had just lost your father and were captured when you finally found a better place to live. That's too much for someone so young."

My eyebrows come together. "I wouldn't have asked you if I couldn't handle it."

Vern takes a deep breath and sighs, "I could hear you crying often in there, and I didn't want you or the rest of your family to feel worse because of me."

I look at Baldwin's self-assured face and say, "You knew it was Vern in that cell the whole time. Why didn't you tell me?"

Baldwin pauses before answering, "He asked me not to." He tilts his head to the side as I let that sink in, and then he walks away to talk to other people.

I think about the timing of Zane Chesterton being found guilty and our arrest. Vern should have been released at about the same time as when we got there.

I am curious. "Why didn't you go home sooner, Vern?"

Vern shrugs. "I didn't have anyone to go home to. I wanted to make sure your family could get out. You lost your dad, and I didn't want you to lose anyone else. I asked if I could stay a little longer to help pay off your debts."

I didn't know selflessness of this magnitude existed in Layland anymore. It takes me a moment to find my words. "I can't believe you chose that. I wouldn't have been able to endure it. I would have been so mad at everyone."

Vern wipes his mouth with a napkin. "Oh, I was angry at first, but it did nothing but poison me, so I gave it up."

The emotion running through my body overwhelms me. "Can I hug you?"

Vern smiles as brightly as he did years ago. "Sure, young lady."

I should probably let go after 10ish seconds, but I just hold on to his thin frame as long as I can. I turn toward his ear and say, "Thank you for helping my mom and sister get out."

He releases me and says, "You're welcome."

I feel so ashamed of when I stormed into the detainment center and told Vern off. "And thank you for not hating me when I accused you of killing my dad."

Vern's hand shakes as he puts it in his pocket. "I hoped that truth would prevail, but I wasn't sure if it would, considering who framed me." He looks down at his feet. "I learned a lot about myself in that cell, and I decided that I would be at peace with whatever happened, either way."

I shake my head. "You should have left as soon as Zane Chesterton was sentenced."

Vern nods. "I almost did, but I was having good talks with Mr. Yesterly each day as we fixed furniture, and I was almost dried out from my alcohol addiction, so I decided to stay a little bit longer just to be sure it was behind me. I don't want that ruling my life anymore."

I do not expect to hear this. "Did it work? Are you sober?"

Vern nods proudly. "Yes, I am, young lady. I've been over six months without a single drop of alcohol."

I clap him on the back. "That's great, Vern."

He leans back on his heels. "Yep. You know, I don't think I could have done it without being forced to go without it, so in a way, I'm kind of thankful I was falsely accused." Vern looks around the room warily and whispers, "Don't tell anyone I said that."

I grin. "Don't worry. I won't." I look at Vern's scruffy clothes and ask, "Did your job take you back when you got out?"

Vern nods. "Yes, I'm back working at the dump, and I have Baldwin and all his friends checking in on me and teaching me how to do other things with my time. You know, rather than... drink."

I hadn't thought about how awkward it would be for him to fill empty hours without a bottle in his hand. "Vern, my family owes you so much. Please call the Mettys your friends, too."

Vern grins. "You always have been, little lady, and you always will be. The truth would never have come to light without your help."

I give him one more hug. "I am so thankful for your kindness to my family, and I'm glad your name is cleared." I smile to myself as I realize that Vern's addiction is nothing but dust now.

Chapter 27

AT SCHOOL, I FILL CONRAD IN about everything he missed at Baldwin's party while writing an essay by hand. He seems particularly interested in when Patrolman Darius made his entrance and exit.

He takes the bag of clothes I borrowed back and says, "You can keep these, you know."

I shake my head. "I couldn't. I probably won't be invited to another fancy party for a long time."

Conrad frowns at me and says, "Yes, you will. I will take

you to a dinner party tonight." He hands the bag back. "You'll need these. I'll pick you up at 8:15."

I lean closer to him as the teacher walks toward us. "Where is the dinner party at?"

Conrad whispers, "My uncle Ty's house."

I sit up straighter. "Ty? The uncle who helped pay for my release?"

"Yep."

My eyebrows come together. "I do want to thank him. Okay, I'll go."

Conrad smiles at me. "Perfect. It's a date."

The bell rings, and he gives me a quick peck on the lips as he heads to work.

I try to imagine what Ty's dinner party will be like as I eat my lunch. Baldwin looks at the crust I ripped off my sandwich and asks, "Are you going to eat that?"

I shake my head. He stuffs the pile of crust into his mouth with an arm that has a GroCom wrapped around it. My jaw drops.

I point at it. "I cannot believe my eyes, Baldwin."

He rolls his eyes at me. "I don't have a choice. The mayor himself gave it to me a couple days ago and wouldn't leave me alone until I put it on."

I grin and yell at his watch, "Hello, Mayor Monroe! How are you today?"

Baldwin scowls at me and puts a finger to his lips. "I've

asked around and taken it apart. I don't think this model is listening in on me. I need to ask Conrad and his engineers some questions, but it appears that the button has to be pushed in to transmit any sound to anywhere else. That is the only reason why it is on my wrist right now."

I raise my eyebrows. "Is it helpful at work?"

Baldwin tilts his head. "Actually, it is. Don't tell any gamers I told you, but it saved the city hall janitors at least an hour of time yesterday afternoon since we could talk to each other from all three floors of the building."

I shake my head skeptically. "If you say so. Your secret is safe with me."

Chapter 28

MY OUTFIT LOOKS JUST AS NICE the second time I put it on. I have a few more minutes to spike out my hair and put on a fresh coat of makeup this time though. I like the way Conrad's eyes light up when I open the door. "Wow! You look amazing!"

I blush. "Thank you."

He touches a flowy red sleeve and asks, "You wore this last night, too?"

I look down at my fancy red shoes. "Yep."

My boyfriend shakes his head. "I should have been there."

I nod. "You really should have. Let's go."

Everley blocks our way to the door. "You two look kind of like twins with your hair spiked out."

Conrad smiles at her. "Which color of spikey hair do you like better? Blonde or black?"

She looks at me briefly and then lights up when she looks at him. "Black spikes are way better!"

Conrad laughs and gives her a hug. "If you help your mom tonight, I'll bring you a treat from the party."

She grins. "Okay! Don't forget!" Everley watches us out the window as Conrad helps me into the car.

I check out the leather seats and ask, "Whose car is this? Milo's?"

Conrad checks twice before pulling out. "No, it's mine."

I frown. "Yours? When did you get it?"

He shrugs. "Milo bought a brand-new limited-edition sedan when he was in charge of the business without Dad's permission. Dad got mad and said the new car would be for himself when he gets out, and he said I could have this one."

I cringe as Conrad slams on the brakes. "When did you get your driver's license?"

Conrad's knuckles are white on the steering wheel. "Uh, last week."

I am intrigued. We always walk everywhere at my house because gas is expensive. "What did you have to do? I haven't even looked into it because we don't have any money right now."

Conrad shrugs. "So, I just showed up to one of the city buildings, and Patrolman Darius took my picture and came back with this." He points to a red card dangling from his rearview mirror.

I take the red card with Conrad's picture and the city of Tifton insignia on it and examine it. "I thought it took study and tests to get one of these."

Conrad bites his lip. "I think it usually does, but my dad has, you know, connections."

I drop the red card like it's hot. "Oh."

Conrad's driving proves that the usual study and tests are important. We almost get in a wreck no less than four times as he takes us out of the city to a big house on the outskirts of town. My whole body relaxes as he stops the car and opens my door. "Welcome to Uncle Ty's house."

I find my smile. "Thank you."

Uncle Ty greets us at the door. "Welcome to our little gathering, Dandra and Conrad!"

I look around at the tables of food and walls of people. Little gathering? I smile and say, "Thank you for inviting us."

Ty takes my hand and says, "I would do far more for my favorite of the United Nine."

I smile sheepishly "Thank you so much for helping me get released. I'm working hard to get you repaid."

"Don't worry about it. I know you are good on your word. Relax. Get some food and enjoy the party."

Conrad whispers in my ear as we walk away, "I told you he thinks you're a celebrity."

I snort, "He's the only one." I feel silly as I realize that I don't recognize any of the food that is being served. Conrad looks at my indecision and starts loading up a plate. "Here, Dandra. I think you'll like these." I take the plate gratefully. He loads up a second plate for himself and leads me to a table.

We sit down next to a fancy couple. "Hello, Conrad. Who is your lovely date?"

Conrad puffs out his chest. "Hello, Felix. This is my girlfriend, Dandra."

Zane Chesterton's business partner reaches out and shakes my hand. "Oh, that's right. I recognize you now. I guess I assumed the United Nine might be on different paths by now."

Conrad forces a smile. "Well, we are in many ways, but Dandra has always been my best friend, and she is more than that now."

"Oh, isn't that sweet?" Felix's female partner says. She takes my hand. "I've heard about you, Dandra. I don't care what anyone else says, I think you are a strong and impressive young woman. I'm Felix's wife, Adele Houston."

My eyes dart from Conrad's mortified face back to Adele's. What do I say? "Um, thank you. It's nice to meet you, Adele."

Felix immediately starts talking about GroComs with

Conrad, and he isn't done talking after I've eaten all my food and had a couple of awkward conversations with Adele about shoes and clothes. The look on her face makes me think she knows that I have no experience with fashion. I finally excuse myself to use the lavatory.

The lavatory is bigger than the first floor of my house. I am afraid of leaving smudges on the marble floors and vanity. I'm about to leave when a couple barges through the door, glued to each other's lips, spilling champagne as they go. I jump out of the way. The man pulls away briefly and looks at me. "Oh, Dandra. I was hoping to bump into you again." It's Uncle Ty. What am I doing here?

I practically sprint back to the table with Conrad and Felix. Conrad squeezes my hand and whispers, "I missed you."

I squeeze his hand back and am about to tell him about Ty's drunken escapades, but Felix suddenly stands up and pulls Conrad out of his seat. "If you are so sure it's working, prove it to me. Let's go count the devices. I'll count GameComs. You count GroComs. Let's go." Felix turns to his wife and says, "This is important. Keep Conrad's girlfriend company for an hour."

An hour? Conrad's eyes are apologetic as he's dragged away. I slump into my seat as Adele starts telling me about her favorite purse designer. This is going to be a long night.

Chapter 29

CONRAD APOLOGIZES OVER AND OVER again over the next few days at school. I think he knows how awkward I felt and how I don't really fit in with that crowd. He says he has late meetings, so I won't see him after school for a while. It takes several days to convince him that I'm fine, but really, I hope Conrad doesn't expect me to do that again. I would rather dust the library without pay than sit through another dinner party like that. Conrad was wanted and needed by almost everyone there, but I felt like less than a zero.

He was super sweet when he dropped me off, but when he

brought up going on another date, I told him it'll have to wait. Obviously, I need time for homework and Everley.

After Conrad fails to stop by seven days in a row, I know it's because of his meetings, but I sort of worry that my lack of desire for another date has discouraged him from visiting me all together. I want to be around him, but I don't want to be around his family and business partner.

Male visitors keep arriving though. Baldwin stops by once in a while when he thinks Patrolman Darius is following him. Patrolman Mark even starts stopping by late in the evening.

Knock, knock. I open the door and grin as a gigantic vase of flowers greets me. I can't see who is carrying them until I dodge out of the way. "Oh, come on in, Mark."

Patrolman Mark grins at me. "Thanks, Dandra. Is your mom here?"

I force a smile on my face. "Yep. She's in the kitchen making dinner."

Mom is cute as she takes the flowers and gives Mark a quick hug while eyeing Everley and me. This is going to be a long night.

I turn to Everley and whisper, "Hey, do you want to play spies after dinner? We haven't done anything fun together in a long time."

Everley lights up. "Yes!" She runs to Dad's old office and brings back a pair of binoculars. "I'm ready when you are!"

I grin at her enthusiasm. "We have to eat with Mom

and Mark, but if we're quick, we could be on our way in 12 minutes."

"Deal!"

I'm not sure who is more uncomfortable as we eat our rice and gravy around the table, me, Mom, or Patrolman Mark. Everley shovels her food in her mouth without stopping for breath, but I try to eat quickly yet respectfully.

Mom tears her eyes away from Mark when I say, "I want to show Everley the buildings we've painted recently at work. Is that okay, Mom?"

Mom hesitates. "Yeah, sure. Don't stay out too late though."

I push my chair away from the table. "We won't. Should we wash the dishes?"

Mark clears his throat. "No, I'll do the dishes. You girls go have fun." He pulls a few coins out of his pocket. "Get yourselves a treat while you're out."

Everley and I jump out of our seats excitedly. Everley snatches the coins and says, "Thank you, Patrolman Mark!"

He grins. "You're welcome. Have a fun time, girls." His eyes immediately go back to my mom's blushing face.

We don't need telling twice. Everley and I grab our coats, a flashlight, the binoculars, and are out the door. Relieved that I don't have to watch my mom have an awkward date, I ask, "So, sis. Who do you want to spy on? You pick one place, and I'll pick another one."

Everley rubs the coins together in her hand as she thinks. She turns to me and says, "I want to spy on Conrad."

I stop walking. "Uh, are you sure? He comes over a lot. You can spy on him from our house."

Everley rolls her eyes. "He used to come over a lot. I want to know why he isn't coming over much anymore."

I sigh as I feel that same thing. "Okay, but I don't want him to see us. That would be awkward."

Everley shrugs. "Okay, we will be sneaky. Who do you want to spy on?"

I am curious about the looks I saw Patrolman Darius and Mayor Monroe sharing at Baldwin's party. So, my decision is easy. "I want to spy on city hall."

Everley sneers, "You don't want to spy on Baldwin, do you?"

I hold up my hands. "No, I don't care what Baldwin is up to. I want to know what Patrolman Darius is up to."

Everley shoves the flashlight at me. "Fine. Can we get ice cream afterwards?"

I shine the light into her eyes. "Yes."

Everley forgives me for blinding her and tells me all the options for spending our coins and why ice cream is the best choice as we walk to Conrad's house. When we arrive, we squat down in the bushes to watch the door and big front window like the spies we are supposed to be. The porch swing creaks as the wind blows it.

I remember all the times I've seen Conrad on that swing smiling at me as he sees me walking down the street. Conrad is not in the swing of course, but I'm pretty sure I see him and Milo through the window having a heated discussion. I rip Everley's binoculars off her eyes to confirm that I am right.

"Hey!" she complains. I ignore her as I wonder what the fight is about. We sink down as Conrad storms out of the house and zooms out of the driveway in his car in the direction of the detainment center.

Everley looks at me and says, "I think Conrad is having a bad day."

I nod my head absently. "Yeah, I think you're right, sis."

She jumps up, steals back the binoculars and says, "Well, we've spied on my place, now let's spy on your place and then get ice cream."

I grin and follow my sister's lead to city hall. I am shocked to see so many cars there this late at night. We squat down behind one of the cars parked on the side of the road, so we have a good view of the lit-up city council window. I pull the binoculars off my sister's neck and look at the room full of people.

"Hey! Stop taking those!" she exclaims again. I push her hands away as I see that Mayor Monroe is there with Patrolman Darius by his side. All of the city council members, including Baldwin, are there. Secretary Hansley is there, and for some reason, they are all looking at their GroComs nervously, even Baldwin. What are they all so nervous about?

Everley suddenly pulls on my arm and says, "We need to move. There is a weird car coming down the street, and the driver can see us."

I follow my sister to a more discreet location behind some large garbage cans and hope that my eyes don't pop out of my head as a limousine flying two green and gold Layland flags on its front antennae pulls up to the city building followed by two other big black cars. Who could this be?

The front doors of city hall swing open, and Mayor Monroe approaches the back door of the limousine. The door opens and Mayor Monroe greets the bald, middle-aged man who steps out. "Welcome to Tifton, President Penn!"

Chapter 30

JED IS MORE ON-EDGE than I've ever seen him. The international convention is tomorrow, and the city isn't as clean as it should be after a month of non-stop cleaning and painting. The water tower is almost completely painted, but we all need a break. I purposefully splash some of my water on my face and hands, hoping to clean my painted skin up a bit. Gordon and Adamar lay down on a clean patch of grass and look up at the water tower. Adamar smacks Gordon on the shoulder and says, "I vote that you do the last bit of ladder work."

Gordon snarls, "What are you going to do?"

Adamar looks up. "Paint 'Tifton' in red across the tank."

Gordon smirks, "Won't you need a ladder to do that?"

Adamar shakes his head and smiles. "No. I'll be on the lift."

Gordon rolls his eyes. "Whatever."

Jed keeps looking at his watch and the movement of the sun in the sky. "Break's over. Let's get back to work."

Neil whines, "What? That wasn't even 20 minutes. I need a rest."

Jed frowns at him and says, "You can rest tomorrow after the international convention starts."

I look at all the litter still blowing down the streets and ask, "What are we going to do about the litter that is dropped in the next 24 hours?"

Jed runs his hands through his hair. "Can any of you skip school tomorrow? I will pay you double if you can work the whole day. If any of you have friends who are willing to skip school to pick up litter all day, I'll pay them extra, too."

I hate to skip school, but I could really use double pay. Mom looks at me enthusiastically and says, "We should bring Everley. She could work circles around Neil, and we need the money."

Adamar exclaims, "My girlfriend could probably come, and probably a couple of my friends can make it as well."

Jed looks relieved. "Perfect. The more the merrier tomorrow. We can't get every piece of litter, but we'll do the best we possibly can."

I look at Adamar's smiling face and think to myself: if Charlisa is going to come, maybe I should ask Conrad to come, too. I sure miss him.

Conrad is more than happy to skip school in the morning to pick up trash with me. I giggle to myself as I watch him in his fancy work clothes picking up wrappers and rotting food off the road like the rest of us. We try to top each other in finding the grossest garbage. He thinks no one can top his black banana peel, but I win when I find a couple of rotten eggs in a tub of moldy yogurt. It's fun to laugh and steal glances at each other again. My only competition for his attention is Everley. She's never more than an arm's length away from him. I warn her not to mention us spying on him, and she keeps her promise.

Beep. Beep. "What is that sound?" I ask an hour into our shift.

Conrad frowns as he looks at his GroCom. "It's an emergency message from work." He shakes his head and closes his eyes. He opens them and looks right at me. "I have to take care of something right now in order to present an idea at the international convention tomorrow. Will you forgive me if I leave?"

I feel my shoulders droop, but I give him a hug and reassure him, "Of course. You don't get to talk to Brock Hamble

189

every day of the week, do you? I'll see you soon." He gives me a kiss and runs to the black company car that arrives to pick him up.

Jed watches our parting and then walks up to me as soon as Conrad disappears. "I didn't get the chance to pay him."

I am still staring at where I last saw my boyfriend. "I don't think he cares. He just wants to help."

Jed looks at me and then at Everley who is working like a girl on a mission. "I'll give his share to your sister then. They seem to have a close bond."

I smile as I look at my sister. Everley is not thrilled to be skipping spelling test day at school, but Mom promised her cookies and time with Conrad if she helped pick up trash today. She has been an exceptionally hard worker so far.

I grin. "Yeah, give it to Everley."

"Okay." He notices Neil wasting time and whistles loudly to bring us together. He points down the road. "The most important areas to have litter-free are the park, the Tifton Elite Hotel, Tifton City Hall, and the roads connecting all three things. Anything else besides that is a bonus." We all nod. He continues, "Let's focus in and get to work." With our augmented crew, the three important properties are done before lunch.

As I pull my sack lunch out of the truck, I ask Jed, "Why didn't we paint the trims and signs at the library? It's a city-owned building."

Jed frowns at me and says, "The work order said to clean and paint all city properties except that one."

I glare at my lunch sack. "But why? It looks horrible compared to everything else, now."

Jed slams the truck door shut and says, "I have no idea."

After a quick sandwich and juice break, we clean the roads from the hotel to the park. When we get to the park, I am disgusted with how messy it is already. I just cleaned this place up. A group of four patrolmen are having a late lunch at a picnic table when we get there. I don't pay much attention to them and start filling yet another yellow bag with trash.

A deep, hateful voice interrupts my reverie. "I'm so sorry to interrupt your yellow bracelet, I mean yellow bag filling, but I accidentally spilled vinegar from my lunch all over this picnic table. The paint is peeling off, and it looks horrible."

Patrolman Darius smiles as he points to the picnic table he and his cronies have just vacated. There is trash all over it and the ground around it, and the newly painted surface is bubbled and coming off in big chunks. I ask through gritted teeth, "What do you want me to do about it?"

He smells like vinegar, and his voice sounds just as bitter as he says, "I know your supposed hero Brock Hamble will be landing his helicopter right here in a few hours. I just don't want his first glance of Layland to be that picnic table. You've worked way too hard to have a bad first impression. You might want to fix that up. Have a good day." Patrolman Darius turns around and walks away with his fellow cronies laughing beside him.

I'm about to run after him and give him a piece of my mind when Adamar and Charlisa hold me back. Charlisa cautions, "He wants a reaction from you. Don't give it to him."

I fume, "He can't treat people, especially people of his own country, like this."

Adamar waves off the retreating patrolmen. "He's just angry that Baldwin is on the city council and is about to talk to Brock Hamble. We need to do our part to make sure it happens. Stay focused. I'll repaint the table."

I shake their hands off me. "Okay, okay. I get it."

Chapter 31

THE SUN IS SETTING as I wipe my dirty hands on my pants. The park and the picnic table look good as new, and just in time. Everley grabs my hand and gapes at the helicopter about to land in the open meadow of the city park. This is the exact spot where Baldwin took me stargazing forever ago.

The man who emerges from the aircraft is as tall, fair, and handsome as ever. I hope he is here to bring us good news. I smile and wave at the man who makes things happen in the United Cities: Brock Hamble.

He has two bodyguards glued to his side as he approaches

his welcoming committee: Mayor Monroe, President Penn, Baldwin, Secretary Hansley, and several other fancily dressed people whom I assume are the mayors of neighboring cities. I want to run up to Brock Hamble and say hello, but Jed shakes his head at me as I gravitate toward the helicopter.

Jed gathers all of us employees, temporary or otherwise, around him and says, "We have done the job the city hired us to do. Are these streets ever going to be perfect? No, but this is the most respectable I have ever seen Tifton look in my entire life." I nod my head in agreement. The city looks so much better. We all clap and cheer.

Jed goes on, "The City of Tifton doesn't want us interfering with this important meeting, so everyone can go home early and rest up." Adamar claps loudly to that. Jed continues, "I couldn't have asked for a better crew today, so thank you. Thank you so much for the time and sacrifice you made to be here today." He turns his head to the left then looks at us. "I can see my mom on her way over here to pay everyone. For you regular employees, we have lots of stocking and inventory waiting at the hardware store tomorrow if you would like to keep working for us. Good work, everyone." We all clap again and then form a line to get our double pay from Sharry.

Everley is all smiles when she pockets her big stack of coins. Mom gives me a look because Everley isn't going to get to keep more than a coin of it. She has a fine to pay off, too.

194

Mom takes Everley's hand and starts moving in the direction of our house, but I stop them. "Is it okay if I go to city hall and listen in?"

Mom's eyebrows come together. "No, Dandra. You heard Jed. We do not need any more trouble. You can wait a day or two for Baldwin to tell you all about it himself."

I frown, but relent, "Fine." As we walk, I keep thinking about the group of people who met the helicopter. I turn to Mom and admit, "I'm kind of surprised that Baldwin is the only city council member walking into that meeting."

Mom looks back at all the dignitaries walking toward city hall. "I'm not." When I give her a curious look, she explains, "I don't think the mayor wants him there, but I bet Brock Hamble requested him by name."

Everley and I are just finishing the dinner dishes when we hear a knock at the door. "Conrad!" my sister exclaims as she runs to the door. I can hear her tone change from the kitchen sink. "Oh, you. What are you doing here?"

I hear the door shut and Baldwin laughing humorlessly, "I have someone tailing me today, so I'm going to have to rent a room for a bit."

Mom says, "That's fine. Make yourself at home."

I hurry into the living room and ask, "Who? Who is tailing you? Is it Patrolman Darius?"

Mom gives me an exasperated look. "Let him sit down."

I shrug. "Sorry. Please sit down, Baldwin. Everley, will you get him a drink?"

She growls at me but obeys.

Baldwin takes the glass of water from Everley gratefully and drinks the whole thing down. "No, it's not Zane or Darius. Not directly anyway. It's the mayor's doing. During our meeting tonight, he made a condescending remark that went something like, 'homeless pretenders should have no authority to speak during this meeting.' The President of Layland reprimanded him about his remark, which I'm sure made him feel foolish then Brock Hamble suggested that if my respectability is really being called into question, it would be easy enough to resolve it by having me followed home for the remainder of the week. So, here I am."

I smirk. "So, we should be blaming Brock Hamble for this."

Baldwin taps his fingers on his knee. "No. Blame is not the right word. He told the council of leaders that he saw and heard great things from me while I was presenting at the academic assembly in the United Cities, and that my words triggered his desire to take down the border wall between the two countries."

I narrow my eyes at him. "But now you're being followed."

Baldwin shrugs. "He was just trying to take the doubt Mayor Monroe was spouting out of the equation."

My nose wrinkles. "Well, I hope it works."

Baldwin looks around the room. "I think it will. I just wish I had packed a bag. Is the cot in the office still an option?"

Mom nods and elbows me. I stand up and look at the office door. "Yeah. I'll go set it up right now. If you're hungry, there's leftover soup in the fridge."

His eyes light up. "I am actually starving. I'll take you up on that."

As I watch Baldwin scarf down two bowls of soup and several slices of bread and butter, I ask, "Does the city pay their janitors much?"

Baldwin nods. "Yeah, they pay just fine. I'm just paying off my debt to the detainment center and Conrad, and I've had to upgrade my wardrobe, so I'm broke. I usually eat one meal a day."

I feel for him, but we're not doing much better. I swallow my pity and say, "The cot is set up for you."

"Thanks."

Ring, ring. Everley answers the phone, "Hello?" She looks at me and mouths the name Conrad at me. "She's right here. See you soon."

I take the phone and say, "Hello?"

Conrad's voice sounds stressed. "Hey, I planned to come over tonight, but my dad and mom are acting like they are getting a divorce right now, so I'm going to stay and play peacemaker. Is that okay?"

My face droops. "Yeah, absolutely. I'm sorry to hear that."

Conrad sighs, "It'll be fine. They do this every week lately, but I'm sure it will blow over."

I feel for Conrad. "Okay. I miss you. Will I see you at school tomorrow?"

"Yeah."

I pause. "Okay. See you then."

"Bye."

"Bye."

Baldwin eyes me curiously. "Is everything okay?"

I shrug. "Um, I guess things are a bit tense in the Chesterton cell tonight."

Baldwin grins. "I'm sure Zane hates being locked away while the international convention is going on."

I rub my hands on my legs. "Do you think the wall will come down?"

Baldwin fidgets with a napkin. "Uh, not the whole wall. That was decided today for sure." He stands up and puts his dishes in the sink and washes them.

I follow him into the living room, saddened that the border wall discussion isn't continuing. "What are they going to talk about tomorrow?"

He plops down onto the couch. "Whether to create an entry point between the countries or not."

I sit on the opposite side of the couch and hope he'll keep talking. "What does the President of Layland want?"

Baldwin rubs his eyes with his hands. "President Penn thinks things are fine as they are. He's not completely against the idea, but he is refusing to provide any money for the construction of an entry point."

I think about the size of both countries and frown. "One entry point is all they are willing to consider? We need more than one!"

He nods. "We do, but one is a big first step, and if it happens, it'll be easier to build more entry points later."

I worry suddenly that nothing will happen from this meeting. "What do you think Brock Hamble will do if President Penn refuses to help?"

Baldwin shrugs. "He'll bring the information back to the president of his country, but more than likely, President Murrey won't endorse doing all the work and paying the whole cost."

I frown. "So, it probably won't happen."

Baldwin pauses before answering, "Well, not until Brock Hamble wins the United Cities Presidential election..."

Everley sits next to me and lays her head on my shoulder. She asks, "When is the election?"

"Next month."

I feel hopeful again. "He needs to win."

Baldwin yawns, "I agree. That could change everything. I also have some ideas on how to convince the current presidents to get the project started." Baldwin looks longingly toward the office door. "It's been a long day. I think I'm going to turn in for the night." He stands up and yawns again.

I stand up and pull Everley up with me. Mom takes Everley's hand and guides her to the stairs. I look at my ex-boyfriend as he opens the office door. "Thanks for filling us in. Good night."

He smiles at me and yawns. "No problem. Good night."

Chapter 32

I WAKE UP BEFORE EVERLEY for once. I couldn't sleep last night, and I want to skip school and peek through the windows at city hall at the international convention so badly. Mom will kill me if I do it. I'm also wondering if I should make Baldwin breakfast. It feels like he's a guest—but he's not. He's a paying renter. So, what does that mean foodwise? I should probably talk to Mom and him about that. I prepare a speech about food expectations, but I don't get to give it.

Baldwin is already gone when I enter the kitchen. I ask my

sister who is making designs with her oatmeal, "Did Baldwin eat before he left?"

"No. He said he never eats breakfast, then he left."

I'm not sure if I feel shame or gratitude, but I'm glad I don't have to give my food speech. I pack a quick lunch and choke some of my favorite food, oatmeal, down in record time. "Let's get to school, sis."

As I walk out the door, I see another pink flower on my shoes—the shoes that used to have a paint stain on them, but the paint stain has been scrubbed off. "Everley, when did Baldwin leave this morning?"

"An hour ago."

I pick up the flower and examine it. "Was he acting funny?'

"Yes."

I sit next to Conrad in math class, but my eyes are on the back of Baldwin's head. I lean over and ask, "Conrad, how are your parents?"

He yawns, "They're fine. They worked it out."

I smile at him. "I'm glad. Are you coming over tonight after work?"

He sighs, "I wish I could, but I'm going to have to fire some people tonight as they get off work."

My eyebrows come together. "Why?"

Conrad whispers, "They are stealing money from the Gaming District."

I whisper back, "Are you sure?"

He nods. "I'm positive. Someone told me about it, and then I witnessed it myself."

My nose wrinkles. "That's rough. Good luck."

Work is such a change now that we're at the hardware store. I'm not complaining. I've filled enough yellow garbage bags to last a lifetime. Mom and I have stocked shelves, watered plants, and are now doing inventory on everything the store sells. I'm using my brains instead of my hands, and it is kind of nice. Jed seems much less stressed, too. He even cracks a joke when we're counting the levels on the shelf. "How does a level stay calm?"

I give him a sideways look. "I don't know."

"It keeps a balanced perspective."

I grin and shake my head. "Of course."

After work, I wait on pins and needles for Baldwin to arrive. I want to know how the international convention went today. I also want to see if Baldwin acts funny around me. I'm really starting to wonder if he is the one leaving the flowers instead of Conrad. Does he still have feelings for me?

Knock knock. Everley flies to the front door. "Conrad!"

I yell, "Conrad isn't coming over tonight, sis."

She growls, "Oh, it's you again."

Baldwin patiently answers, "It's nice to see you, too, Everley," He looks at Mom and admits, "I need to rent the cot again."

Mom nods. "I figured you would. Make yourself at home."

I hope I don't look too eager as I welcome Baldwin and lead him to the kitchen table. "Are you hungry? I made hot ham and cheese sandwiches."

He grins. "Thank you. I'm starving."

I watch Baldwin scarf down two sandwiches before I ask, "Did Brock Hamble leave tonight?"

Baldwin points to the ceiling and listens for a second. "Yep. He's flying over our heads right now." I can hear the rumble of a helicopter faintly.

I tap my fingers on the table impatiently. "So, how did it go?"

Baldwin shrugs. "Well, not a lot was set in motion, but talks are the first step."

I slump into my chair. "Nothing is going to happen, is it?"

Baldwin winks at me. "I wouldn't say that. I just think Brock Hamble wants this more than anyone with power in Layland wants it, and he can only do so much right now. He can't be hasty, or he'll lose the presidential election on his side of the border."

I shake my head. "Ugh. What a waste."

Baldwin sits forward. "No. This meeting was huge. Our countries haven't talked like this since the border wall went up."

I sigh, "I was so hopeful that Brock would waltz in and take down the wall."

He sits back in his chair. "Unfortunately, Mayor Monroe asked Patrolman Darius to show up today and give testimony on how we all escaped. Those two kind of set the tone for the Layland side of the conversation."

I bury my head in my arms. "Oh no. What did President Penn do after that?"

Baldwin shrugs. "He voiced his concerns about our countrymen leaving in droves if we create an entry point, but Brock Hamble handed out his plans for border security which includes sliding steel doors, guards at night, and an interview process by guards during the day. He wants the first phase of opening the border to be giving citizens of either country day passes, the second phase to be week passes, and the third to be month passes. He said that at that point, people might want to change their citizenship to the other country, and more discussion on that will need to be decided, but that is years down the road."

I imagine getting to spend a month with Shasta and Ernestine and getting to visit Mr. Bronson at Casswell's. "I love that idea. Too bad no one else did."

Baldwin shrugs. "I think visiting passes did intrigue some of the mayors, but no one wants to pay for the infrastructure it would take to make it or enforce it. I did get to talk to Brock one-on-one for a while before he left though."

That brings a smile to my face. "What did he say?"

Baldwin sits up taller. "He said I should keep an eye on Mayor Monroe. He thinks he has too much influence on President Penn, and he doesn't trust the mayor's alliance with Patrolman Darius."

I give him a sardonic smile. "Well, an outsider wouldn't know that they are both on Zane Chesterton's payroll."

Baldwin nods. "Zane can't do anything himself from the detainment center, but he can get those two to do his bidding. I just need to catch them in the act."

I look at him sideways. "What will that do?"

Baldwin grins. "The general opinion of Mayor Monroe is actually not good. If I can catch him doing something illegal, the people won't reelect him and maybe even demand his resignation." Baldwin takes a drink of water. "I'm going to meet with Patrolman Mark tomorrow to see if he will help me.

Mom comes into the kitchen dressed in a nice outfit with fresh hair and makeup. She takes a deep sniff of her newest flower bouquet. I roll my eyes. "You will probably get a chance to talk to him tonight."

Baldwin watches Mom leave the kitchen and smirks. "I don't want to interfere with their date."

I scowl. "It's not a date. They just talk."

Baldwin shrugs. "If you say so." He grins, and that makes me grin, too.

I'm sure Patrolman Mark will help, and I can imagine Ed and Baldwin listening in on conversations as they mop floors and empty garbage cans at city hall tomorrow. If Mayor Monroe does anything out of line, they'll catch him. I give Baldwin an encouraging smile. "It sounds like your job at city hall just got more demanding."

Chapter 33

SLEEP TRIES TO STEAL ME AWAY as I soak my legs in the tub after a long morning of community service. *Knock, knock.* "Dandra, do you have time to take me to the library today? I want to get a book or two since I'm bored after school every single day."

The image of my sister sitting on the couch by herself looking through the window, waiting for us to come home from work breaks my heart. "Give me one second." I hurry out of the tub and get dressed. Everley is waiting by the lavatory door when I open it. "Come here, sis." Everley follows me into my room and sits on the edge of my bed. I wrap her in my arms. "I—uh, I'm sorry, Everley. I need to spend more time with you, and I think we should definitely go to the library together."

Everley disentangles herself from my arms and jumps to her feet. "Yay!"

I take Everley on a circuitous route to the library. I stop at every city property that we have cleaned and painted, so she can see that Mom and I are doing good things for the city while we're away from her. She laughs out loud when she sees the painting of Mayor Monroe. She points to his sleeve and asks, "Who wrote 'Mercenary' on his sleeve?"

I have to tilt my head and stand closer to see it, but there it is, our mayor being called out, and he hasn't even done anything about it. I chuckle, "It was Baldwin."

Everley raises her eyebrows. "Baldwin did that? Hmm. Do you think he would help me write secret words into my art homework?"

I smile at her. "You should ask him. He would probably like that."

As we walk down Main Street, I see Jed setting up a display of garden seeds through the hardware store window. He sees me and waves. I wave back. It's funny to watch someone so muscular be so gentle with tiny, little seed packets.

Everley pulls my arm in the opposite direction. "Oh no! Dandra! Look!"

My head swings around to see what my sister has spotted across the street. There are boards on all the library windows, and a big sign that says, "Library Permanently Closed from Lack of Use."

Agatha and Zelma are sitting on the front steps sobbing. I rush to them and throw my hands in the air. "When did this happen?"

Agatha whimpers, "This morning. I got a call from the mayor last night telling me to meet him here."

Zelma nods. "I got a call from him, too."

Agatha continues, "When we got here, the windows were already boarded up, and the mayor was standing by the front door with this sign. He said we had five minutes to gather our things before he locked the doors forever."

I think about all the books that will never see the light of day again, and then I think about the people secretly living in the basement. "Were there lights and heat on when you went in there?"

Zelma kicks her box of belongings. "No. All power has been shut off. The library is finished."

I thought they had until winter before this was going

to happen. Is this early closure a coincidence? Was it the international convention that spurred this? Or maybe the mayor saw the words on the paintings after all.

I hug my librarian friends and then wander around the building to see if all the windows are really boarded up. It appears that the worker assigned to do the job was scared to climb a ladder more than two stories tall, so the top windows are still visible. It will keep kids from breaking the reachable windows at least.

I notice that the board over the basement window that the antigamers use as a door is sitting loosely in place. The screws have been taken out.

I think the crypt is still in use but just got ice cold.

Chapter 34

EVERLEY IS SURPRISINGLY KIND to Baldwin at dinner. She even gives him the last slice of bread. Mom puts a hand on his arm as he eats. "Should I take the truck to the library and bring your friends and all their stuff here?"

Baldwin glares at his soup and fidgets with his napkin. "No. We've talked about it. They want to sleep there tonight to see how bad it is without lights and heat." I shake my head at the unnecessary suffering. He continues, "I don't want them to come here. I'm still being followed, and if they join me here, I'm sure Patrolman Darius and Mayor Monroe will find some way of bringing up my legitimacy of staying here to the city council."

I wonder out loud, "Do you think Patrolman Darius did this?"

Baldwin sighs, "Maybe, but I'm leaning toward Mayor Monroe."

"Why?"

Baldwin's eyebrows come together. "The mayor is treating me differently lately. Closing the library feels personal." Baldwin pauses before going on. "The antigamers agree with me. They're keeping their distance from me while we're being watched."

I think of how depressing sitting in complete darkness and the cold cement floors must feel for hours on end. I insist, "Our friends can't stay in a dark basement, Baldwin. Where else can they go?"

Baldwin's knee bounces as he thinks. "I'm going to ask Vern Craigstaff if they can stay with him for a while, but we should probably start saving up for a place of our own."

I watch helplessly all weekend as Baldwin calls apartment buildings. There aren't many vacancies, and the ones that do have an open unit are way too expensive. I touch his hand gently. "I wish I could help, but we're barely paying our fines and bills."

"I know." He runs his hands through his hair in frustration. "Letting me stay here is the best thing you can do right now. I've made a few friends on the city council and at city hall, and more importantly, I know everyone who hates the mayor in that building. Things are about to get messy."

Conrad finally gets some time off and comes over for dinner and card games. I greet him at the door with a kiss. He hugs me like it's been a month since he's seen me. The bag of pastries he brings for dessert gets squished in the process. "Sorry I'm late. Our maid quit this week, so I had to do a week's worth of laundry and dishes on my day off."

Baldwin rolls his eyes as he looks through the newspaper's apartment ads from the couch. I almost say that I had to do the same thing on my day off, but I don't want to make him feel worse. "Well, I'm sure you'll find another maid, and if not. I know plenty of people looking for jobs."

Conrad gives me a sad smile. "I wish I could hire you or your mom, but I asked my dad about it yesterday, and he gave me a firm no."

I shrug. "It's fine. The hardware store is working out

great," I lie as I lead everyone to the kitchen for yet another thin potato soup. At least the dessert will be good.

Baldwin is silent and gruff as we eat dinner and play a round of Sevens, my favorite card game. I try not to let his frustrations affect my night with Conrad.

As we settle into the softer seats in the living room, Baldwin suddenly gets talkative. "I assume you heard that Mayor Monroe permanently closed down the library this week. Did your dad have anything to do with that?"

Conrad looks at his GroCom warily and says, "I don't know for sure, but I don't think so."

Baldwin's voice gets more aggressive. "I know you and your dad are patching up your relationship and everything, but don't delude yourself. He still has Patrolman Darius and Mayor Monroe in the palm of his hand, and they are trying to stop everything Brock Hamble and I are trying to do."

Conrad's nostrils flare. "I'm not an idiot. I know what he is. I just wish you knew that I'm not him and would actually trust me."

Baldwin shakes his head. "I'm trying to. I just know that the mayor is insisting that I wear one of those spy devices on my arm, and suddenly the library closes, and we are out of a home."

Conrad holds up his watch. "GroComs are not spy devices. I can show you the blueprints and take one apart with you if you want."

Baldwin raises his eyebrows. "I've already done that, but I'd like to do it again, just to be sure."

Conrad scowls, "Fine. Meet me in my office at the Gaming District tomorrow at 8:00 pm."

Baldwin throws the paper down. "Fine."

I close my eyes and take deep breaths. Will these two ever get along? I hope their little meeting fixes their rift. I'm losing yet another night with my boyfriend, and I hope it's worth it.

Chapter 35

BALDWIN HAS LEFT for school before Everley and I have finished breakfast every day that he's stayed with us so far. I wonder what he does that early.

Everley glares at me as we walk out the door. "I don't like how Baldwin makes Conrad act when they are both at our house."

I give her a knowing look. "I don't like it either..." I stop midsentence because there is another rare pink flower sitting on my shoes.

Everley picks it up and walks it into the house to replace

the dying one in the vase on the kitchen table. It is becoming a routine for her to do that as I lace up my shoes on the porch.

I purposely sit by Marcella in math class. "How are you?"

She rolls her eyes. "How do you think?"

I squeeze her arm. "I don't care what Baldwin says; you are always welcome to stay at my house."

She looks at the back of Baldwin's head at the front of the classroom and says, "Sleeping in the cold dark basement for a night *was* the worst, but I don't want to ruin things for B."

My eyebrows come together. "*Was* the worst? Where did you sleep last night?"

She gives me a sideways look. "At Vern Craigstaff's house."

I nod. "The library basement must have been frigid. You guys made a good choice."

Marcella frowns. "Oh, it was, but that wasn't the worst part That's not why we left."

The teacher is walking toward us. I wait until he leaves to whisper, "What was the worst part?"

She leans toward me. "Patrolman Darius was waiting by the entrance to the crypt last night. He asked what we were doing at a permanently closed city building late at night."

My jaw drops. "No way."

Marcella yawns, "Yeah. We had to lie and say we were just

passing through. We walked to Vern's house, but left Ed to keep checking for when Patrolman Darius left. He didn't leave. He sat there all night."

I shake my head. "He totally knows then."

Marcella nods. "Yep. At least we have Vern. He only has two bedrooms, so I got the couch. It'll be fine for now, at least it's warm."

I look at her slightly disheveled appearance. "Do you have any of your belongings?"

She wrinkles her nose. "We have what was on our backs last night, and Ed is there now sneaking out more of our clothes."

I whisper, "Seriously, stay with me."

Marcella smiles at Gordon and then whispers, "No. It will be fine. We are saving for a place of our own. We did it in the United Cities; we can do it here."

I raise my eyebrows. "Baldwin says that everything available is too expensive."

Marcella shrugs. "Yeah, it's true, but there are cheaper places available in a couple of months. We can last that long."

Chapter 36

IT'S A ROUGH FEW WEEKS for the antigamers. I
wish I could do more, but we're all struggling to make it by.
Baldwin is still being followed, so he has to keep sleeping on the
cot in the office. Conrad is barely tolerating the arrangements.
He isn't coming over much, and he insists that I visit him at
his house instead. I finally take him up on it when I realize that
there isn't enough bread and meat for all four of us, and we can't
buy more groceries until we've paid the next fine installment.

Conrad is happier than I've seen him in weeks as he pulls
a sizzling pan of pork chops out of the oven. Milo cheers as the

cream on the fancy pink drink he's making holds up the cherry he places on top. I feel like a queen as I look at my plate covered in mushroom salad, rice pilaf, and a glazed pork chop. "I didn't know you two could cook like this."

Milo laughs. "I make a pretty mean strawberry quencher, but our new maid Lexis made everything else."

"Is there anything else you two need before I go?" A pretty blonde girl maybe a year or two older than me asks as she peeks in the kitchen door.

Milo smiles at her. "I think this fabulous dinner is all we need. Have a great night, Lexis."

She smiles and waves goodbye, "You too, sir."

Milo grins as he turns back to his pork chop. "Lexis is definitely an improvement from Gertrude in more ways than one, but I wish she wouldn't call me, sir."

I watch Conrad's face as he watches Lexis walk past the window. He thinks she's pretty, too. I'm sure of it. I narrow my eyes at my pork chop. "Who hired her?"

Conrad pauses before taking a bite of salad. "Uh, I did." He suddenly stands up and turns on the television on the kitchen wall.

My eyebrows come together. "Since when do you watch TV during dinner?"

Conrad shushes me as he flips to the local news station. The news anchors on the television screen seem like they've had too much coffee. "This just in: Brock Hamble has won the

United Cities Presidential election by a 51% majority. It doesn't get any closer than that, folks."

My jaw drops. "How did you know their election was today?"

Conrad cuts into his pork chop. "Baldwin told me."

I push my plate away. "Since when are you and Baldwin close?"

Conrad shrugs. "Since we started caring about opening the border to the United Cities."

I take a sip of my fancy drink while watching Conrad's uncomfortable face. "Are you referring to your meeting to take apart a GroCom?"

Conrad offers me more salad. "Um, yeah."

I frown when I realize Conrad is not at school. I want to talk to him about a thing or two. Baldwin is more than happy to sit next to me, though. He leans close to me once the teacher stops teaching. "So, good news. Did you watch the news last night?"

I scribble a picture on the corner of my paper. "As a matter of fact, I did."

Baldwin grins. "It was so close, and I knew it would be, but he made it."

I smile back. "I'm glad he won."

Baldwin leans closer. "Me, too. I have more good news. One of the city's junior bookkeepers quit yesterday." He finishes a math problem in his notebook as he continues, "Apparently the mayor asked him to fudge the numbers on how much it costs to heat the library."

The thought of the boarded-up library makes my nose flare. "Which part of that is good?"

Baldwin looks at me like I'm dense. "Two parts of that are good and one part is bad. I'll miss Trevor, he was a good, honest bookkeeper, but I'm glad there is an opening."

I roll my eyes. "What makes you think that Mayor Monroe will give you the job?"

Baldwin shrugs. "He won't be in favor of it, but he doesn't do all the hiring at the city, and I just so happen to be friends with the person who does."

I turn toward him. "Isn't that a full-time job? You still have school during the day."

He grins at me. "They have both full-time and part-time bookkeepers. I am going to apply for a part-time position."

I smirk at his excitement. "Okay, maybe it will work out, but what is the last bit of good news?"

Baldwin raises both wrists and flaunts their nakedness at me. "We have more than Patrolman Mark as a witness to Mayor Monroe's corruption now."

I grab his bare wrist and demand, "How did you get your yellow bracelet off?"

He grins suspiciously. "My fine is paid in full, obviously."

I jolt back in my chair. "What? Who paid it?"

"Conrad."

My chest starts heaving as I look at my own bracelet. "Why would he do that for you before he does it for me?"

His eyes soften as he sees the confusion in my face. "I—uh, we made a deal."

Chapter 37

I GO STRAIGHT from the hardware store to the Gaming District after work. Conrad is in a meeting when I get there, which irritates me. His secretary offers me a drink while I wait for him. I take the cherry soda gratefully, but why is this secretary so pretty? Does Conrad only hire pretty females? My irritation grows.

I hear his laughing voice before I see him exit his office door. "Thanks, Mayor. I will have another 100 units delivered to you in two days."

My face is still as stone as Mayor Monroe's sneering face

walks past me. I remain a statue until the door clicks behind him. Conrad moves a stray strand of hair behind my ear. "Are you okay, Dandra? Come into my office."

I am a robot as I follow him into his office. As soon as the door clicks behind us, I explode, "What is going on? Why are you friendly with the mayor?"

He puts a hand on my shoulder. "Dandra, I know that seemed suspicious, but I have to play nice with him if I want him to listen to me."

I scowl, "Okay, whatever. But why did you pay for Baldwin?—" I point to my yellow bracelet.

His face falls. "I meant to tell you before he did."

My eyebrows come together. "So why didn't you?"

He sighs. "You don't have a GroCom, or I would have this morning."

I look him straight in the eye. "Or you could have shown up to school and told me."

He holds up a hand. "I had no choice this morning. I have been in critically important meetings all day."

I slump into my chair. "Fine. You couldn't get out of your meetings. Why did you pay Baldwin's fines?"

Conrad twists his hands hesitantly. "He is trying to get a better job at the city..."

I growl, "Yeah, so? You want him to have a better chance at getting the job? Have you considered that Mom and I are in the same boat? We would like to get respectable jobs too, but our yellow bracelets are holding us back, just as much."

Conrad runs his hand through his hair. "Dandra, I am working on that as fast as I can."

I shout, "Then why did you..."

He interrupts me. "Dandra, he offered me a deal I couldn't refuse."

I can't believe our tight little United Nine have come to this. Why are they making deals behind my back? I look into my boyfriend's eyes as I ask, "Did that deal have anything to do with me?"

Conrad looks down at his hands. "Well...yes."

Chapter 38

I SPEND THE REST OF THE NIGHT in my room. I have no words for anyone, especially not Baldwin.

The next morning Everley and I get ready together as usual, but there is no flower on my shoes when I slip them on.

Conrad is in class, but he sits as close to the door as he can, and his eyes never leave his GroCom.

I guess I left him with no questions about how I feel last night.

I'm fine with the silence. I slide into a seat next to Marcella and pull out my notebook. The silence doesn't last. "I got the job! I am officially a bookkeeper instead of a janitor. I wanted to tell you last night, but you never left your room!" Baldwin exclaims.

I keep my eyes on the teacher, but I say out the corner of my mouth, "I had a headache. Congratulations, Baldwin."

He grins. "I finally feel like my luck is changing."

I pause before asking, "Does your deal with Conrad have anything to do with your luck changing?"

He looks startled. "Uh, maybe. This isn't the time to talk about that."

I roll my eyes. "Fine. Does this new job mean you'll be wearing more suits?"

He grins. "Yeah, probably. I need to make a friend at the frugality store."

The hardware store is slow today. Mom hands me a broom and asks, "Dandra, are you doing okay?"

I shrug. "Yeah."

She pulls out a dust rag and starts attacking the nearest shelf. "Are you happy for Baldwin and his new job?"

I keep my eyes to the floor as I sweep. "Yeah. It's great news."

Mom stops and squeezes my arm. "What's the matter?"

I flick the dirt pile with the broom with more force than I should. "Nothing...and everything."

Mom takes my broom. "What do you mean by that?"

I take Mom's dust rag and start dusting the shelves, doing what I always end up doing. "I am just watching Baldwin and Conrad get more and more responsibility and leadership."

Jed walks over to us and hands us cold water bottles. Mom thanks him and takes a drink. She looks at me. "Are you happy for them?"

I smile and nod as I take a water bottle from Jed. "Yes. I'm very happy for both of them. I just feel left out sometimes."

Mom starts sweeping. "That happens. It's pretty natural."

I throw the dust rag on the shelf and say, "I don't want to be jealous or petty. I want them to have these opportunities, but I kind of wish I wasn't picking up trash all day and hearing about their awesomeness each night."

Mom gives me a knowing look. "I feel the exact same way." She sweeps the dirt into a dustpan. She elbows me and says, "I just keep hoping that since Baldwin and Conrad's respectability is moving up that the rest of us are gaining respectability as well."

I sigh, "I hope so."

Mom squeezes my shoulder. "Is that everything?"

I think about it for a minute. "No."

Mom puts her arm around me. "What else is bothering you?"

I try to put my swarm of thoughts and feelings into a sentence. "I'm so busy and surrounded by so many good people and good projects, but I just feel lonely."

Chapter 39

I KEEP HOPING that my loneliness will change, but it doesn't. It actually gets worse. Conrad has late meetings almost every night. Baldwin is trying so hard to learn his new job that he is staying late every night too. I have no idea what is going on anymore.

At least I have my sister. She still likes me for some reason.

We trudge to school but stop as soon as we hear something overhead. The helicopter flying over the border wall toward the city park is not like the one Brock Hamble arrived in last time. This one is twice as large and twice as flashy. This is how the president of a country arrives.

We take the long route to school just so we can watch Brock Hamble and his bodyguards walk to city hall. A black limousine is already parked outside the city building.

Baldwin is going to be so excited.

Baldwin actually gets in trouble in both of our morning classes today because he keeps talking while the teacher is talking. I keep putting a finger to my lips to cue him on how loud he's being.

Conrad risks my wrath and sits by me during English. "I feel like I haven't talked to you in forever. Are you okay, Dandra?"

"I'm fine."

He leans closer. "You don't seem fine."

I turn and look at him. "If you would come over once in a while, you'd probably understand why."

He sighs, "I'm sorry. I'll come over tonight. I'll even bring beefy patties."

I shrug. "That will make Everley's day."

He whispers in my ear, "Will it make yours?"

I see the yearning in his eyes and say, "Um, maybe."

Both Conrad and Baldwin leave after second hour and don't come back.

Conrad is good on his word. He brings double the food we need, and he doesn't leave my side. I love holding his hand and stealing glances with him.

My boyfriend's focus changes a bit once Baldwin comes home, though. I mean, I get it. We all want to know what Brock Hamble came to say.

I shove a beefy patty into Baldwin's hands and ask, "So, is President Brock Hamble ready and willing to build an entry point in the border wall?"

Baldwin takes a bite and mutters, "Yes."

I clap enthusiastically. "I saw the helicopter and the limousine this morning. Has the president of Layland changed his mind? Will he donate money or workers to the cause?"

Baldwin takes another big bite. "No."

I should be patient, but we all want to know, "Is Brock Hamble willing to do the whole thing himself?"

Baldwin swallows and takes a drink. He narrows his eyes as he thinks. "I think he personally would, but the rest of his country doesn't agree. They voted on it, and the result is that the United Cities will only agree to the entry point if both countries contribute equally to it."

I sit back in my chair. "Oh, no."

Baldwin sighs, "Yeah."

Conrad looks at Baldwin sideways. "You are a bookkeeper. Is there any money to spare from the city budget?"

Baldwin shakes his head. "Not much."

Chapter 40

THE NEXT DAY IN MATH CLASS, Conrad is absent again, and Baldwin gets his assignment done in literally five minutes. I guess being a bookkeeper is a good job for him. I can't figure out the problem I'm working on. I'm too distracted. I throw my pencil down. "I think we should give up on the border wall entry point idea. It's not going to happen."

Baldwin narrows his eyes at me. "I can't, and I won't give up on it."

I pick up my pencil again and sigh, "Well, what can be done about it if our country refuses to donate any money?"

Baldwin shrugs. "President Penn said he was fine with an entry point in the border wall as long as he didn't have to pay for it. Brock Hamble and I think there are ways to fundraise without angering the powers that be."

I look around the room at all of our broke friends and ask, "How?"

"Gaming tournaments."

I shake my head. "No. Anything but that."

Baldwin leans closer to me. "I don't like gaming any more than you do, but there are more gamers in this country than antigamers, so I think we need to find a way to get the gamers to contribute to our cause."

I look at a kid sitting across from me poking at his GameCom instead of doing his homework. Baldwin suddenly makes so much sense. "I hate it, but I like it."

Baldwin leans back in his seat and stretches. "I think I'm going to talk to Milo to get his ideas on what people will pay to play."

When Baldwin gets home from work, I still haven't seen Conrad today. I hope he's all right. I scrape the last of our fried potatoes onto a plate for Baldwin and sit down to talk to him while he eats. He isn't quite as ravenous as usual. Maybe the bookkeepers get fed at work more than the janitors do.

Baldwin finishes his food slowly and then looks at me. "Dandra, I have an idea. What if we organize a volunteer work force?"

I look at him skeptically. "Well, I am sure the United Nine would be more than willing to volunteer, but nine people can't do it all."

Baldwin takes a drink of water and sets down his cup. "You're right. Brock Hamble says if we can provide 40 workers from 8-5 for four months straight, and—a million coins, he'll provide the rest."

The wheels in my head start turning. I'm sure I can recruit every friend we have to the cause, but that would only be half the workers we need, and it would require us all to quit school or quit our day jobs. I'd be willing to quit my day job and work all night to get this accomplished, but I'm not everyone. And even if I could find that many people, how do we come up with a million coins? Conrad is the richest person I know, but with his current paychecks, it would still take him over five years to come up with that much money to give.

I throw my hands in the air. "It's impossible, Baldwin. We can't find that many people, and I don't know anyone with that much money."

He taps the table with irritation. "Don't give up before we've even started! Things are changing. I'm seeing more people in the parks now that they are clean. I have seen people

243

show up to community events more than I ever have in my lifetime. I believe in miracles. Do you?"

I look down at my scruffy work clothes and say, "I don't know."

Baldwin lifts my chin with his finger and looks me in the eye. "I want to make you a deal."

I cringe. "No way. I'm tired of you and your deals."

He looks genuinely hurt. "How have my deals ever hurt you?"

I pound my finger into the kitchen table. "I'm not making a deal with you until you tell me what your last deal with Conrad was."

He avoids my eyes. "I don't know what you are talking about. We are working together a lot these days."

I scowl, "You know which deal I'm talking about. It's the one where he paid to take your yellow bracelet off."

Baldwin doesn't look happy. "That deal hasn't hurt you; I promise."

I fold my arms. "Tell me, or I'm not agreeing to anything."

Baldwin rolls his eyes. "Okay, fine." He sighs, "I told Conrad that if he paid my remaining fine, I would pay him back as soon as I can, and I would promise to never think of you romantically ever again."

I feel taken aback. "That was your deal?"

Baldwin nods. "Yes, and then he made me promise to find you a job at the city as soon as possible."

I sit back in my chair. "That was worth 5,000 coins to him."

"Apparently."

I close my eyes and pause before asking, "Why don't I get a say in my own relationships?"

Baldwin looks amused. "You do, but I just gave away my chance at getting back with you again." He looks at me for a minute before continuing. "Conrad didn't like the idea of me staying in the same house as you, and it didn't seem like I had a chance to get back with you anyway, so I thought, why not try and calm his mind and get something I want out of it."

I try not to feel like a commodity to trade with as I say, "I'm glad you got what you wanted out of the deal." I swallow and then growl, "What deal do you want to make with me?"

Baldwin finds his confident voice again. "I think we can make the entry point happen even if the mayor and the President of Layland don't want to pay for it. It will take a ton of work though. I am willing to work for it, and I think you are, too. This is my deal. I'll start raising funds for the entry point, and you start finding volunteers."

I quickly add how many hours it would take 40 people a day to donate. I shake my head. "No one, not even me with my detainment center debt can give five days a week to a service project."

Baldwin puts his hand on mine. "I don't expect you to. I

think I can convince the detainment center to count working on the border entry as the community service we still owe."

I shrug. "That would help, but it's still not enough. I could give one day a week, maybe two, but that's all." I wave my hands around the kitchen. "We still have to eat and pay our debts at this house."

Baldwin nods. "That's all I'm asking. See if you can find people who want access to the United Cities to donate one or two days a week. I'm hoping to start this project June 1st, so three out of the four months will be summer break."

I forgot about summer break. I could donate more time during the break. I could still even give one or two days when school is in session. The question is, how many more people can I get to join me?

I shrug. "I'm catching your vision, Baldwin. I think it's possible, but it won't be easy."

He smiles and sits back in his chair. "Nothing worth fighting for ever is."

One thing I know for sure, he's decided I'm not worth fighting for.

Chapter 41

CONRAD PLOPS DOWN IN A SEAT next to me in math class. I whisper out the corner of my mouth, "You didn't come over last night."

"Yeah, I know. I meant to, but the second round of the international convention got my dad all stirred up, and he wouldn't let me leave the detainment center until midnight."

I think back to the deal he made with Baldwin. "So, Baldwin has made our relationship very business-like lately."

Conrad lights up. "Really? Does he have a job for you?"

I shrug. "Uh, sort of. He wants me to recruit volunteers to work on the entry point in the border wall."

He looks at his GroCom distractedly. "Huh, that's great." The teacher frowns at us and decides to finish his lesson from right next to us. I guess our conversation is over.

English isn't much better. Conrad rushes through his assignment and then types a long message into his GroCom. I try to get his attention, but his eyes never leave his wrist. I look at my own wrist with its yellow bracelet and sigh.

Work is a blur. Mom keeps asking me if I'm okay. Jed keeps offering me drinks and snacks. I appreciate their kindness, but I don't think I'll have peace of mind until I have a heart-to-heart talk with Conrad.

As soon as we clock out, Mom heads home to Everley, and I head to the Gaming District.

I knock gently on my boyfriend's office door. "Hey, Conrad. Do you have a minute?"

He looks up from the papers on his desk and smiles. "Uh, just a minute, unfortunately. I've got an important meeting in five."

I look around at his fancy office and all the devices sitting on shelves hoping to become the next GameCom. "Conrad, I am so proud of you."

He blushes with the compliment. "Thank you. Sit down and have some chocolate."

I take a shiny wrapped chocolate out of the velvety box he offers me. I wait until he's looking me in the eye and proclaim, "You have stood up to your dad even when you've had so much to lose, and you've done more good than your dad could ever dream of."

He stacks the papers on his desk into a neat pile and says, "Thanks. I'm not sure my dad agrees, but I appreciate it."

I look around the office and say, "Conrad, this company needs you."

He looks at me curiously. "Yes..."

I set the chocolate on his desk. "The city of Tifton needs you."

He looks at the chocolate suspiciously. "Okay..."

I point to the calendar on his wall filled to the brim with appointments written in bright colors. "The entire gaming community of Layland needs you."

He tilts his head as he looks at me. "I guess you're right."

"But I need you, too." Conrad finally gets where I'm going with this.

He jumps up from his chair and sits next to me instead. "I can cut out some meetings and turn some things over to other people. Don't say anything else, Dandra. You are more important than all of this."

I give him half a smile. "I love you for saying that, but the truth is, I'm not. I'm just an average girl who needs an average boy with an average amount of time to be there for me." I hold up a hand as he tries to interrupt me. "I know I could demand more time with you, and you would give it. I've been tempted to demand it, but I don't think that is the right thing to do."

He frowns and takes my hand. "Dandra, don't..."

I pause and look into his chocolatey brown eyes and say the hardest thing I've ever said. "I think I need to give you back your time, so you can do what the rest of us can't. You can change this country. I can't."

"Don't say that. You are my inspiration. You make me want to be the best I can be."

I give him a peck on the cheek and say, "I am giving you your time back."

He blurts out, "I don't want my time back! I want you! Do you have any idea what I've done to be able to have you to myself?"

His reference to his and Baldwin's deal sickens me. I push my repulsion down. "I know you mean well, Conrad." I inhale and exhale slowly. "Keep working on communication devices for our country. Make them affordable and less distracting. Maybe when the border wall opens, you can sell your GroComs in the United Cities." Conrad's head tilts sideways as he hears me say this. I continue, "Give generously to the border wall entry point so that can happen. This is what I want."

He visibly droops. "But I want you."

I shake my head. "You can't have it all, Conrad. Your work is more important right now. It's more important than me. It's more important than us."

He takes my hand. "I'll miss you."

I squeeze his hand. "I'm not going anywhere. You know where to find me."

His voice gets hard. "Are you going back to Baldwin? I knew sleepovers were a bad idea. I did everything I could to keep you two from getting back together. He gave me his word—"

I interrupt, "No. I am not going back to him. You both will always be part of my heart, but he has important work to do, too. I don't want to distract him, just like I don't want to distract you."

Conrad's eyes are despairing. "Dandra, you deserve a protector, someone who will make your life better. You've never had a fair life. You deserve more."

I shrug. "I'm just an average girl who wants an average life. If I'm in trouble, I know you have my back, but most importantly, the work you and Baldwin are doing will make my life and the lives of all the citizens of Layland better. Who knows what the future holds, but for the next five years, Layland needs you."

Conrad grabs my shoulders and looks me in the eye. "I'm going to hold you to that. Five years from now, we'll revisit this."

I stand up and give him a hug. "Okay. See you around, Conrad."

His eyes sink to the floor. "See you, Dandra."

Chapter 42

ENGLISH CLASS IS AWKWARD with Conrad
looking like a hurt puppy, sitting in the opposite corner from
me. Seeing him hurt kills me. Am I the biggest jerk alive? He'll
never believe I'm trying to do the right thing for everyone.

Baldwin startles me by tapping on my desk. "Dandra, did
you see the news?"

He knows I work late and don't have the time or interest
for it. I sigh, "No, what happened?"

Baldwin grins ear to ear. "Patrolman Mark has accused
Mayor Monroe of tampering with city funds, receiving bribes

from Zane Chesterton, and unrightfully shutting down the library."

I like the sound of that. "Really? What does that mean?"

Baldwin leans closer. "It means his chances of winning the election are slim."

I roll my eyes. "But no one is running against him. He's still going to win."

Baldwin doesn't bat an eye. "There is someone running against him."

I scoff, "Who?"

"Me."

I turn to look him square on. "Aren't you too young? You're only on the city council because they were desperate after an unnaturally long vacancy. Even if you were old enough, you don't have the means to run a campaign."

He pretends to write something down so the teacher won't get mad at us. "I am too young, but I've found a loophole in the law."

I whisper, "What is the loophole?"

Baldwin practically cackles with delight, "You have to be age 20 or older to run for mayor unless the current mayor is recalled. If that happens, any of the current city council can run against him."

My eyebrows wrinkle together. "What are the chances that we can make that happen?"

Baldwin grins. "Well, step number one is happening right

now. I think we have enough evidence to recall him. I just need to keep other unsavory people from running against him."

I see another problem. "But what if good people decide to run against him?"

Baldwin shrugs. "Then we'll vote for the good person."

I whisper out the corner of my mouth, "I'm sure Mom will be willing to help out, but I don't think she'll love making our house campaign headquarters."

Baldwin looks at me cautiously. "It won't be. The anti-gamers and I are moving into an apartment tomorrow."

I feel my jaw drop. After several seconds, I force my jaw shut and ask, "How can you guys afford it with all your debts?"

Baldwin answers slowly and carefully. "Well, being a bookkeeper pays more than being a janitor, and Conrad is giving me a good deal on it."

"Conrad?" I shoot a glance across the room and catch Conrad looking at me. He immediately turns around.

Baldwin continues, "Yeah. He met me at the bookkeeping office late last night. He wants to fund my campaign."

I shake my head. "And he just happens to have an apartment for you, too."

Baldwin shrugs. "His dad owns a two-bedroom apartment on Main Street. He used to sleep there when he and his wife were having troubles, but he won't be needing it for a while, so the rent is cheap, and I'm taking it."

I wonder if this decision by Conrad is more about helping

Baldwin run for mayor or getting the entry point done sooner or stopping him from sleeping over at my house any longer.

Chapter 43

THE OATMEAL LOOKS EXTRA GOOPY and tasteless this morning. A quick spoonful proves I'm right, and the sugar bowl is empty. *Knock, knock.* I wipe the sleep out of my eyes as I open the front door. An overweight patrolman with a pleasant face is standing there.

I address him cautiously, "Hello? How can I help you?"

He smiles and says, "Are you Dandra Metty?"

I answer warily, "Yes..."

He nods. "An anonymous donor just paid off your remaining fine to the detainment center. I was sent by said

257

anonymous donor to pick you up and take you to get your yellow bracelet removed."

Everley suddenly pushes her way into the doorframe. "How do we know this isn't a trick by Patrolman Darius?" I try to shush her, but she is determined to confront the man.

He raises his eyebrow at my sister but pulls out an official document signed by the Fines Patrolchief. Everley and I look it over. It looks legitimate.

I push my hair behind my ears. "I don't know what to say."

The patrolman smiles at me. "I would suggest getting your shoes on and coming with me quickly, so you aren't late for school."

I grab my jacket and backpack, but when I reach for my shoes on the porch, I see a pink flower laid across them again. What is Conrad up to? Is he trying to get me back? I look at the patrolman and say, "I'm afraid I cannot accept this donation. The donor has other places he should spend his money. I will not be going with you."

The patrolman's forehead wrinkles. "He said you would say that, and my instructions are to tell you that he will not donate another coin to Baldwin Kole's campaign unless you get your yellow bracelet removed today."

My jaw drops. Only Conrad can come up with a way to do a kindness through blackmail. "I—I guess I will come with you then."

Chapter 44

MOM AND I STACK the last of the mulch bags on the sale floor and look around. There isn't much else for us to do here. With the city cleanup job done and the store stocked and ready for summer, I'm pretty sure layoffs are coming. Just the thought twists my stomach in a knot. My fines are paid off, and my bracelet is gone, but Mom and Everley still have theirs, and I fully intend to pay Conrad back every coin for mine.

We sweep and dust and make grammatically correct signs for the walls and windows until closing time. As we are about to leave, Jed's mom calls us around her favorite cash register.

She sighs, "I'd like to thank you all for your hard work the last few months. We couldn't have completed our city contract without you. Unfortunately, we don't have enough work to do at the hardware store for this many people. We are only going to keep Gordon and Adamar on for the rest of the summer. Unfortunately, today is your last day. Thank you, everyone."

Neil collects his coins from Sharry and says, "Thanks for nothing. You won't be seeing me ever again." He trips on his own feet as he marches out the door. Sharry rolls her eyes.

Mom smiles at Sharry and says, "Thank you for several months of solid employment. I appreciate it so much. Dandra and I are available tomorrow if you think of anything else we can do."

Jed approaches us as Sharry gives us half a smile and says, "This happens every year, and I feel bad every time, but I just can't pay people if I don't have work for them to do. I'll call you if I think of anything. I wish you both the best."

Mom is understanding. "Thank you, Sharry, and thank you, Jed."

Jed nods at us and insists on walking us to the door. He lowers his voice and says, "I tried so hard to convince Mom to keep you two, but Mom is pretty old-fashioned, and she thinks males can work circles around females when it comes to manual labor. She insisted that we keep Adamar and Gordon."

I wave him off. "It's fine. We understand. We'll figure something out."

Jed stares at my wrist. "Your bracelet is off."

I look at my bare wrist and rub it with my other hand. "Yeah, an anonymous donor paid off my fine."

Jed looks like he is battling whether to say something. "Do you love him?"

I feel my body twitch in surprise. I look at Jed sideways. "Love who?"

Jed's eyes are hard to read as he says, "Conrad Chesterton."

My cheeks feel like they are on fire. "How do you know he is the anonymous donor?"

Jed looks at me and then looks at his shoes. "There are rumors about you two, and I've seen the way he looks at you."

Mom gives me a hard nudge with her elbow, and I give her a hard nudge right back. I look at Jed and insist, "Conrad will always have a spot in my heart, but we broke up."

Jed raises his eyebrows. "I—I'm sorry to hear that, and I'm sorry Mom and I just added to your troubles."

I reassure him, "It's okay, really. It was my idea. Conrad and I parted as friends. Being without a job is tough, and I will definitely miss working here with you. Maybe I'll see you when we start working on the border wall entry point though. I'm in charge of recruiting volunteers."

Jed nods. "Yeah. I hope so. See you around."

Chapter 45

MOM WALKS HOME SLOWER than she ever has. Not even the reminder that Everley is waiting for us puts pep in her step. She moans, "What are we going to do, Dandra? We still owe thousands of coins to the detainment center, you are out of work, I am out of work, and our room renter is leaving us."

I sigh, "We have to find other jobs, obviously."

Mom flicks her yellow bracelet like it's an annoying bug on her arm. "Do you remember how hard it was to find this job with these bracelets?"

I lift my bare arm and say, "I don't have one anymore."

Mom blurts out, "I know, but I do!"

I put my arm around Mom's slumping shoulders and reassure her, "I say we just do our best and apply for everything we can, and I guess if worse comes to worst...we can always get a job at the Gaming District."

Mom sighs with relief. "I'm so glad to hear you say that. I feel better about applying other places already."

I feel taken aback. "Is my gaming attitude that bad?"

She opens her eyes as big as they can go. "Yes."

I try not to let that remark sting too much. "Maybe tutoring will pick back up; you never know."

Mom concedes, "More educational jobs will open up if, and only if, Baldwin becomes the mayor."

Chapter 46

I TRY TO SMILE as I help Baldwin move his things from my dad's old office to the front door. We pause awkwardly as we set down the last two bags. I smack him on the arm. "I wish you the best of luck with the election. You have my vote."

My ex-boyfriend smirks. "Thank you. If you can convince a few more people to vote for me, that would be great."

I frown. "Is anyone running against you? And is Mayor Monroe going to be recalled for sure?"

Baldwin raises his eyebrows. "Dandra, you really need to watch the news."

I throw my hands in the air. "What did I miss?"

Baldwin drops his bags. "Patrolman Mark took the case to recall Mayor Monroe to Judge Lemons today, and he won."

I shake my head in confusion. "Who won?"

Baldwin squeezes my arm. "Patrolman Mark obviously. Mayor Monroe is officially recalled and only working as an interim mayor until the election."

I squeeze the bridge of my nose with my fingers as I process how much I've missed. "But he can run for mayor again?"

Baldwin nods. "Unfortunately, yes."

Mom forces a smile as she listens in. She hasn't seen Patrolman Mark in a while, and it makes sense why now. She's still stressed about money. I find my smile a bit easier than she does. "If you need help making signs, I made some pretty nice ones at work today."

Baldwin snaps his fingers and points at me. "Actually, yes. I do need help making signs. I'll even pay you for it."

I look at Mom eagerly. "Perfect timing because Mom and I got laid off today." Mom's head raises hopefully.

Baldwin's eyebrows come together. "Really? Well, I'll tell you what. If you let me borrow your truck tonight, I will bring it back tomorrow filled with sign-making materials. I'll pay you for each sign made."

My heart leaps with excitement while Mom gushes,

"Absolutely, Baldwin. I'll go get the keys for you. I've always believed in 'If I scratch your back, you scratch mine.'"

Baldwin looks happy. "I couldn't have said it better myself." He takes the keys from Mom. "I will bring her back with a week's worth of work tomorrow."

I am truly grateful for these green and gold "Vote Baldwin Kole for Tifton Mayor" signs that have stained my hands the wrong color. They gave us one more week of work and one more payment to the detainment center for Mom and Everley, but they are done now. They just need pounded into the ground around town. Since we need the money, I offer to help with the sign placement, and Baldwin takes me up on it.

While we are placing a sign in front of the post office, he says, "I owe Patrolman Mark so much. He got Mayor Monroe recalled just in the nick of time."

I try to show even half his enthusiasm. "Yeah. It's perfect timing for you."

He looks at my worry-filled face and asks me, "Do you want to help with the border wall entry point?"

I raise one eyebrow. "Yes, obviously. That's why I've been recruiting volunteers."

Baldwin finishes pounding the wooden peg of a sign in front of the library. "You aren't getting what I'm saying.

I appreciate your free service, but it turns out that we need someone to be in charge of the volunteers. Someone to organize them and assign them jobs. Someone to keep them working hard even through the heat of the day. President Penn is insisting on it."

I pick up some discarded signs off the ground and say, "I would love to do that for you, but I still have bills to pay..."

Baldwin stops what he's doing and waits until I'm looking him in the eye. "I'm offering you and your mom a paid job."

I am flabbergasted. "How is that possible?"

Baldwin grins. "I'm a good bookkeeper, and I've cut out unnecessary waste and now have enough extra money to pay you two for four months."

I wonder what Baldwin cut to make this possible. "Will we get in trouble?"

Baldwin waves me off. "No. I've tried to give the job to four other people, but no one is willing to work outside in the heat of the summer with only a tiny shed for an office for only four months of pay."

I scoff, "Mayor Monroe can't stop us anymore, but I bet President Penn doesn't want us in charge of it."

Baldwin looks pleased as he picks up his bags. "Actually, he is quite impressed with what the United Nine have done since coming back to Layland."

I smack Baldwin in the arm. "Has he been spying on us?"

Baldwin laughs humorlessly. "Uh, yes, kind of, but the

reports have been good because he has put me in charge of the Layland side of the border entry point project. He approved hiring you and your mom just this morning."

I am overcome with shock and gratitude. "I can't believe it. Mom will be so relieved. Thank you so much!"

Chapter 47

SCHOOL IS ALMOST OUT for the summer, and Conrad and Baldwin are barely showing up anymore. I hope they pass their classes. I feel like a third wheel sitting with Adamar and Charlisa. When I can tell that I'm getting on their nerves, I switch to sitting with Gordon and Marcella, and then I eventually switch back. Ed tries to get me to join the chess club during lunch, but I don't do it. I would rather bring a book and read under the apple tree out front.

After checking and double-checking what President Penn's engineers have designed for weeks, we have a list of what volunteers can do and what paid professionals will have to do to make the border entry point a reality. The gaming tournament was a success, and Baldwin has found more donations for our cause. President Penn has given us a thumbs up to start phase one: buying necessary supplies.

I leave school with my feet on autopilot. I can't believe I'm back at the hardware store again, but I have a whole list of supplies to get for our volunteer work force. Mom and I stayed up late with Baldwin making this list. She has an interview with a potential tutoring client, so I tell her I'll order the supplies by myself.

I'm disappointed when I see Sharry behind the register instead of Jed.

She barely looks up from the catalogue she's flipping through. "Hello, Dandra. What can I help you with, today?"

I lean against the counter and slap my list down. "Hi, Sharry! Mom and I just got new jobs as the volunteer crew managers for the border wall entry point, and I need a whole bunch of tools and supplies."

Sharry looks over my list. "I'll say you do." She whistles as she reads. "I'm not sure I have this much in stock, but I can get an order in right away." She looks me over slowly and says, "Aren't you a bit young to have this job?"

I twist my hands together nervously. "Well, technically, Mom got the job, and I'm her assistant. I knew you'd have to order more, so that's why I'm here two weeks early."

Sharry looks at my shabby clothes and says, "I have about half of what you need, and I can have the other half in about 10 days, but I will need payment first..."

I whip out a work order form and paper check from The Country of Layland Infrastructure, and say, "That won't be a problem."

Sharry smiles at me like she's finally realized I'm a good person. She says, "I never thought I'd say this, but I'm glad you worked here and want to do business with me."

I grin. "I think we will both benefit from this transaction." I look around the empty store and ask, "Is Jed here?"

Sharry nods as she starts making calculations on a piece of paper. "Yeah, he's out back watering the plants."

I look down at my feet. "Do you think he'd help me take the supplies you do have to the border wall?"

Sharry grabs the keys to Jed's truck. "Absolutely."

I can't hide my grin as Sharry takes my arm like we're best friends and escorts me back to where Jed is watering flowers. He is such a contradiction with his big muscles being so gentle with the tiniest flower blooms. I remember watering these plants myself.

Jed sets down his watering can as soon as he sees me. A smile erupts on his face. "Dandra! Did you miss me or something?"

I grin at his happy face, but then hand over my list. "I

actually have a new job and need some help getting these things to my job site."

He takes the list and gives it a quick glance. "Well, I'm your man."

I chuckle. "I—uh, thanks."

Baldwin wasn't kidding when he said my office would be a small shed without electricity. I get a bit nervous when I see how small the old shed on the vacant lots really is. I need to lock all the shovels, work gloves, hard hats, and sledgehammers I just bought in there. I guess I won't be sitting at a desk.

Jed jumps out of his work truck and opens my door before I've even closed my gaping jaw. "Should we put the lock you bought on the door before we do anything else?"

I am still in shock at how much work I have ahead of me as I answer, "Yeah, that is a good idea, but you don't have to help me. I can put it on after everything is unloaded."

Jed looks at me like I have two heads. "I'm going to help you."

I shut the truck door and say, "No. I'm taking you away from your other work. I've got it."

Jed unwraps the new, heavy-duty lock I just bought and fits it to the door. "I'd much rather do this than anything else today."

My heart leaps with his willingness to help. His assistance will save me hours.

Jed is more knowledgeable about stacking tools than I am, and I am happy to be wrong about the amount that this shed can hold. Every single tool I bought fits inside thanks to Jed's expert stacking prowess. He hardly even breaks a sweat. I wish I could say the same. I need to go home and shower.

I collapse against the truck. "Thank you so much, Jed. I really owe you one."

He smirks, "Naw, it was no problem."

I look down at my list. Half of what I need is officially checked off. I just need my order to come in and the rest of my volunteers. I look at Jed sideways. "So, while we're here imagining what is ahead, I have a question for you. Are you willing to donate a day a week so we can unlock our country?" My sales pitch sounds silly as I say it.

He throws his work gloves in the truck and smirks. "As a matter of fact, I'll donate two days a week."

That is not the answer I was expecting. "Really? Will your mother be able to handle the store without your?"

He waves me off. "She'll be fine. She doesn't own me, and I want to help."

I am thrilled to hear this. He is the hardest worker I know. "I will call you to put you on my schedule."

He nods at me. "I look forward to it."

I stand there awkwardly for a second. "Well, I better get home. Mom might worry."

He pats the hood of his truck. "Can I give you a ride?"

I look at my worn shoes. "It's only a 10-minute walk. I'll be fine."

Jed walks over and opens the passenger door of his truck. "But I'd like to drive you home."

I look inside the truck I know so well and say, "Okay then. You've convinced me." He smiles and shuts the door behind me.

I've ridden in this truck with Jed dozens of times, but this time feels different for some reason. It's probably because Neil isn't taking half of my seat or because Mom isn't looking at me hoping that we get home before Everley starts to worry, or maybe it's because Jed and I are alone.

I suddenly become hyper aware of how many inches apart our legs and hands are and how much quicker my breathing is than his.

We get to my house in what feels like 10 seconds in one way and 10 hours in another. Jed turns to me and asks, "Do you have all the volunteers you need?"

I frown. "No. I have asked all my friends and acquaintances, but I am still only a third of the way staffed. I am heading to the gaming district tomorrow. I'm hoping for a miracle to get some of the gamers to volunteer."

Jed looks at me skeptically and says, "Sign me up for the first day of construction."

I look at the schedule on my clipboard and then at him. "Are you sure? It's the first Monday of June. You'll probably be missed at the hardware store."

Jed looks at me. "It's fine. I'll take the day off if I have to."

I look away. "I can schedule you for the weekend..."

He insists, "I want to be there the first day to help you out."

His words are music to my ears. I used to assume he was all business, but he has a thoughtful side, too. "Thanks, Jed. That means a lot to me."

He shrugs. "Yeah, well, you helped me get through my city project. Now I'm going to help you through yours."

He jumps out of the truck to get my door again. Was he really this gentlemanly when we worked together? It's kind of nice to see hard work and thoughtfulness come together.

Chapter 48

I SHUDDER DESPITE THE HOT SUN above as I approach the Gaming District. This place literally makes my blood boil, but I have no choice but to beg the gamers inside to help make my dream a reality.

The heat of the 12 o'clock sun brings a bead of sweat to my forehead. The huge automatic doors make the hairs of my arms stand up as I approach them, but they swing open so invitingly. No wonder people keep coming back. I could have been here earlier, but what's the point? Gamer's morning starts at noon. So here I am to convince the zombie-like gamers to do something they don't want to do.

The posters on the walls of the entryway advertise a week-long gaming tournament called "Master of the Great Wall," which catches my eye. As I look closer at it, I see that it is over but there is a second tournament coming up, and Milo is the person to contact to sign up. Proceeds will be donated to the border wall entry point. That brings a smile to my lips.

As I walk in, I am greeted by a man in a red suit. He asks, "Can I help you find the game you are looking for? Or would you like to buy a gaming card?"

I put on a fake smile and say, "I am actually not here for gaming. I am trying to recruit volunteers to build an entry point into the United Cities."

The worker folds his hands in front of himself and looks at me condescendingly. "Well, this is a gaming facility, not a city recruitment center, so I'm afraid you can't do that."

I challenge him. "Who says I can't do that?"

He doesn't back down. "The owner, Zane Chesterton."

I pull out my Tifton ID with my name on it, so the man will know I'm one of the United Nine. "I know for a fact that Zane Chesterton is in the detainment center, so that excuse doesn't work."

The man in red doesn't blink. "His son is here though, and he won't agree to it either."

I look him in the eye. "Let's find out, shall we? Take me to him."

The man in the red suit marches me to the main offices of the Gaming District. I am taken to the waiting area where I can see Zane Chesterton's empty office and right next to it, the all-too-familiar door that says, "Conrad Chesterton, managing director."

I have to wait in the waiting area with the pretty blonde secretary for 20 minutes before I am invited into Conrad's office. It is the same as it was when I broke up with him, but he isn't the same. For one thing, his hair isn't spiked anymore. He has cut it short. It makes him look older. He looks at me with such a strange emotion on his face. He looks at my wrist and then at my face. "Hi, Dandra."

I swallow. "Hi, Conrad."

He pushes all the papers on his desk to the side and looks at me. "I hear you are planning to disturb the peace here today."

I smirk. "I have no intention of disturbing the peace. I just need 40 workers a day for 4 months straight so we can build an entry way into the United Cities."

His eyebrows come together. "Why is this your job?"

I shrug. "Because President Penn told Baldwin to hire someone, and he hired me to do it."

Conrad nods. "You two are working together?"

I wrinkle my nose at his response. "Uh, he hired me, but I only see him to discuss the border wall project."

281

Conrad lowers his voice. "Are you two together?"

I roll my eyes. "No. He's over me, Conrad. He is nothing but business with me. It's almost like someone paid him to be over me."

Conrad looks down at his hands uncomfortably. "Well, he may just miss Josie. All of us United Nine have people we miss on the other side of the wall."

I try to decide if that statement is true. Who does Conrad miss from the United Cities? Certainly not Mrs. Abbot, maybe Mr. Bronson? I look down at my clipboard and decide to try out my sales pitch. "Does that mean you'll sign up as a volunteer one day a week until the border wall entry point is completed?"

His eyes bore into mine. "Will I get to work with you?"

I nod. "It is my job for the summer."

He shakes his head. "I'll only sign up if I get to work near you every shift."

His eyes are so intense, I can't look away. "I can arrange that."

He leans forward. "I miss you."

I smile at him. "I miss you, too."

He stands up and moves to a seat next to me and touches my wrist. "It's nice to see your bracelet off."

I blush as I feel the warmth from his fingers on my wrist. "Thank you for that."

His fingers slowly work their way down to my fingers. "You know I would do more."

I pull my hand back as my heart rate jumps. "I know you would, but we are needed in different places right now. I don't want you spreading yourself too thin."

He reaches across me. "Give me your clipboard. I want to sign up, so I at least get to spend eight hours a week with you."

I hand it to him but insist, "You are always welcome for dinner; you know that. Everley misses you."

His eyes lure me in, again. "I'm glad someone misses me. I will stop in randomly for her."

I close my eyes and refocus my brain. I didn't come here to reconnect with Conrad. I clear my throat. "I would enjoy a random visit, too, but the reason I'm here is to ask people to volunteer one day a week to open the border wall." Conrad nods, and I continue, "Do I have any chance of success here, do you think?"

Conrad walks to his desk and sits down. His eyes look sad, but he responds, "Yes. You definitely do. I would start with the games of skill area. They will like the idea of learning about new people and their customs. I'd probably go to the games of whimsy after that. Those people are movers and shakers. Appeal to their opportunities to game in another country. Go to the games of chance last. Those people are risk takers, and they may see visiting another country as a risk worth taking.

I try to memorize what he just said. "Thanks, Conrad. This is so helpful. You really are good at what you do." I move to leave, but he comes around his desk to hug me.

He holds me for a long time and whispers in my ear, "Please, don't forget me."

I lay my head on his shoulder. Missing this connection. I say into his shoulder, "How could I? You've always been my best friend, and you always will be."

His voice chokes up. "What if someone else takes my place?"

I let go of him and shake my head. "We need each other. It's what friends do. We'll never desert each other. See you around, Conrad."

He squeezes my arm. "See you around."

I walk quickly away so I don't turn back to him. I have to slow down my heart and my breathing if I'm going to do my job today.

He recommended going to the games of skill first, so I march straight ahead until I get there. Conrad's advice is spot on. I decide not to walk around with the sign I made asking for volunteers. I set it to the side and just start talking to people.

It's amazing how many people are willing to talk to me. They ignore their GameComs and GroComs and look me in the eye. They are surprisingly hungry for a change in this country. It doesn't take much description of the United Cities for them to want to see it, too. I get six people to sign up for one day a week in the games of skill section.

The games of whimsy section has a different feeling in the air. These people know me. A guy named Mick asks me so many questions about my escape. "Miss Metty, what is it like on the other side of the wall?"

I grin at him. "It's so clean, and so amazing."

He nods and asks, "What is it like in the detainment center?"

I shake my head. "I don't recommend it. It would take me all day to tell you the horrors of that place." I can't tell if I'm a celebrity or a freak show to Mick and his buddies, but I do get 10 people to sign up.

The games of chance people look the least groomed, but they like the idea of mixing things up. A gamer named Maggie flips her messy hair out of her face and says, "I think the entry point will be risky. What if we all leave and don't come back?"

I reassure her, "We can't all leave. We can only visit if we have a visitation pass." She looks like she's about to walk away, so I say, "The gaming is amazing on the other side of the wall!" Heh, heh. It probably is, right?

Maggie stops and looks around the Gaming District. "The gaming is getting kind of lame around here. I want to try gaming somewhere new." She grabs the pen out of my hand and signs up to help one day a week. I'm shocked, and the shock continues when twenty more people sign up to do the same. I literally can't believe it. Why have I been so negative toward gamers my whole life?

My legs are so tired of standing that I have to sit down and rest and marvel for a bit. I'm getting so close to the amount of people I need, but more importantly, I feel like these people are my people, my countrymen, my neighbors, and my friends. I never thought I could have positive feelings toward gamers, but I am so grateful for them today. So many of them have signed up for Milo and Baldwin's fundraisers, too, and they are willing to do some manual labor for a positive change around here. I smile with a new kind of patriotic pride as I walk home.

Chapter 49

THE BELL RINGS on the last day of school, and I realize as I stuff all my belongings in my backpack that I only have one more year of mid level schooling left.

Baldwin is stopping by the house tonight to update Mom and me on what the Layland Entry Point Committee's mandates are for the construction. This happens a few times a week.

He looks tired when he walks through the door. I ask, "Is everything okay?"

Baldwin nods and plops onto the couch. "I got all the

inspections arranged and all the forms filled out. We are on schedule to start on Monday."

Mom claps her hands. "That is great news. Did you pass all your classes? I hear you've been missing a lot of school lately."

Baldwin gives me a side eye. "Yes, Conrad and I both passed all of our classes, by some miracle."

Mom offers Baldwin a glass of water and asks, "Will you be back next school year? I know you and Conrad have adult jobs now, but there is still another year of learning ahead of you."

Baldwin shrugs. "I can't speak for Conrad, but even for me, I can't say for sure at this point."

Mom nods sadly. "I see."

Baldwin sits up in his seat and says, "I had a fight with Interim Mayor Monroe and Patrolman Darius yesterday."

I move next to him on the couch. "What was it about?"

Baldwin smirks. "Well, two things technically, but you two failing to get the last bit of the volunteer work chart filled out by the deadline was his main concern."

I scowl, "I literally went door to door, but I just ran out of volunteers."

Baldwin waves me off. "I know you did. I reached out to the mayor of Chester and got the remaining workers we need. Everything will be fine."

I sit back on the couch with a huff. "I'm glad the city

next door cares about opening the border wall unlike Mayor Monroe. What was his other concern?"

Baldwin opens his mouth then shuts it. He opens it again and says, "Mayor Monroe told me that I can't just waltz into city hall and ruin all of his hard work." He folds his hands in his lap and continues, "He said he would do whatever it took to stop me from ruining anything else."

I take a deep breath and exhale. "I'm sorry about Mayor Monroe. He is the most pathetic mayor our country has ever seen. His threats are probably just talk. Thank you for calling the mayor of Chester and fixing my volunteer problem, Baldwin."

"No problem."

Mom is thriving in this job, and she is an amazing organizer and liaison with the government inspectors, but she does not want to be the voice of our volunteer operation. She insists that I have to do all the talking when the volunteers show up.

All forty people show up today, the first day of volunteer construction, and I am so relieved. I am not sure that all of them showered before arriving, but beggars can't be choosers. I whistle loudly to get everyone's attention. "May I please have your attention?" I gather my smorgasbord of volunteers around the large sign Mom made to show who will be working in which area and with which people.

I swallow the frog in my throat and say as confidently as I can, "I can't tell you how happy I am to see you all here today. This is history in the making." I wipe a tear from my eye and continue, "I have been on the other side of that giant concrete wall, and I know that opening the border between our countries is going to open the eyes of people from Layland and open the eyes of the people from the United Cities." I see people I know mixed with people I just met smiling and nodding at me. I think this is going to work! I clear my throat. "Please focus your attention on this work distribution diagram that City Councilman Baldwin Kole is about to explain."

Baldwin jumps up with a big smile like the politician he is and gets everyone pumped up. "Hello, Tifton! Are you ready to open the border?"

The crowd cheers, "Yeah!" and hangs on his every word.

I am kind of proud of Baldwin and his real-life speech. He is every bit as impressive as he was at the educational assembly in the United Cities. I'm also proud when I don't have to answer very many questions after Baldwin's presentation. Mom and I must have done a good job on the work distribution diagram.

I wasn't sure what managing a crowd of 40 people would be like, but the energy this group of volunteers brings is absolutely electrifying. Why haven't I felt this kind of energy with paid employees before? Even in the United Cities?

A smile comes to my face when I see a tall muscular person I know walk toward me. Jed gives me a crooked smile and asks, "Am I really working as your partner today?"

I look at my shoes. "Uh, yes."

Jed takes a shovel from my mom and looks at it. "It's almost like the crew manager knows how well we work together or something."

I grab a shovel and chuckle, "Yep."

I placed myself in the digging group. Why did I do that? Well, to be honest, I think I have more experience with a shovel digging under the border wall than anyone else in this group. Well, there may be one person here who has more experience with a shovel than me, and I made him my digging partner.

I look at all the supplies stacked around the shed and say, "It feels like we just dropped this stuff off, right?"

Jed looks thoughtful as he responds. "Kind of. It's been nine days since we unloaded your second load of supplies."

My eyebrows come together. "Uh, yeah. That sounds about right."

Jed pats my hands as they grip my shovel. "I see you still have the work gloves I gave you."

I lift up my hands to admire my gloves. "Yeah. I hope they save my hands from blisters."

Jed's eyebrows crease. "I've never met a girl like you before."

I puzzle over his statement as I keep handing out shovels to the digging group. "What do you mean?"

Jed helps me distribute tools. "You are willing to work hard and get blisters. Most girls don't want to ruin their fingernails."

I look down at my well-worn jeans and shoes. "Well, I was raised with a shovel in my hand. In fact, I'm pretty sure the first time we met was when I was buying a shovel at your hardware store."

He grins. "You're right. You were wearing a purple jacket."

I can't believe he remembers that day from before my dad died, before I snuck out of the country. I raise my own shovel and say, "I hope I can dig as fast as I could that day. Let's find out, shall we?"

His grin turns to determination. "Yeah. Let's get to work." We work as a team and get our assigned area dug out before the rest of the digging teams finish their areas. We help the other diggers get caught up with the wheelbarrow runners. I look at how wide our eight-lane border crossing is going to be. It's going to take a lot of road fill to get these empty lots where they need to be.

When it's lunch break, I blow the whistle to signal it's time to stop and then make sure the water coolers are full. Mom and Baldwin are deep in conversation, but they wave me away when I try to join them. Once everyone is settled on the grass, I pull out a book and a sandwich and find a shady spot to sit down.

Jed sits down a few feet away and pulls out cheese and crackers like the kind he always had in his truck. I look at the all-too-familiar box of crackers and ask, "Do you like those crackers, or are they just what your mom buys?"

Jed holds a round salty cracker up and says, "I love these, but they are also my mom's go-to. I don't think I've ever met a cracker I didn't like."

I shake my head and start reading my book. When lunch is over, I blow the whistle again and get everyone back to work. It's not as hard being a crew manager as I thought it would be. I don't have to pay everyone at the end of the day, so that helps. It feels good to be working for a cause that I feel so passionate about. To think, in four months, I could be on the other side of this wall hugging Shasta and Ernestine. I smile and walk amongst the crew giving encouragement. I didn't think we could get enough people to volunteer, but here they are!

Some of my gamer workers look like lost souls, but most of my volunteers, like Maggie, are figuring things out quickly and working up a sweat. I don't know what I would do without Jed and Mr. Yesterly. They are the hardest workers I've ever seen, and they have foresight about why we're doing what we're doing, and what needs to happen next. They even give pointers to the struggling workers around them.

Jim Yesterly pats a frowning Mick on the back and asks, "Is that your first blister?"

Mick cringes. "Yes. I've never seen my skin rip open like this before."

Jim pulls his work glove off and shows the young man his callused hand. "Be proud of that blister. You earned it today. Remember to wear gloves next time, and remember the more you use your hands, the tougher they'll get."

When it's water break time, Jed grabs my water bottle and hands it to me. "Thanks." I look at Jed as he takes a drink himself and ask, "Are you planning on taking over the hardware store?"

Jed smacks some dirt off his work gloves and says, "Well, yeah. That's what my mom wants me to do."

I drink too fast, but it's so refreshing on this hot day. "Is it what you want to do?"

Jed shrugs, "No. Not really. It's fine, but I've always wanted to be an engineer." He eyes the blueprints to the border wall entry point on the table behind us longingly.

I tap the blueprints and say, "You could still do that."

Jed looks unsure for the first time. "I don't know. I've been out of mid level school for a couple years now, and I was okay, but not great at school. English was my worst subject, but I did pretty well at math." Jed shakes his head. "I've been using my hands and not my brain for too long. I think it's too late to go to high level school now. Plus, Mom wouldn't pay for it."

My heart sinks for him. "It's never too late, Jed." I smile at him encouragingly. "My mom has done some of her high level schooling a class at a time in the evenings. You could do that."

Jed shakes his head. "Mom would never allow it."

I raise my eyebrows. "Does she have to give her permission? You're old enough to decide for yourself."

Jed looks at me like he's never considered that possibility. "I don't know. Ever since my dad walked out on her, I've tried to be there for her. I hate to make her mad."

The wheels start turning in my head. "Well, what if I brought you a book on general engineering? Would you read it?"

Jed looks at the book in my hand and then looks into my eyes. "I don't know where you'll find one with the library closed, but if you bring it to me, I'll read it."

I grin. "Deal."

It looks like I might have to visit the crypt tonight.

Chapter 50

"IS THIS EVERYTHING you left behind, Adamar?"

"Yep."

I look around the empty library basement. "Well, it won't take too long to get these loads to your new apartment, then."

He starts handing boxes through the open window to Ed. "I'm surprised you came to help."

I pick up a bag of clothes and shove it through the window to Gordon. "Jed told me you were planning to move more stuff to your apartment tonight, and you know me. I love to help—and I kind of want to break into one of the book rooms upstairs..."

Adamar rolls his eyes. "Oh, I see how it is. You only come to visit if you want something."

I tilt my head to the side. "Hey, let's be fair now."

Adamar grins. "I'm just kidding. Which book room do you want to break in to?"

I answer as I peek into the holes in the walls. "Math and engineering."

Adamar hesitates. "Okay, well, that is a trickier one. You may have to climb all the way up to the attic and stomp on the trap door until it opens."

I frown at that plan. "What if it doesn't open?"

Adamar shrugs. "Then you have to climb all the way back down empty handed."

"Ugh. Do you have any engineering books laying around here?"

Adamar picks up a book out of a box. "Just this one. It's pretty advanced though."

I examine it carefully. "Yeah, that's too advanced. All right, I guess I better start climbing."

This is arguably the worst decision of my life. I feel like a rat trying to go through a dark 100-year-old maze made for ants. I thought dusting the finished side of these walls was the worst thing ever, but I was wrong. The inside of the walls of this library is ten times worse. I am choking on the dust as it coats my mouth and nostrils. It takes all my strength, determination, and willpower to suppress any claustrophobia I have and wiggle-climb up four flights of wall like a mouse. When I get to the attic and look in a discarded mirror, I look like a fuzzy, gray rabbit. Blech! I wipe the dust out of my eyes and shake like a dog to get the blanket of dust off me. It takes a second to locate the dusty trap door, and I stomp on it for 10 minutes straight before the latch gives and I get it open. But—I get it open.

The library I worked so hard to clean and make more inviting is definitely creepy again. The hair on my arms stands up as I walk the dusty, creaky halls to the math and engineering room. I come to a stop when another room label grabs my attention: the botany room. It's not likely that I'll put myself through the torture of getting in here again, so I take a little detour. I wipe the dust off a row of books at a time looking for books on flowers. When I find the flower books, I flip through the pages of several books hoping to find the picture I'm looking for. I finally find it.

The pink flower that I've found lying across my shoes several times is a tropical flower called the Pride of Hankins Hibiscus. Conrad never ceases to amaze me.

I drop six engineering books and 6 mysteries down the

secret hatch in the detective and mystery novel room, so I won't have to carry them down with me from the attic. It's all I can do to force myself down into the wall again. The things I do for... Jed's...education?

Everley looks at me funny. "What's the matter with you, Dandra? You are so jumpy."

"Uh, nothing," I say as I set my mystery book down.

The second day as volunteer crew manager went well enough. I only had one no-show. My digging partner today was not nearly as good as my partner from yesterday. My eyes keep wandering to the stack of books on the table. These engineering books I...borrowed are burning a hole in my pocket. Can I really last until Saturday before giving them to Jed?

Apparently not.

I twist the phone cord around my finger nervously as I call the hardware store. I have to see if Jed is there before I pack the heavy books all the way across town. A female voice answers the phone. "Hello, Tifton Hardware, this is Sharry speaking."

My shoulders slump in disappointment. "Uh, hello, Sharry. This is Dandra Metty, and I was wondering if Jed is there. I found the book I promised to lend him."

Sharry snorts. "He wants to read a book, huh. Well, he's

not here. His sinuses were acting up today, so I told him to go home early and take some medicine."

I swallow the lump in my throat. "Oh, okay. I'm sorry to have bothered you."

Sharry tsks me. "You aren't bothering me. In fact, why don't you take the book to him at the house? I'm sure it will make his day."

My shoulders straighten. "Oh, okay. What is your address?"

"371 Cyprus Street. Have a good day, Dandra."

"I will, Sharry. Thank you."

I don't want to overwhelm Jed with six books, so I just grab the two easiest level engineering books and walk out the door. But after a couple of steps, I decide to change my outfit into something less scruffy. I should look presentable when visiting a neighbor, right?

My short-sleeve purple shirt somehow gets sweaty on the short walk to Jed's house. It must be the rising summer temperatures. When I get to the door, I pause an uncomfortably long time before knocking. What's wrong with me? It's just a coworker's door. Knock on it.

When Jed answers the door, his jaw drops, but not as much as my own. Jed is in a tank top and pajama pants. I've never seen this much skin exposed on him. He always wears long sleeves to protect his skin from the sun. The muscles I've noticed with his shirt on are hard to look away from with his shirt off. Jed wipes his red nose and asks, "Dandra, what are you doing here?"

It takes me a second to realize I need to respond to his question. "I—uh, brought you the engineering books I promised you."

He smiles at me. "Oh, thanks, come on in."

My feet feel like they are glued to his porch. "I hear you're sick, so I don't want to bother you."

Jed tilts his head slightly. "I'm not that sick, and sinus problems aren't contagious. Come on in."

I don't need telling twice. I'm sure I look like a little kid in a toy store with wide eyes and a grin on my face. I've never been here before, but Jed's house has a familiar, comfortable feeling to it. It is about the same size as my house, but it's in considerably better repair. It's not decorated much, but it's cozy and clean. I finally find my voice. "You have a nice house."

Jed looks around quickly. "Thank you. Have a seat in that easy chair. It's the best seat in the house. Would you like a drink?"

"Um, sure."

He rubs his bare arms distractedly. "We have several sodas and juices, what would you like?"

I smile and shrug. "I like all juices. Surprise me."

Jed comes back from the kitchen with two glasses of purple grape juice which I spill on myself during my first sip. Jed grins. "That's why I chose purple grape juice. You spill a lot when you're taking a drink."

My face turns insta red. I'm not sure if it's embarrassment for today's spill or embarrassment from all my previous spills, but either way, I wish I could hide. "I will try to slow down." I grab a tissue from the box on the coffee table and try to mop up the purple juice on my purple shirt.

Jed suddenly turns red, too. "Should I go change my clothes? I don't usually wear this when guests come over."

I shake my head. "No. It's fine. You deserve to be comfortable when you're sick."

"Okay." Jed seems awfully nervous as he sits down.

I try to find clues to who Jed is as I look around the living room. "So what do you like to do when you finally get some time off work?"

Jed grabs a tissue and wipes his nose quickly. "Well, sometimes I read, or tinker around in the garage. I spend at least a half hour in my flower garden every day."

I raise my eyebrows. "You have a flower garden?"

Jed gets defensive. "Uh, yeah. It's good for business."

I feel a grin creeping onto my face. "Can I see it?"

Jed runs his hands through his hair and starts to fidget. "Um, okay."

I ask, "Why are you nervous?"

Jed takes another quick sip of juice and sets down his glass. "I, uh, I've never shown my flower garden to anyone but family before."

I try to keep my face neutral. "I can keep it a secret if you want me to."

He won't look me in the eye. "It's not that. It's...well, whatever. Come have a look."

I don't think I could be more curious as I follow Jed's muscular figure to his back door. When he opens the door, I don't just see a little flower garden, it is an enormous, immaculate, takes-up-the-whole-yard flower garden.

My jaw drops as the fragrant blooms fill my nostrils. Every color of the rainbow is represented and then some. "Jed, this is the most beautiful garden I have ever seen." I touch the biggest orange blossom next to me. "You must be so proud."

Jed tries to hide his smile, but I can tell he likes the compliment. He takes me through the entire garden one flower bed at a time and tells me the story behind each flower. Some of them are the usual varieties for our climate like snap dragons, roses, and daisies, but some of them are rare and exotic like poppies and purple passiflora. Jed waits patiently for me to smell each type. When my tour is almost done, I notice a tiny green greenhouse that is only big enough to hold a single vase of flowers in the farthest corner. He doesn't offer to open it up.

I point at it and ask, "What's in there?

He hesitates to answer, "Oh, just a rare flower that I have to keep warmer than the rest."

I inquire, "Can I see it?"

Jed's eyes dart from side to side. "Um, it's not that pretty, and it's unusually sensitive to our climate, so I'd rather not. *Achoo!*"

I touch his elbow. "Are you okay?"

He pulls a tissue out of his pocket. "Yeah. I just need to take more sinus medicine."

I insist, "Go take some then. I don't want you to suffer."

He looks hesitant. "Are you sure? It's in the lavatory in the house."

I lead him by the elbow toward the house. "That's fine. Go take it."

He shrugs. "Okay, I'll be right back."

I know it's wrong. I know I could cause some damage to a precious flower, but I can't help myself. As soon as Jed goes into the house, I sneak to the corner of the garden and open the little greenhouse lid. Inside, I see a pink Pride of Hankins Hibiscus flower with several blooms cut off.

Chapter 51

I AM SO SURPRISED that I almost don't shut the lid before Jed comes back. I was so sure that Conrad had given me the flowers.

That means it was Jed who cleaned the dirt and paint off my shoes all those times as well. Did he give me the red dress shoes? What does this mean? Is he just a nice florist, a nice boss?

Jed's eyes and nose are redder than ever when he comes back to the flower garden. I feel like I need to go now that I've intruded on his privacy. "Jed, you look very sick. I think you need to lay down and sleep."

He frowns. "No, I feel fine. You don't have to leave."

I look at the beauty around me and say, "I would love to visit this garden again. Could I come again when you feel better?"

He smiles. "Yes. Absolutely."

As we walk to the house, I say, "I can't wait for my next visit. Should I take you off the schedule until you're better?"

He shakes his head forcefully. "No. Don't do that. I'll rest up today and tomorrow. I'll be ready to work by Saturday."

I open the back door. "Okay, get lots of sleep, and I'll see you soon."

Jed ushers me into his kitchen. "Let me walk you out."

I follow him and nudge the books I brought as we enter the living room. "I hope you like the engineering books."

He smiles at me. "I will. I don't know how you found them, but thanks for bringing them."

I shrug. "It was no problem. I'll see you soon."

Chapter 52

I AM AS NERVOUS AS A FOX in a hen house as I get ready for work Saturday morning. Does he know that I know? Should I tell him? Should I pretend like I don't know?

I almost forget to aloe my legs, and I put on my fanciest shirt instead of a work shirt for some reason. I have got to get it together. When I open the door to collect my work shoes, there is a pink Pride of Hankins Hibiscus flower lying across them. A smile erupts on my face. It's been a while since my last one, but instead of putting it in water, I put it behind my ear. I can't wait to see Jed's reaction.

Mom smiles at me as we walk to our work site. "Have you figured out who has been leaving you those flowers?"

I try to hide my smile. "I think so."

She touches one of the tender petals. "Do you think you'll see your secret admirer today?"

I blush. "Yeah. I'm pretty sure."

When we get to the border wall entry point, Mom and I set up our volunteer job chart for the day and set out tools in organized rows. I made Jed my digging partner again. I keep looking over my shoulder as I hand out tools, but I don't see him. Is he not coming? Is he too sick after all? I'm about to write *no show* on his name on the job chart when I hear his congested voice. "Sorry I'm late." I grin, excited to see his reaction to the flower in my hair.

I turn around and stare at Jed. He looks a bit surprised when he takes in my hair, but I'm even more surprised. His nose is still red, but he is holding an entire vase of pink Pride of Hankins Hibiscus flowers.

His whole face becomes as red as his nose as he extends the vase toward me. I take it, letting my fingers linger on his. I feel my cheeks turning red as well as I say, "Hi."

He steps forward and touches the flower in my hair. "Hi."

I am at a loss for words.

He puts his hands in his pockets and says, "Surprise."

Mom walks toward me and winks. "Those flowers are lovely, but you two need to get to work!"

I nod obediently and pull the flower out of my hair and stick it with the rest of the blooms in the vase. I look up at him shyly. "Thank you."

He takes the vase from me and sets it in the shade of the shed then picks up a shovel and says, "You're welcome."

I pick up my shovel and follow him to our assigned spot. We are behind the rest of the digging crew for once. I know we'll catch up quickly, but I can't make my body move very fast. I can't take my eyes off my secret admirer. "Jed?"

"Yeah?"

"Did you see me peek at your Pride of Hankins Hibiscus flowers when I was at your house?"

He gives me a sideways grin, "Yes. I was watching you from the lavatory window."

I want to disappear. "Did I damage them? Is that why you're giving them all to me?"

Jed stops digging and leans on his shovel. "You didn't damage them. I'm kind of glad you looked. It's been a hard secret to keep, and a hard flower to keep alive."

I stop digging and ask, "Why did you do it?"

He pauses before answering. "Pretty girls deserve pretty flowers."

He starts digging again, and I feel my cheeks getting red again. How can this guy be so simple yet so complex at the same time?

After I blow the whistle for lunch, I sit down next to my

vase of flowers and soak in their fragrance. Jed sits next to me after he blows his nose and washes his hands. He looks at the flowers and then looks at me. "Do you like them?"

I grin. "Yes, I love them!"

He takes a bite of sandwich and then asks, "Did you have any idea it was me before you visited my flower garden?"

I feel foolish as I shake my head. "I thought it was either Conrad or Baldwin."

He grins. "Do they usually clean your shoes?"

I laugh out loud and smack his arm. "No, definitely not. I've been kind of confused about my relationships lately."

He looks at my work shoes and says, "I'm glad the red shoes fit."

I blush at how much I love those shoes. "Why did you give me shoes?"

Jed runs his hands through his hair nervously. "I felt bad that working for me made you ruin your shoes. They're too extravagant, aren't they?"

"No! Well, maybe." We both laugh. I clear my throat. "I love them, and they were just what I needed to go to Baldwin's swearing-in. Thank you."

Jed looks into my eyes and then off into the distance. "You looked beautiful that day." He looks at the vase again and asks, "What kind of relationship do you think we have?"

I look down at my shoes. "I don't know." I look at Jed. "I do know that those engineering books were not easy to find, but

I was determined to get them for you, and once I had them, I couldn't think about anything except giving them to you."

He nudges my foot with his. "Would you be okay with getting to know me better?"

I try to hide my smile as I say, "Yes."

Chapter 53

I AM ALL SMILES THE NEXT DAY, and Conrad seems to think he is the reason. "Good morning, Dandra. You look happy this morning."

I try to wipe the grin off my face. "I am. It's good to see you, and in different clothes than your usual."

Conrad pats his brand-new work clothes proudly. "I want to dress like the rest of the volunteers."

I swallow my laugh as I look around at the much scruffier crew forming around the shed. "Well, you just need one last touch, Conrad." I pick up some dirty work gloves and wipe them on his brand new "work shirt." He scowls at me as I say, "There, now you look like the rest of us."

Conrad wipes the dirt off annoyedly and looks at the work chart. "I am digging for four hours straight today?"

I hand him a shovel and say, "Yep. Be happy I didn't make you dig all day."

He takes the shovel and forces a smile as the rest of the scruffy-looking volunteer work force crowds around us. I give out my usual instructions, and then show Conrad how to do what I've been doing all week. He is determined to keep up with me, and he is pretty exhausted by the time I blow the whistle for lunch.

He plops down on the ground next to me and pulls out the biggest sandwich I have ever seen and offers me half. I take it reluctantly. "Did Lexis make this for you?"

He leans back against the shed and says, "Yes, she made it yesterday. Sorry if it's stale."

I take a bite and shrug. "I think it tastes great."

He smiles and nudges me with his elbow. "I've been looking forward to today."

I smile back. "Really? Most people dread doing this kind of work all day."

He rubs a spot on his arm and says, "I'm sure I'll be feeling it tomorrow, but it's worth it to spend the day with you."

I take a bite of sandwich and grin. Once I swallow, I ask, "How's the family? Are you and Milo getting along?"

Conrad gives me a noncommittal shrug. "Mom is not doing well. She wants a divorce, but she has suddenly realized how hard her life will be without Dad's money and connections."

I ask sarcastically, "Did she visit my old cell or something?"

Conrad bites his lip. "Actually, yeah. Something like that. She demanded to be removed from Dad's 'cell,' but after one night in a regular cell with the regular food, she came crying back to him."

I don't know whether I should laugh or cry as I imagine Jerika Chesterton's predicament. "Well, at least there are two giant beds in your parents' cell."

Conrad looks at his feet and nods. "Yeah, and there is a row of bookshelves between them now."

I hate to see my best friend suffering. I squeeze his knee. "There is nothing you can do to fix their relationship, so don't torture yourself about it."

He nods. "I know. They just like to vent to me, a lot."

I try to change the subject. "How is Milo doing?"

Conrad perks up a bit. "He is still making money by unlocking game advantages at the Gaming District. He hates visiting Mom and Dad though, so that is adding more responsibility to me, but other than that, the first gaming tournament went well. Master of the Great Wall brought in 250,000 coins."

I pick my jaw up off the ground. "No way!"

Conrad grins. "Milo turns out to be awesome at running gaming tournaments. Who would have thought, huh?"

I look at the equipment sitting all around me and say, "We needed a million coins though. How has Layland paid for all this equipment, and the specialists I have coming in the next few weeks?"

"Hasn't Baldwin told you?"

My eyebrows come together. "No, he just said he fundraised all the money we needed."

Conrad grins, "Well, I told him I'd match any amount that he could fundraise, so I donated 250,000 coins after Master of the Great Wall was over."

"Where did the rest come from?"

Conrad grins and shakes his head. "Milo got so many compliments on his gaming tournament that he decided to do a second one: Master of Layland."

I ask curiously, "Did it bring in another 250,000 coins?"

Conrad answers proudly, "Yep."

I look at my friend in admiration. "Did you match that as well?"

"Yep."

I stand up and hand Conrad my shovel. "You should keep this."

He looks at me funny. "Why?"

"You, Milo, and Baldwin paid for all of this. You made this

happen. These supplies are here building this entryway because of you."

Conrad sets the shovel down and says, "I'm done carrying shovels to this border wall for you, Dandra."

I feel silly and look down at my shoes. "I just thought it would be a nice souvenir."

Conrad's eyes look determined. "I'd rather have a different souvenir." He leans forward and wraps me in his arms.

I am surprised, but I hug him back. His arms are so familiar and comforting. Right until I see Jed walking toward me with two ice cream cones in his hands.

Chapter 54

I LET GO OF CONRAD and awkwardly blow the whistle to signal everyone back to work. I answer a few questions from my volunteers and then take an ice cream cone from a shocked Jed. Conrad looks at me funny and says he needs to use the lavatory. I send him off and then take Jed a ways away to have some privacy.

I smile at him and lick my ice cream cone. "Thank you so much for this!"

He just stares at his own cone as it melts over his fingers. "Sorry I interrupted you and Conrad."

I feel bad, and I dread having another rivalry start up amongst all the important males in my life. It took a long time for Baldwin and Conrad to get along. I squeeze his arm and say, "Conrad has been my best friend since low level school, and he will always be my friend. He is doing so much good that no one knows about right now, and yet he's up late every night because his mom wants to leave his dad. I can't abandon a friend when he needs me. Can you accept that?"

Jed looks at his melting cone and then at me. He answers slowly, "I've kind of watched the two of you for years. His feelings toward you haven't ever changed, I don't think. But, I have seen your feelings, or at least your actions change. If you say that you are only friends now, then..." I hold my breath as he answers, "I believe you."

I sigh with relief. "Thank you. Thank you for believing me and thank you for the ice cream cone." I take a big bite and laugh as Jed licks his fingers. "I need to get back to work, but I will see you soon!"

"Yeah. See you soon." He looks like he wants to hug me, but he changes his mind and walks away.

Conrad frowns as we start leveling out where the road is going in with levels, rakes, and shovels. "Who is that guy? He seems familiar."

I shrug. "He's my friend and my old boss from the hardware store."

Conrad's eyes narrow. "I remember him now. He brought

the ladder and moved the desk at the library when you worked there. Why did he bring you ice cream?"

I avoid his eyes. "Because he knows how hot and miserable this job can be, and he's just a nice person."

Conrad pinches his mouth together. "If you say so."

Chapter 55

I AM KIND OF GLAD to have a volunteer shift without anyone I know well after my uncomfortable afternoon with Conrad yesterday. Now that the dirt is removed, it's time to put in gravel road fill. Dump trucks bring it in, and tractors smooth it out, but my volunteers keep the edges straight with shovels and rakes in hand, and they fill low spots and dig down high spots.

Baldwin and the head engineer stop the tractors and insist on more gravel several times throughout the day, but by the end of the shift, we have an 8-lane gravel road from the border wall to the existing Tifton roads with space for the foundation of a building right in the middle.

I'm terribly curious how things are going on the United Cities side. I can hear machines and voices quite often. Baldwin assures me, "I'm in daily contact with Brock Hamble through the GroCom that Conrad gave him." He rolls up his personal copy of the blueprints and sticks them under his arm. He looks at the wall and says, "The United Cities are keeping a similar schedule with us, but their workers are not volunteers. Don't worry, Dandra. Everything is going to work according to our plan."

It takes an extra day for the head engineer to approve our road base and let us start paving the road. I get a weird sense of satisfaction when the light gray gravel turns black with tar and oil. I think the initial black layer is deep enough, but the engineer insists on quadruple thickness. I sure hope we don't run out of money.

Jed finishes his first engineering book in a week. He asks me questions while we work side-by-side during his volunteer shifts. I can answer his simple questions, but I ask the project engineer from the city to answer some of his harder questions. I love seeing his mind behind his muscles.

Jed gathers his things and sighs, "Maybe I should take an evening engineering class."

I grin at him. "Yes! Do it! I just hope they offer one at the right time for you at the high level school."

Jed shrugs, "If they don't, maybe I can take one in the United Cities when the wall opens up."

I squeeze his arm. "Yes! I'd be tempted to take it with you just so I could go back to school over there."

Mom approaches us as she is pouring over her clipboard. "You should go home, Dandra. I have to meet with Baldwin and the engineer who just pulled up."

I frown. "What about?"

She shrugs. "Oh, just about the steel doors being made for the opening of the wall."

"Okay, see you later, Mom."

"See you later."

I walk Jed to his truck, and he of course tells me to hop in. When I do, he turns the wrong way. "Hey, Jed. I live in the opposite direction."

Jed's eyes twinkle. "I know. You said you wanted to see my flower garden again. Why don't we go see it now?"

I grin. "Okay, but I better be quick. Everley has been home alone all day."

Jed slows down the truck. "We could go pick her up."

I shake my head. "Well, we could, but she probably won't be very friendly. She misses Conrad."

Jed's eyebrows come together. "Oh, well, maybe we'll pick her up next time. I'll have to think about how to approach her first."

I grin. "Sounds good."

When we get to Jed's house, his mom is not home from the hardware store yet, and I suddenly feel hyper aware of how far away he is from my body again. He takes my hand gently and leads me to his backyard.

It is as beautiful as I remember it with fragrant blooms leaning in from every direction, but this time there is a table and chairs set up under the wooden gazebo. Jed pulls a chair out. "Take a load off."

I sit down gratefully. "Thanks. It smells heavenly out here."

Jed doesn't sit down with me. He asks, "Are you hungry or thirsty?"

My stomach growls almost like it heard its cue. "Um, well, both."

Jed grins. "I'll grab you a juice before I dig up dinner."

I sit there stumped for a minute. Is he really going to make me a dinner from scratch right now, when I said I couldn't stay long?

He is back in a second with ice cold apple juice, plates, silverware, and some oven mitts. I ask, "What are you going to do with the oven mitts?"

"I told you I was going to dig up dinner. I buried it this morning in a pit of hot coals."

I am overcome with curiosity as Jed walks over to a circular fire pit area with his oven mitts. He uses a shovel to uncover a giant metal...milk can? He uses the oven mitts to pick the milk can up and unstoppers it. A heavenly aroma of pork

328

and vegetables hits me in the face. Jed grins at me. "Bring me your plate."

I grab two plates and watch in wonder as Jed pours mounds of meat, potatoes, carrots, and onions onto them. "Wow. I've never seen anything like this before."

Jed shrugs and grabs the plates to walk them to the table. "It's an old family tradition. I like it because I can add the ingredients and then walk away."

"I can't wait to try it." Jed watches me anxiously as I put the first bite in my mouth. The pork is so juicy and flavorful I sigh with satisfaction. "I haven't had anything this delicious in a long time. It's absolutely amazing. Thank you!"

Jed blushes and takes a bite himself. "I'm glad you like it."

Chapter 56

THE ROADWAY to the city border wall is finally done. The road is the required thickness and spans the needed lanes. My volunteer crew has not been the most skilled of workers, but they have shown up, and our hard work has paid off. It's kind of beautiful to look at.

President Hamble notified President Penn that the United Cities had cut through the wall on their side of no man's land, and they are just waiting for us to cut through our wall to continue the construction. Our volunteer work crew is a few days behind the United Cities crew, but it's finally the day to cut a hole into the city border wall itself.

The concrete is three feet thick, so average concrete saws and drills won't get all the way through it. Sharry had to order industrial strength concrete saws with diamond blades for me. I also had to hire the best concrete cutters in the country to attempt this. No one, especially in Layland, wanted to take on a task this big. Two brothers from Concrete Forever in the neighboring city of Chester took the job. They were not cheap and were unwilling to use their own equipment, so I am crossing my fingers that this works today. I am also hoping like crazy that I will see some familiar faces on the other side of the wall.

Ten patrolmen are standing ready for when the wall is breached. The presidents from both countries don't want a wild free-for-all to happen as soon as citizens can see what's on the other side. It will take the enormous steel sliding doors we've special ordered and six patrolmen posted here around the clock to keep this opening secure.

Joe and his brother Matt from Concrete Forever fire up the diamond blade saws to thunderous applause. I shove my fingers in my ears from the noise and bounce on the balls of my feet in anticipation.

Unfortunately, the blades don't even touch the wall. An uninvited visitor pushes his way through the crowd of volunteers.

"Stop! Stop! Stop!" Patrolman Darius insists as he marches to the wall and stands in the way of the cutting blades.

I can't believe he thinks he has any authority here.

What is he thinking? Mom, Baldwin, and I have done everything that the International Building Committee has asked us to do. He has no right to stop this.

Mom immediately confronts him. "You have no authority here."

Patrolman Darius hold up a piece of paper. "Actually, I do. Zane Chesterton has pulled his funding for this project."

Baldwin and I join Mom as we look daggers at my personal enemy. I proclaim confidently, "Zane Chesterton has left the management of the Gaming District to Conrad Chesterton, and Conrad has agreed to pay for half of this project."

Darius smirks. "Actually, Zane Chesterton is revoking that decision as of today and is revoking all money decisions Conrad has made in the last month."

I look at Baldwin, hoping to see a contradiction to this statement. He grabs the paper out of Patrolman Darius' hand and reads it to himself. "If this is really Zane Chesterton's signature, then he's right."

People groan in outrage all around me. I am not willing to trust Patrolman Darius' word without proof. I clear my throat. "Joe, Matt, put the saws away for today. I need to verify this information before we continue."

Everyone around me groans and starts cleaning up our job site.

Mom, Baldwin, and I are left alone with Patrolman Darius. Baldwin growls, "Why can't you just leave us alone?"

Patrolman Darius grins. "I am but a humble servant of the city of Tifton. I do what I am asked to do."

Mom puts her hands on her hips and frowns, "You mean you do what you're paid to do."

He scoffs, "Is there a difference?"

Mom nods. "Yes. There is."

I turn to Baldwin. "Call Conrad on your GroCom. I want him to tell me if this is true."

He frowns as he pokes at his GroCom. "On it."

Patrolman Darius eyes Baldwin's wrist warily. "Stop trying to lie to yourselves. You have seen the document." He waves the paper in our faces. "You don't have the money to finish this entry point. Just go home and start living a normal life. If you feel overly connected to this roadway you've made, make it a picnic area."

Baldwin calls Conrad on his GroCom. "Conrad, is it true that your dad has fired you?"

Conrad's voice sounds distraught coming from Baldwin's watch. "A patrolman just delivered an official letter to me. I can't believe it. I just saw Dad yesterday, and we had a small disagreement, but he never said anything about this."

Baldwin answers into his wrist. "Go confront your dad, Conrad. We'll figure this out."

Conrad answers, "I'm leaving now." The GroCom goes silent.

Baldwin turns to me. "Let's go talk to Zane at the detainment center, Dandra."

Patrolman Darius steps in front of me. "There is no need for that. Just look at this signed document. This is the proof."

Baldwin wrinkles his nose and reaches for the document. "Paper documents can be forged."

Patrolman Darius pulls the paper back and barks at us, "It's not. I swear it's not."

Baldwin glares at him. "Then why are you trying to stop us from talking to Zane Chesterton?"

Patrolman Darius shrugs. "I'm not. I just know what's done is done, and he doesn't want to be bothered by the likes of you."

I look at my emptying work site and say, "Zane was perfectly cordial to me the last time I was in his cell. I'm sure he'll be fine explaining this to me."

Baldwin reaches for the paper in Patrolman Darius's hand. "I'd like to take this with us."

Patrolman Darius pulls the paper out of reach. "Absolutely not. This is the property of Mayor Monroe."

Baldwin scoffs, "You mean Interim Mayor Monroe."

Chapter 57

BALDWIN AND I MARCH to the detainment center while Mom sends the volunteer and paid crews home. We are huffing and puffing when we approach the information desk. "We would like to see Zane Chesterton, please."

The patrolwoman behind the desk frowns at us. "Visiting hours are almost over. I will have to get special permission."

Baldwin pulls out his city id card and says, "I am City Councilman Baldwin Kole. I have urgent business to discuss with Mr. Chesterton that cannot wait."

The patrolwoman recognizes him and says, "Oh, yes sir. I'll take you right to him."

I give Baldwin an impressed look. "Wow. Look at you!"

Zane looks genuinely surprised to see us as we enter his cushy cell. He offers us a seat, and after he sits down in a comfortable chair, asks, "To what do I owe this honor, Councilman Kole?"

Baldwin rolls his eyes. "Drop the pleasantries, Chesterton. Why are you doing this?"

Zane looks confused. "Why am I doing what?"

I lean forward. "Firing your son for one."

Zane looks taken aback. "I haven't fired my son."

Baldwin uses his hands to accentuate his tone. "Is he allowed to donate money from the Gaming District to city and country projects?"

Zane sits back in his chair. "I didn't know he wanted to do that, but I haven't done anything to stop him."

Baldwin leans toward him. "Then why did Patrolman Darius just stop our border wall entry point project?"

Zane shakes his head. "I have no idea. It had nothing to do with me."

Conrad bursts through the door. "Dad, why are you doing this?"

Zane frowns at his son and gestures him toward a seat. "I just got done telling your friends here that I have no idea what you are talking about."

Conrad pulls out a replica of the same official letter Patrolman Darius flashed at us. "Why did a patrolman deliver this letter to me tonight?"

Zane takes the letter and reads it slowly. He flips the paper over and examines the signature. "I didn't write this."

Baldwin says through his teeth, "Obviously you had someone type it up for you, but you signed it."

Zane throws his hands in the air. "This is not my signature. This is a stamp of my signature."

Conrad's eyebrows come together. "Why do you have a stamp of your signature?"

Zane sighs, "Son, you know how many documents I have to sign at the Gaming District. I actually told your mom this week that you should get a stamp of your signature, too."

Conrad demands, "Where is your stamp?"

Zane stands up and gets busy finding us all drinks before he answers. "I, uh. I used to keep it at my office, but I believe I lent it to someone right before I got locked up here." His ears turn red.

Baldwin scoffs, "Who? Who did you lend your stamp to? Was it Patrolman Darius?"

Zane hands him a soda. "No. It was Mayor Monroe."

Chapter 58

I'M NOT SURE IF CONRAD IS RELIEVED the document is a forgery or having a sugar crash after his soda, but Conrad slumps further into the sofa beside me and asks, "Dad, do you want to fire me?"

Zane sighs and rubs his eyes with his hand. "No, son. I don't."

Conrad points to the forged document. "Are you going to revoke the financial decisions I've made in the last month?"

Zane holds up a finger as he reads a message coming in on his GameCom. His defeated voice suddenly goes hard. "Is it true that you donated 500,000 coins of Gaming District money to open the border wall?"

Conrad looks down at his feet for a moment. Then he sits up and looks his dad in the eye. "Yes. It is true that I have promised the country of Layland 500,000 coins for the building of an entry point in the border wall, but some of that is my own wages, and the rest has come from the sale of GroComs. GroComs were on your 'do not pursue' shelf when I took over. I'm donating money that I made without you, Dad. I hoped you wouldn't mind."

Zane Chesterton slams his drink down on the coffee table and storms off to the bedroom section of his cell.

Baldwin looks at me uncomfortably, but Conrad looks defiant. I can't believe he didn't tell his dad. My mom would kill me if I did something like that. But, Conrad has just proved that he isn't just riding on his dad's coattails. He marketed a product, I suspect with the help of Felix, and is using the money made for good, just like he said he would.

Zane eventually comes back in a huff and plops down in his chair. "Conrad, I did not authorize that large sum of money to be spent on anything." Conrad nods at his dad. Zane continues, "I definitely didn't authorize any sum of money to be spent on something I don't believe in."

Conrad leans forward. "Dad, I learned so much in the United Cities. I want to go back there. I want you to meet Mr. Bronson and Rocky and the Hambles. I know that our country will benefit in many ways if we open the border. I gave Brock Hamble a GroCom on his last visit, and he said that as soon as the entry point is done, he will order 1,000 GroComs for his staff."

Zanes eyebrows come together. "Really?"

Conrad continues, "Do you like being locked in a closet?" Conrad gestures to the cell walls. "Dad, Layland has been locking us in our own closet for over 100 years. I want what's best for both countries, and I made enough money with my own investment to make that happen. I thought you might hate it, but I also hoped that you would be proud of me."

Zane folds his arms and glares at the ceiling for a while. I bite my fingernails to the quick wondering what is about to happen.

Zane's mom coughs pointedly from the bedroom area, and Zane exhales. "Conrad, I wish you had not kept this a secret from me. I trusted you with millions of coins."

Conrad drops his head. "I know, Dad. I'm sorry. It was wrong of me."

Baldwin and I exchange worried looks.

Zane sits forward on his chair and admits, "But, if you had told me your intentions, I would have stopped you. These GroComs wouldn't have come into existence." Conrad's head perks up. Zane continues, "Since the money you have promised to the country border wall was made by you without interfering with the income from the rest of the business, I approve of you giving it to whatever cause you want."

Conrad exhales, "Really? Thanks, Dad!"

Zane looks down at his shoes. "Unfortunately, my former business partners have gone rogue on me. My signature stamp needs to be reclaimed, and this fake document needs to be brought before a judge."

Conrad nods eagerly. "How do we do that? Do you want me to spy on Mayor Monroe and Patrolman Darius?"

Zane's eyes open as wide as they can. "No. Absolutely not. Stay away from them at all costs. Stick Patrolman Mark on them."

Chapter 59

CONRAD GIVES BALDWIN AND ME RIDES home in his car. He pulls out of the detainment center faster than he should in his exhilaration. "I'm so glad I'm not fired!"

I lean back into my seat. "Me, too."

Baldwin grins. "This is actually excellent news for me. Mayor Monroe just put the final nail in his coffin with this mistake. He hates me, but I can't believe he would dare to stop our project like this. I didn't believe Ed's report on how much Mayor Monroe is drinking these days, but I believe it now!"

We laugh about it. It's surreal to be in a car with these

two important people in my life and all be laughing together. I like it. As we approach Baldwin's apartment, which I haven't seen until now, I sigh, "Patrolman Darius is just rotten whether someone is whispering directions in his ear or not, but if Mayor Monroe is the leader, things are going to get interesting for all of us. Are you ready for that, Baldwin?"

My friend who looks like he has aged in the last few months with his dark goatee says, "Yes. As long as you two stand beside me, come what may. Are we united in this? Will you stand beside me when everyone else complains about my age and lack of experience?"

Conrad stops the car. "I will. The worst that could happen to me for supporting you just happened tonight, and I survived it, so I'm all in."

I look at Baldwin's earnest face and see a leader I can support and feel excited about the future with. I squeeze his shoulder and say, "I am with you 100%. Who knew we would be here now, doing this a year ago?" I sigh, "Do you ever miss being average teenagers, sneaking around passing secret notes and having meetings with just antigamers?"

Baldwin sighs, "Life was simpler then, but I wouldn't trade my journey the last year for anything, and I owe so much of it to you two."

Conrad looks at me longingly then nods at Baldwin. "I wish things were simpler and happier now, but we've got this."

I shrug my shoulders and say, "Unfortunately, I'm pretty

upset. I am going to have to contact 40 volunteers tonight to tell them not to come to the border wall tomorrow." Both guys look at me with concern for a second, then we all laugh again.

Baldwin insists, "I can help you make the calls if you want, but first I need to schedule a meeting with Patrolman Mark for first thing in the morning."

Baldwin opens the car door and climbs out. I follow behind him and give him a big hug. "Thanks for this job, Baldwin. I can make the calls myself. You and Mark just get Mayor Monroe."

He smiles at me and says with a twinkle in his eye, "Oh, I will."

I should have just brought him home with me because Patrolman Mark's car is sitting outside my house when I get there.

After another hug and reminiscent goodbye with Conrad, I walk into the house feeling so proud of my guys. They are such good people. We just have to figure out what to do with Patrolman Darius and Mayor Monroe.

Mom dishes me up some dinner as I relay all the information I received while we were in Zane Chesterton's cell. Patrolman Mark is all smiles. "I suspected Mayor Monroe was forging documents, but I hadn't found any tangible proof yet."

I smile. "Conrad has your proof."

Mark squeezes Mom's hand and says, "I guess I better schedule a meeting with Conrad and Judge Lemons tomorrow."

Chapter 60

I AM A MESS ALL DAY not knowing whether Patrolman Mark got permission to search for the missing signature stamp or not. I almost—almost wish I had a GroCom today so I could get updates from Conrad, Baldwin, and Patrolman Mark.

Everley braids my hair and does my makeup, which is fun for a while, but my feet get antsy staying home all day. I decide to visit Jed at the hardware store since I'm unemployed until this misunderstanding is cleared up.

Jed looks at me sideways as he waters flowers. "Are you sure you're okay?"

My leg won't stop jittering. "I think so. I just hate not knowing." He is a good listener as I tell him everything that is going on with the border wall and Mayor Monroe.

Jed looks at his watch, his real watch, not a GroCom. "The evening news will start soon. Maybe they will have an update on the case."

I slap my leg. "You're right. I'm going to run home and watch it with Everley."

"Before you go..." Jed slips a large white daisy behind my ear.

Jed is right. There is a breaking story on the news. Mom is already watching it at home. Everley digs her nails into my hand as we watch a video of Patrolman Mark barging into Mayor Monroe's office. Interim Mayor Monroe is handcuffed and hauled to the detainment center by a patrolman I don't recognize. Patrolman Mark searches each drawer in the mayor's desk.

He doesn't seem to find anything important, but then Patrolman Mark lays on the floor and reaches for something out of sight under the desk. He pulls out a rubber stamp and a file full of papers. Patrolman Mark pounds the stamp down on a piece of paper and holds it up. It says Zane Chesterton in swirly handwriting. Patrolman Mark says to the camera, "I think this is enough evidence to remove Interim Mayor Monroe from office immediately."

Everley cheers, "Yay, Mark!"

Mom blushes and repeats my sister's sentiment, "Yay, Mark."

We all start dancing around the house. Mom makes us stop long enough to eat some soup.

I can't stand not knowing anything. I don't think I can wait until tomorrow. "Mom, can I stop by Baldwin's new apartment really quick to see if he has any more news about our job site?"

Mom shrugs. "Sure, but don't stay out too late."

I walk to Baldwin and the antigamers' apartment on Main Street and knock on the door. Marcella answers it. "Oh, hi, Dandra. Long time no see. Come on in."

I smile as I walk into the first-floor apartment with much nicer furnishings than our apartments in the United Cities. There are more females in here than I expect to see. "Hello, Charlisa."

My red-headed friend is snuggling with Adamar on the

couch. She looks up long enough to say, "Hi, Dandra. Did you watch the news? Are you excited for B?"

"Yes and yes!"

Marcella elbows me. "Do you want to see my room?"

"Sure."

Marcella marches me past the kitchen to a small bedroom with a single bed and a huge desk covered in green and gold posters advertising Baldwin's campaign for mayor. She motions with her hands to the posters. "Since I get my own room, I get to share it with the campaign."

I chuckle. "There are worse roommates out there."

Marcella scrunches her nose. "Yeah." She looks at me and pauses before she asks, "Did you come to see us, or B?"

I fidget with the corner of my shirt. "I'm thrilled to see you guys of course. It's just that I saw the news, so now I have some questions for Baldwin. I'm kind of out of work until this gets cleared up."

The sound of the door opening and closing makes Marcella turn her head. "I think B just got home, so you're in luck."

It looks like Baldwin had a long day. He grabs some bread off the kitchen counter and plops into a chair by the kitchen table. He says through a mouthful, "Hello, Dandra. How do you like our new place?"

I admire the art on the walls and the matching furniture. "It's very nice, but Zane will want it back when he finishes his full-time detainment and gets his work release. If you didn't notice yesterday, his marriage is not going well."

Baldwin shrugs. "I know. We'll cross that bridge when we get there."

I sit close to him at the kitchen table. "So, what is going to happen to Mayor Monroe?"

Baldwin swallows a bite of bread and grins. "He is in a cell at the detainment center and will be facing Judge Lemons tomorrow at his trial."

I am suddenly unsure. "What happens if they don't find him guilty?"

Baldwin leans back in his chair. "Then he will keep being the crummy mayor that he is, well, until election day. If I don't win after all the evidence that has been brought to the public about his corruption, I don't know if this country is savable."

I nod. "What happens if they do find him guilty?"

Baldwin smiles. "Then he goes to the detainment center for many, many years and the election will be immediately moved up."

I hope that happens. I look around the room and ask, "When can I go back to work?"

Baldwin raises his eyebrows. "The only people who said you couldn't work are now behind bars. So, you can act as you were before Patrolman Darius' interruption."

Chapter 61

I HAVE TO CALL all my volunteers again to tell them that we are back on track.

I am distracted throughout my first shift back. My concrete cutters can't make it back here for a few days, so the volunteers clean up the never-ending trash and work on the framing to put up the giant steel doors. Going all day without talking to Conrad, Baldwin, or Jed is lonely. I yet again almost—almost wish I had a GroCom.

As we clean up for the day, an alert sound rings through

my gamer volunteers. They all stop what they're doing and look at their GameComs and GroComs.

I look at Mom who shrugs and wish I wasn't out of the loop. I sneakily look at every volunteer's wrist as they hand me their equipment to put in the shed for the night. A lady who volunteers twice a week named Faith hands me her hammer and then sticks her GroCom in my face. "I can tell you're curious. Just read it yourself."

I blush at being caught. "Thanks." The message on the little screen says that Patrolman Darius and Mayor Monroe's trial starts tomorrow at 10:00 am.

I know that since I have a government job, I should be more responsible and show up to work, but I insist on going to the trial. Mom says she'll cover for me at the work site.

I arrive 20 minutes early hoping to get a good seat, but the place is packed! I've never seen citizens of Tifton show up in these numbers to a trial before. Hardly anyone was at our trial, and the United Nine were big news for a long time.

Luckily, Baldwin has a seat near the front and lets me sit by him. Right before the doors to the judge's chamber are closed, Conrad slips in, so we squish him in, too.

The patrolman by the door yells out, "All rise for the enforcer of Layland justice, the honorable Judge Lemons."

We all stand up and watch Judge Lemons march through the overflowing benches in his red robe and yellow hair.

I lean toward Baldwin. "We're lucky it's Judge Lemons again."

Baldwin whispers into my hair, "Judge Hoage is on trial, as well."

Patrolman Mark is sitting in the little desk nearest us, and a patrolman I don't know is sitting in the other little desk by Mayor Monroe and Patrolman Darius, who look like the villains they are in their yellow jumpsuits.

Baldwin nods toward the patrolman I don't know. "That is Patrolman Victor. I've had to interact with him a few times, and he is actually very good with his words and will probably do a convincing job with Mayor Monroe and Patrolman Darius' defense."

I frown. "Great."

Judge Lemons takes his time reading and organizing the documents on his desk before he addresses the room. "Interim Mayor Monroe, you have been accused of the following crimes against the City of Tifton: illegal imitation of a person with power, tampering with a judge, tampering with city funds, closing a city building under false cause, and hindering international affairs." People behind me gasp at the list of grievances. Judge Lemons continues, "Patrolman Darius, you are accused of being an accomplice but not the mastermind behind all these same crimes." Patrolman Darius doesn't bat an eye. Judge Lemons looks at Patrolman Victor and asks, "What do the accused plead?"

Patrolman Victor stands up and motions to Mayor Monroe with his hands as he speaks, "Judge Lemons, Mayor Monroe has been an honorable mayor supported by the people of Tifton for three voting cycles. The City of Tifton has never looked more beautiful or had such a blooming economy. It is shocking and appalling that he has been accused of these crimes." Baldwin shakes his head at Mayor Monroe taking credit for all the hard work we've done to the city.

Patrolman Victor turns to Patrolman Darius before he continues, "Patrolman Darius is the most determined and hard-working patrolman in the City of Tifton. He has caught illegal activity taking place by the border wall and has been honored for his efforts. He does what he is asked to do without question and with every fiber of his being and is thus not an accomplice so much as a loyal city employee."

Judge Lemons turns to Patrolman Mark. "I have heard and seen evidence you have collected against Mayor Monroe for several days. Do you have anything you would like to add to your accusations?"

Patrolman Mark stands up and says, "I don't as long as Judge Hoage is brought in to testify that he was bribed by Mayor Monroe to tamper with your coffee and also bribed to give the harshest penalty available to the United Nine."

Conrad looks at me as everyone around us gasps.

Judge Lemons holds up a hand for silence. "Judge Hoage requested and was granted a private audience with me this morning. He confessed to every accusation you have placed before him, and he wishes not to be in the same room as his former malefactors. He has been relieved of his civic duties and is packing up his office now. Since he gave testimony to being bribed, he has been granted community service instead of detainment for his crimes."

Patrolman Mark nods his acceptance of this explanation and walks tall and assuredly to Judge Lemons desk. He presents the forged letter given to Conrad and the city bookkeeping records regarding the library. He turns to the audience and says, "I have been investigating Mayor Monroe for a year. He was in cahoots with Zane Chesterton before he was sentenced for murder, and that relationship has continued since Zane Chesterton's detainment." He hands a folder of documents to Judge Lemons. "This is a record with pictures of these men at 27 meetings that have taken place between Mayor Monroe and Zane Chesterton in the last year." Judge Lemons opens the file. Patrolman Mark points to something in the file. "You will notice that the usual biweekly meetings that happened after Mr. Chesterton was locked up started to dwindle once the United Nine were brought back to this country."

Judge Lemons nods. "So they do, what is significant about that?"

Patrolman Mark rubs his hands together. "I believe that

Mayor Monroe decided to break his agreements with Zane Chesterton and do his own thing once Conrad Chesterton was given the managing director role at the Gaming District."

Judge Lemons gestures to the evidence on his desk. "What evidence led you to believe that?"

Patrolman Mark opens a small evidence box and sets it on Judge Lemons desk. "This is Zane Chesterton's signature stamp, and it is used on multiple documents that Zane Chesterton did not approve its use on. I found this is a hidden compartment of Mayor Monroe's desk."

The judge looks the stamp over and then says, "I watched your discovery of this stamp on the news."

Patrolman Victor stands up. "There is a logical explanation for why Mayor Monroe had that stamp."

Mayor Monroe stands up and insists on speaking for himself. "I was told by Zane Chesterton that I was allowed to use his signature stamp for anything that would benefit the City of Tifton during his full-time stay in the detainment center."

Judge Lemons frowns and addresses Patrolman Darius. "Is this true?"

Patrolman Darius sneers, "Yes, your honor."

Judge Lemons holds up Conrad's forged note. "Well, the word of several witnesses say that Zane did not give permission to fire his own son. Why don't we ask the man himself?" Judge Lemons looks at the patrolman by the door. "Patrolman Kevin, go collect Zane Chesterton from the detainment center and bring him here."

The patrolman by the door says, "Yes, Judge Lemons."

When Zane arrives in his yellow jumpsuit and handcuffs, Judge Lemons seats him on the opposite side of the chamber as Mayor Monroe and Patrolman Darius. He asks him, "Did you give permission to Mayor Monroe to create this document and fire your son and revoke all money decisions he made in the last month?"

Zane Chesterton shakes his head. "No, Judge Lemons, I did not. I have not given my permission to use that stamp for months. I regret giving it to him in the first place."

Mayor Monroe throws his hands in the air in exasperation.

Judge Lemons looks at the city bookkeeping record. "Zane Chesterton, did you convince Mayor Monroe to close the library through the artifice of false bookkeeping?"

Zane looks at me guiltily for a moment. "I did come up with the idea of closing the library, yes." Everyone around me breaks into whispered conversations. "I was a power-hungry and money-greedy man before my detainment. I knew that the only people who opposed my plans with the Gaming District and the GameComs were the few people who still used the library. I thought that shutting down the library would benefit my business."

"Did you come up with the false bookkeeping idea?"

Zane lifts one shoulder as he finds his words. "I did suggest that method, yes, but I haven't talked to Mayor Monroe about the library since I was sentenced months ago. I hear from my son that the library was permanently closed down after the international convention. That was all Mayor Monroe's doing."

Patrolman Victor clears his throat. "Judge Lemons, this man is a murderer and a criminal mastermind. This case has become a game of who do you believe. Zane Chesterton was the mastermind of all of these schemes from the beginning. He ordered Mayor Monroe to do everything he has done including the closing of the library and firing the son he was too chicken to fire himself."

Conrad visibly jerks beside me. He looks at his dad who is shaking his head at us.

Patrolman Mark smiles at Patrolman Victor and says, "Judge Lemons, if you look in this evidence," he plops yet another thick file folder on the judge's desk, "that I found in Zane Chesterton's office, you will see Zane Chesterton's privately-paid officials payroll."

Mayor Monroe's nostrils flare.

Patrolman Mark continues, "You will notice that Judge Hoage, Mayor Monroe, and Patrolman Darius have been getting paid monthly for years...until the last three months. The payments have stopped in what I believe is Zane Chesterton's attempt to redeem himself to his son." Zane Chesterton turns to us again and gives Conrad a small smile. I pat my friend's white-knuckled hand. Patrolman Mark points at Mayor Monroe. "Mayor Monroe has illegally imitated Zane Chesterton with a signature stamp, tampered with city bookkeeping, closed the city library under false pretenses, and most shockingly, stopped an international compromise with the United Cities. The power he wielded as Mayor of Tifton has certainly gone to his head."

Judge Lemons looks overwhelmed. "I am requesting 30 minutes to review all the new evidence I have received this morning. Is a 30-minute break okay with you, Patrolman Mark and Patrolman Victor?"

Patrolman Mark nods. "Yes, Judge Lemons."

Patrolman Victor's nostrils flare, but he says through his teeth, "As you wish, Judge Lemons."

The audience erupts into a quiet roar as the judge tries to read. Baldwin turns to us and grins. "Conrad, your dad must have given those records to Patrolman Mark. That may lead to another trial for him. I'm surprised he would do that."

Conrad looks at the back of his dad's head. "I think being locked up is changing him. I asked him to make things right for the sake of Tifton, and I really think he is doing what he can now."

Zane turns around and looks at his son for a long time. Zane's humble eyes make me believe that he has many regrets when it comes to Conrad. I can't believe it, but I actually feel bad for my dad's murderer. He was such a bad person for so long, but I think he wants to change. I just hope it isn't too little too late.

Suddenly, the chamber doors burst open, and one of President Penn's personal patrolmen dressed in green and gold runs an official envelope to Judge Lemons. The official looking patrolman leaves as quickly as he came. Judge Lemons opens the envelope and reads the letter inside. He calls Patrolman Victor and Patrolman Mark to his desk for a conference. When the patrolmen sit down, Judge Lemons clears his throat.

Judge Lemons looks at all involved parties and says, "After careful examination of the evidence and considering the personal testimonies I have heard, this does become, as Patrolman Victor said, a case of who do you believe. There are so many moving parts, interpersonal agreements, and personal motivations that have ultimately halted an international agreement. The President of the United Cities and the President of Layland has demanded that this case be resolved today." He waves the official letter he just received as proof.

"After careful consideration, I have reached my decision." Judge Lemons gathers all the papers on his desk into a single pile and says, "Mayor Monroe you have been found guilty of illegal imitation of a person with power, tampering with a judge, tampering with city funds, closing a city building under false pretenses, and stopping international compromises. You are sentenced to 20 years in the detainment center and a fine of 50,000 coins."

The judge's chamber fills with chatter. I sigh with relief.

Judge Lemons goes on, "Patrolman Darius, you are found guilty of knowingly being an accomplice to illegal imitation of a person with power, stopping international compromises, and unwanted harassment. You are sentenced to eight years in the detainment center and a fine of 15,000 coins."

Mayor Monroe jumps to his feet and starts cussing out Patrolman Victor. Judge Lemons raises a hand for silence. Everyone sits down to hear what he has to say. "I am not done here. Since the City of Tifton is now without a mayor and the international agreement about the country border wall resides within the Tifton city limits," Judge Lemons waves the official letter again before he continues, "and there is a candidate campaigning against the former mayor in good standing with the law, the election is won by default. Baldwin Kole is to be sworn in as mayor of Tifton at earliest convenience. This meeting is adjourned."

The applause that follows is deafening. I see people like Maggie and Mick rising to their feet and patting Baldwin on the back and congratulating him, all while former-Mayor Monroe and former-Patrolman Darius are booed and taunted as they are forcefully removed from the judge's chambers.

I am not sure who is more shocked, Baldwin or me. I feel like the last one on my feet as I hug him and ask, "Did you know that they could make you win by default today?"

Baldwin gasps, "I suspected it could happen like that, but it actually did. I am the—mayor."

I squeeze his shoulder. "Yes, you are. Congratulations, Mayor Kole!"

Conrad claps him on the shoulder. "How does it feel to have that title, Mayor?"

Baldwin stares at Conrad like he can't believe he just said that. "Surreal."

Secretary Hansley pushes her way through the crowd and latches on to Baldwin's arm. "It looks like we need to plan another swearing in. Do you want chocolate cake again, or do you want the usual champagne?"

Baldwin laughs, and it's probably because he is the youngest mayor to ever serve the City of Tifton. "I am going to request chocolate cake again, Secretary Hansley."

Chapter 62

SECRETARY HANSLEY IS GOOD, but she can't make giant chocolate cakes appear out of nowhere, so she schedules Baldwin's swearing in for tomorrow morning at 7:30 am. I'm glad to hear it because I definitely want to be there, but I don't want to overburden Mom again at our work site or miss the cutting of the concrete.

As I get dressed the next morning, I'm not sure what to wear. I want to look nice for Baldwin's sake, but I also have to walk to the work site immediately following. Nice clothes or work clothes?

I decide on nice clothes with work clothes in my backpack for later. I hope no one minds that I'm wearing the same outfit as his last swearing in when I hear a knock at the door. When I open it, I see Milo with his usual grin and a bag of clothes for me. I can't help but smile at how Conrad is still thinking about me.

I take the bag and give Milo a hug. "Tell Conrad, thank you."

Milo clicks his tongue. "You can tell him yourself. He's going to be at the swearing in, and so am I, and honestly, I think the whole City of Tifton will be there."

My eyebrows come together. "Why do you think that?"

Milo looks at me like I'm crazy. "This is the coolest thing that has happened in our country in over 100 years! A teenage mayor! A mayor who served time for illegally escaping the country! A mayor who is practically a genius! A mayor who wants to blow holes in the border wall! This is going to be epic!"

I laugh at how ridiculous and wonderful this all is. "Okay, okay, I get it! I'll see you there, Milo."

When I open the bag, I see three fancy outfits. Everley will be so excited. But at the bottom of the bag is one more thing I don't expect to see. It's a GroCom. I look at it for a long time before I pick it up. It doesn't feel heavy or evil—I slip it on my left wrist and fasten it on. A message immediately pops onto the screen. My heart beats rapidly as I read it. *I know how you feel about gaming devices, but I want to feel more connected to you. Please just give this a try. If you don't want to wear it, at least keep it in your bag. I hope you like the dresses. See you soon. Your forever best friend, who misses you so much, Conrad.*

Mom lights up when she comes down the stairs and sees the outfits laid across the couch. "Which one do you want, Dandra? I'll take the other one." She takes my wrist and smiles at me. "It's a communication device, right?"

I tilt my head to the side and smile. "Right."

We're lucky that we are basically the same size. Conrad knows me well. There is a purple ruffly dress and a red silk dress with an exaggerated shawl. I love them both, but the choice is easy. I'll take the red one.

My jaw drops when we get to city hall. Milo was right. It looks like the whole city is here. There is no way all these people will fit in the city council room. Secretary Hansley looks a little frazzled when she calls out, "We will be moving this swearing in to the city park down the street, everyone. Please gather to the park as quickly as possible."

I giggle to Mom, "I hope she ordered enough chocolate cake."

I am thrilled for Baldwin but worried about getting to

work late. Today is an incredibly important day. My concrete cutters are here and ready to work.

My heels slow me down a bit, but Mom, Everley, and I all make it just in time. I can see Conrad and Milo and...Lexis across the park from us. A familiar voice behind me asks, "Is this spot taken?" I turn around to see Jed holding three white daisies. "Here, take one," he says to Everley. She smiles and takes the biggest one. Mom takes another one then Jed slips the last one behind my ear. He says to all of us, "Pretty girls deserve pretty flowers."

I smile at Everley's adoring gaze. "Thank you," I whisper in his ear.

Secretary Hansley clears her throat loudly. "Welcome, everyone, to the swearing in of Baldwin Kole as Mayor of Tifton." We all applaud loudly. It's such a different level of support from when he was sworn in for the city council. She practically yells as she says, "Will all City Council members please join me on the stage for this historical swearing in?"

They all join her obediently. They form a straight line across the temporary stage Ed is literally still putting together in the background. She continues, "I'm sure you've all seen the news about our former mayor and his sentencing yesterday. We have not had a new mayor get the job in this way in over 50 years, and we have never had a city council member this young run against a recalled mayor, ever. This is a historic day." She smiles as big as her face will allow. "Will Baldwin Kole please step forward?"

Baldwin looks confident in his black pinstriped suit as he steps forward to the podium to join Secretary Hansley. She commands, "Place your left hand on the Layland City Charter Rule Book." I swear I see my confident friend's hand shake as he places it on the leatherbound book. This whole thing happened so suddenly. I'm surprised he isn't passing out.

"Raise your right hand and repeat after me. I, Baldwin Kole, do promise to exercise the duties of the Mayor of Tifton..." Baldwin repeats what Secretary Hansley says only stumbling on the title, *Mayor*. Secretary Hansley continues, "honestly and faithfully. I will preserve, protect, and defend the Tifton City Charter and the citizens of Tifton and do so fairly, impartially, and to the best of my abilities." Baldwin repeats everything she says, and then Secretary Hansley proclaims, "May I present to you, the youngest mayor in the history of the City of Tifton, Mayor Baldwin Kole!"

The crowd around me erupts into applause. I even hear air horns and music playing from somewhere behind me. My eyes never leave Baldwin's face. I swear he is getting emotional. He's come a long way from stealing candy and books and living in an abandoned car. He deserves this.

I love the energy in this park. It's like the first day of working on the entry point times ten. As I look at the happy faces around me, I know so many of them. Maggie, Mick, and most of my other volunteers got themselves out of bed to be here to support Baldwin at 7:30 in the morning. I am so happy that I start to get emotional, too.

Jed looks at me with concern. "What's the matter?"

I wave him off. "It's nothing. I'm just happy."

Secretary Hansley definitely didn't get enough cake, but Everley snags one of the last pieces, so I'm going to call it a win.

All the antigamers find us, and I am overcome with emotion again. I hug all of them individually for a long time. This has been a long journey, but we made it! Baldwin made it! We are his team, and things are going to get better in our country. We all know it.

A photographer spots our group and asks, "Can I get a picture of the United Nine for the newspaper?"

Everyone looks at each other nervously yet happily, so I answer, "Sure, if you can get the man of the hour to join us."

It takes a few minutes to get through the crowd, but the giant camera and the press pass around the photographer's neck is enough to get Baldwin over for a quick picture. As soon as it's over, we all wrap our arms around him, even Conrad. We hold each other for a full 10 seconds. Baldwin sounds emotional when he says, "Thank you, my friends. I knew we could do it. Thank you."

Chapter 63

I LOOK AT MY NEW GROCOM, thankful that it shows the time as well as the other things it can do. I have to get to work now! I look around for a place to change out of my dress, but the only thing I can see is the lavatory with a line ten-people-long coming out the door.

I kick off my red heels in the grass and pull my work shoes out of my bag. I'm going to look like an idiot, but I am out of time. I gather my long dress over my arm and say, "Mom, Everley, we need to get to the job site now! The Concrete Forever guys are waiting for us to start cutting!" Conrad looks at us and says, I wanted to say something to your crew anyway, so I'll give you all a ride."

I look at Jed and all the antigamers. "Does everyone want to come? How many of us can fit in your car?"

Conrad bites his lip. "Uh, I can take four plus me."

Milo chimes in, "The rest of you can climb into my car. This party is just getting started!"

I smile questioningly at Milo. What is he talking about? I don't have time to ask. Jed says he'll meet me there in a bit. I give him a quick hug, and then hurry with Mom, Everley, and Baldwin to the car. The other antigamers climb into Milo's car, and somehow, we start a trend. Almost all of Baldwin's crowd follows him—us—to the border wall entry point.

I watch out the back window in awe. I know some of those people are my volunteers for today, but not all of them. I look at Conrad's smiling face and ask, "Why are they following us?"

Conrad taps my GroCom.. "Have you checked all your messages?" Of course I haven't. I look down at the screen Conrad just activated and see the following message that came in 45 minutes ago: *To all loyal citizens of Tifton: The border wall to the United Cities will be breached today, and the new mayor of Tifton, Baldwin Kole needs your support when that happens. Watch his swearing in at 7:30, then be to the border entry point by 8:30. Bring a lunch and your working gloves. Long, Live Layland!*

I squeeze Conrad's arm. "Did you send this to the whole city?"

Conrad grins. "If you have the power to change things, you should, right?"

I grin and give him a one arm hug.

He stops the car at our work site and says, "I want to assure your crew that this project is funded and moving forward since Patrolman Darius scared them the other day."

I squeeze his arm. "Thank you, Conrad." I jump out of the car and look at the shed and my bag and realize I have nowhere to change except the three lavatories on wheels that the volunteers are already lining up to use.

I sigh. Fancy volunteer crew manager it is. Joe and Matt beat us here and are setting up their saws and blades next to the wall. They look a little nervous as more and more people show up. Joe pulls me aside and says, "Could you tape off a perimeter so these fancy people don't get hurt while we're bringing this wall down?"

"Yeah, I'm on it." I grab a roll of yellow caution tape out of the shed, and the antigamers help me set up a perimeter to separate the concrete cutters and the volunteers from the rest of the crowd.

Mom gives me the signal to get us started. So I hide the roll of tape behind my back and say, "Welcome, everyone! I'm so happy that so many of you are here to witness yet another historic event in Tifton today." The crowd cheers, which gives me confidence to keep talking. "If you are on the volunteer work crew today, please look at the job chart by the shed to know where to go. Everyone else, please stay behind the yellow tape, so no one gets hurt while we break through the wall." The crowd cheers again.

Conrad suddenly walks out of the crowd while pulling something behind him. I look at him curiously. He smiles at my surprise and exclaims loudly, "I am here to clear up a little misunderstanding. My name is Conrad Chesterton, and I agreed to donate money to the building of this entry point. I don't want anyone to believe the intruder who showed up last week saying that the funding for this project is gone. Mayor Kole, could you and Laurel Metty please join us?" Mom and Baldwin join me as we look at Conrad questioningly.

He signals to the friendly patrolman who helped me get my yellow bracelet off. He picks up the suitcase Baldwin has been sliding behind him on wheels and opens it up. It is filled with paper $100 bills. Conrad points to the money and says, "Please accept this donation of $500,000 that Patrolman Sam is holding to complete the border entry."

I have never seen Baldwin so giddy with excitement. He shakes Conrad's hand and then pulls him in for a hug.

Baldwin immediately looks at the crowd that followed him here and says, "I spoke with President Penn and the president of the United Cities, President Brock Hamble himself this morning, and President Hamble promised that he would start cutting on his side today at 8:30 AM, the same time that we start cutting on our side. Shall we get started?"

"Yeah!" the crowd cheers.

I gesture to our concrete cutters and say, "Take it away, Joe and Matt from Concrete Forever!"

We all get out of the way and watch as the concrete cutters from Chester take center stage. Mom, Conrad, Baldwin, and I decide to send the money with Patrolman Sam to city hall, so we won't miss the excitement.

Joe and Matt fire up the diamond blade saw and the crowd cheers again. I hold my breath as I watch the saw cut into the concrete wall like it's a knife cutting through a slice of cake. We bring in a lift, so they can cut the top line across. It would be great if we could just slide that huge slice of cake out, but it's way too big and heavy for any of our machinery to move. The huge rectangle has to be cut into smaller pieces so that each piece is light enough for men or our small excavator to lift.

I feel like we're carving a stick with a pocketknife. Each sliver we take out is getting us closer to breaking through the other side. Volunteers keep moving pieces, and the dump trucks keep filling up. I keep holding my breath in anticipation. I don't even notice that Jed has arrived until he puts a hand on my shoulder. His eyes look concerned. "Are you all right?"

I feel silly as concrete dust coats my red dress that's soaked with nervous sweat. I try to explain it to Jed. "I'm a bit disappointed that Joe and Matt keep cutting small pieces all the way down our eight-lane length. I wish they would just cut a

Dandra-sized hole all the way through and then worry about the rest later."

Jed nods and says, "That is frustrating." He looks at my dress. "Do you want to change?"

I shrug. "I want to, but there's always a line for the portable lavatories."

He points to the side of the shed. "I saw you leave in that dress, so I ran home and grabbed a tent for you, so you can change."

I wipe some dust off my dress and sigh, "Thank you." I give him a hug. This is the second hug I've given him today, and he seems to enjoy it. After I let go, I head for the tent. Mom and Everley are just coming out of it when I get there with my bag.

Everley says, "Jed is so nice. He went home and got this tent just so we could change."

I bite my lip. "He is nice, isn't he?"

I feel much less silly once I'm in my work clothes. I join Jed again and wait for the inevitable breakthrough to happen.

Once a couple of feet of thickness has been removed from the entry point, I can hear something on the other side. It sounds like a saw. Suddenly a blade appears in the cave we've hollowed out. I'm so happy, I could hug that thing. Luckily Jed shakes his head at me when I start walking toward it.

A Dandra-sized rectangle appears thanks to the saw blade on the other side, and then it goes silent. We all look at each other and then we hear a loud "*Crack!*" The rectangle falls to the ground. I see the face of some worker in a mask, and right behind him is Brock Hamble.

Chapter 64

BROCK HAMBLE STRIDES THROUGH the hole in the wall, rips off his dust mask, and walks straight to Baldwin. Brock Hamble embraces Baldwin in a handshake hug thing. "We did it. We really did it, Mayor Kole," I hear him mutter.

I ignore Jed's warnings and run to join them. I feel tears streaming down my face without my permission. Brock Hamble looks at me and says, "You're Dandra Metty, right?"

I nod and bounce on my toes like a love-sick celebrity fan. "Yes, President Hamble. I have been looking forward to this moment for a long time.

He takes my hand and says, "So have I, Dandra. So have I."

President Hamble goes back to his side of the wall, and I try to act like a professional, but I still try to peek through the hole. Baldwin insists that we keep our volunteer workers away from it as Joe and Matt keep cutting the rest of it out. Several patrolmen join us as guards while the debris is cleared.

Mom waits by the road for a new set of contractors handpicked by President Penn to show up. They are to secure the sliding steel doors to the wall and to start the construction of the check-in building. My volunteers are happy to trade their shovels and wheelbarrows for hammers, nails, and shingles.

I am practically worthless today. I keep trying to do everything but end up doing nothing. I just can't stop watching the eight-lane hole appear in the wall. When I look through the hole in our wall and through the 15 feet of no man's land to the United Cities side, I swear I can see Ernestine. Some dark-curly-haired woman keeps waving from over there. Brock Hamble keeps talking to her throughout the day.

When the shift is over, 90% of the spectators are gone, the entire hole is cut, the rubble is removed, but the steel doors are not in place. I'm tempted to just send everyone home and insist the patrolmen keep everyone out for the night, but a limousine pulls up as my volunteers are leaving.

President Penn and his bodyguards march straight toward Mom and me. I look at Jed who is stacking tools in the shed and then at Mom. She whispers, "Whatever he asks for, we need to do."

I whisper back, "Okay."

President Penn walks past us to the hole in the wall and looks through it. Patrolmen follow him but don't stop him. He waves to President Hamble on the other side. He seems nervous to walk through like President Hamble did. After a careful inspection of the wall, the hole, the steel doors, and the partially framed walls of the check-in building, President Penn approaches Mom and me. Baldwin jogs up to join us.

President Penn nods to Baldwin and says, "Congratulations, Mayor Kole. You have the beginnings of a border wall entry point."

Baldwin smiles. "Yes, we do, President. It's been a long day."

President Penn looks at the GroCom on his arm. "You were sworn in at 7:30 this morning. It has been a long day for you, but I'm afraid it's about to get longer. I don't want you three to leave this site until the doors are in place. I don't want the mass exodus you were accused of starting to actually happen."

I feel my body slump. I don't want to stay here until the doors are on. I'm so tired. I look to President Penn to see if he is kidding, but I don't think this guy is the kidding type.

President Penn looks at Mom and me. "You two are Laurel and Dandra Metty, correct?"

"Yes, President," Mom mutters.

He looks at our work clothes and sweaty hair and says, "You've done a good job with very limited resources here, and I want you to know that I am very impressed."

Mom repeats, "Thank you, President."

President Penn looks at all the tired workers putting supplies away. "I wish you could go home and rest, but national security is my main concern with this project, so I'm afraid I must insist that the doors are secure before the work site is vacated."

Mom nods, "Yes, President Penn. We will gather as many volunteers as we can and work through the night."

President Penn lets the corners of his mouth curl up. "I'll have some dinner sent for you and your workers, and I'll be back in the morning to check on things."

Mom smiles. "Yes, sir. Thank you."

I watch as the president of our country walks back to his limousine and disappears. I sigh with relief. Baldwin looks at the new batch of President Penn's contractors who showed up later in the day. He sighs, "They seem fresh and ready to work through the night. Now we just need 15ish more volunteers to help them out." He looks at me.

I shrug. "I have maxed out my volunteers for the daily

schedule. I don't know if I can find that many to work through the night with us."

Jed joins the conversation. "I'll stay." My heart fills with gratitude. He continues, "And I'll call Mom. She'll be glad to help while the store is closed."

The antigamers join the conversation. Adamar looks at Baldwin. "What did the big man say, B?"

Baldwin stands a little straighter and says, "We have to keep working until the doors are in place. Even if that means working through the night."

Adamar looks at the other antigamers and nods. "You got it, B. Charlisa will have to ask permission from her mom, but the rest of us are fine with that."

Baldwin starts poking at his GroCom. "I'll ask the Yesterlys if they'll come. I know they have a vested interest in getting on the other side of that wall."

I suddenly make a connection. "Brock Hamble's sister Elira is a Yesterly. I bet her husband is related to Jim."

Baldwin pokes at his GroCom some more. "I think you're right. Either way, they say they are on their way."

I look at Mom's relieved face and sigh. We have enough people. It's going to be all right.

The contractors President Penn brought have us mostly holding things still while they put the sliding frames of the giant doors together. It takes all of us, except Everley who is taking a nap in Jed's tent. I am tempted to join her.

Luckily, President Penn is good on his word. He sends beefy patties and potato wedges and bottles of soda with Secretary Hansley. Relieved to have something to eat, I blow my whistle to signal break time. I find the perfect spot to plop down on the ground and look through the entry point into the United Cities while I eat my greasy dinner.

Jed sits down beside me and looks at the view I've chosen. He grins. "Do you know the dark-haired woman who has been looking through the hole all day on the United Cities side?"

I chuckle as I watch her waving her arms around yet again. "Yeah. I'm pretty sure that's Ernestine. She's the one who helped us when we escaped." I wave back at her.

"She sure is persistent." I nod my agreement. He looks at the tent that is still up and says, "Mom thinks you should sleep in the tent for a few hours so you can still function when your next set of volunteers show up in the morning."

I shake my head. "You have to work, too."

He shrugs. "I'm physically tired, but I think you are physically and mentally tired. You should get some sleep."

I lay my head on his shoulder and say, "Thank you for looking out for me."

His voice is soft. "No problem."

The daylight fades as we finish our food. Jed chuckles as he watches my friend from the United Cities. "She has a flashlight out now. I think she's trying to send us a message. Do you know morse code?"

I sit up and watch the flashlight flashing across the way. "I don't, but Baldwin does."

I call Baldwin over and sure enough he starts writing down letters on his beefy patty wrapping. "We need to get her a GroCom, Dandra."

I chuckle, "Yeah, if she'll take it. What is her message?"

Baldwin grins and shows me his messy scrawl. *Rocky and Josie are waiting for you. Hurry up.*

Chapter 65

I GET A FEW HOURS OF SLEEP thanks to Jed's persistence. He had his mom bring their two sleeping bags and a couple of pillows when she showed up to volunteer. Everley steals my pillow at some point, but I'm tired enough that I barely notice.

The smell of eggs and bacon wake me up more than the sun coming through the thin tent walls. "Dandra, wake up. I have some breakfast for you."

I expect Jed, but when I open my eyes, I see Conrad. I wipe the sleep out of my eyes. "What are you doing here?"

Conrad looks hurt. "I brought you and your whole crew breakfast."

I sit up and give him a big smile. "Thank you! Did Baldwin ask you to?"

"Yeah."

I nod. "How do the sliding metal doors look?"

He hands me a giant scone filled with bacon, eggs, and cheese and says, "They look done to me, but I haven't seen them move."

I scarf my stuffed scone down in an unlady-like way while Everley tells Conrad all about President Penn coming in his limousine and telling us we had to have a sleepover until the door is done.

Conrad laughs and hands us bottles of orange juice. I chug mine down in one minute flat. Everley turns to me and says, "You could use some manners when eating around guests, Dandra."

I wave her off. "Conrad isn't a guest. He's family."

That brings a smile to Conrad's face. He helps me stand up and offers his pocket comb to me. I shake my head and smile. I think it's silly that he carries a pocket comb, but I also appreciate it.

The doors do look done, but the contractors are still working on the gears that make the huge things slide from side to side. Jed runs over to me with a half-eaten scone and says, "They let me help put the gear boxes together while you were sleeping. I'm so glad I read those engineering books. I knew what they were talking about, and the way we put them together made perfect sense to me!"

"That's great, Jed. Go tell them I want to see them move."

He gives me a sideways glance. "Uh, I'll try."

He talks to the engineers for a long time. So long in fact, that my 40 fresh volunteers show up for their shift while he's still talking to them. I guess they're still not ready.

I gather my volunteers together. "Good morning. I'm glad to see so many rested faces. Some of us have been working through the night, so it's good to have fresh recruits. Ten of you will be working on the sliding doors and the rest of you will be framing walls for the check-in building. Find your assigned area on the chart and get to work."

I have Conrad help me clean up the breakfast garbage as a long, black limousine shows up. I wash my hands at the water coolers quickly and run to greet the President of Layland and his guards.

Mom and Baldwin join me. President Penn nods at us and says, "I can see progress was made last night, but do the doors work?"

Baldwin pokes at his GroCom and says, "You came at just the right time, President. We were just about to test them out." He pokes some more instructions into his GroCom, and I watch an engineer send Jed and another strong volunteer to the doors on both ends of the hole.

Jed and the other volunteer start cranking with all their strength on the handles that turn the gears and slide the doors open and shut. The doors start sliding toward each other. I bounce on my feet as I watch Jed and the other guy shut the giant doors for the president. When it's completely closed, I can see the patrolmen guarding the hole physically relax. Mom looks at President Penn and asks, "What do you think?"

He is still for a moment and then asks, "Is that a locking mechanism in the middle where the doors meet?"

Mom nods. "Yes, it is. It was custom made and the strongest and most secure we could find in the whole country."

President Penn nods. "I'll need to look at it closer, but I think that will work. Nice job."

President Penn examines the closed door and the mechanism and asks the contractors questions about how secure the door mechanism is. When he runs out of questions, he approaches Baldwin and says, "When the check-in building is done, send me a message on my GroCom. I want to be here for the grand opening."

Baldwin grins. "Yes, sir."

Chapter 66

JED KEEPS LOOKING at the door gear boxes and then walks back to me several times before he finally confides, "I think the engineers did something wrong. It took all my strength to turn that handle, but it shouldn't be that hard. The engineers told me the problem is in the frame, but I think the problem is in the gear boxes."

I squeeze his arm. "Go tell them your suspicions."

He looks at his shoes and shakes his head. "They are professionals. I've only read two books about engineering. I don't have enough engineering knowledge to give an opinion."

I grab Mom and have Jed relate his suspicions to her. She addresses the contractors about his concern, and what do you know, he is right.

I punch him in the arm and ask, "How does it feel to figure something out that stumped the professionals?"

He grins sheepishly. "It makes me feel like I can become an engineer myself."

It takes us a month to finish the check-in building and the guiding walls through no man's land.

I get caught up on sleep, mostly.

Jed makes me dinner at least once a week and helps me relax in his flower garden after the most grueling shifts. His eyes watch me as I eat the fire grilled chicken skewers he just finished making. He puts a hand on mine. "When will your project be done?"

I swallow and say, "Another day or two."

He pours me some lemonade and asks, "Am I invited to the grand opening?"

I sit up straighter. "Yes! Of course you are! Baldwin promised we'd get front row seats."

Jed pulls a piece of chicken off a skewer. "Will Conrad be there?"

I wish I could read his face easier. I wipe my mouth with

a napkin. "Yes. He paid for most of the project, so he should be there."

Jed swallows and asks, "Do you talk to Conrad much these days?"

I shrug. "No, not much. He stopped by last week to show me how to use my GroCom properly. I said I only needed it to talk to him and Baldwin, but he promised he'd give one to Shasta, Ernestine, and Mr. Bronson. So, I'm actually starting to like this thing." I point to the GroCom on my wrist.

Jed looks at my wrist and says, "Maybe I'll buy one, so you can talk to me easier."

I touch his hand. "I would like that."

He grins and throws his napkin on his empty plate. "I've been impressed with your friend, Baldwin. I thought he was too young and inexperienced to accomplish anything as a mayor, but he is fixing things in the city left and right."

I grin. "I know. He wants Milo to run a gaming tournament to fundraise money to fix up the library and reopen it."

Jed grins. "I bet you'll be the first one to check out a book when that happens."

I blush. "I've missed that place so much."

Jed leans back in his chair. "I hear Baldwin has opened up applications for United Cities Visitation Passes as well."

"Yep."

"Have you applied?"

I frown. "No. I want to, but I've been too busy to get it done. I really want to see my friends in the United Cities again."

Jed stands up and pulls my chair away from the patio table. "Well, if the border entry point is done in a day or two, you'll see them sooner than you think."

After a couple of long days painting, flooring, and sealing every crack and cranny, the border entry point and its check-in building are done.

Baldwin is asked by President Penn to act as co-master of ceremonies at the grand opening, and I couldn't be more proud.

Everley, Mom, and I are wearing the fancy clothes Conrad gave us and are sitting in front row seats next to Jed, Conrad, Milo, and the antigamers. I guess knowing the mayor has its perks.

Baldwin taps the microphone to test it. "Can you hear me?"

We all nod, so Baldwin steps back and lets President Penn take over.

President Penn puffs out his chest and says, "Welcome, everyone to this historic event. The border between the United Cities and Layland is open for the first time in over a hundred years!" The enormous crowd behind us erupts into applause. After we quiet down, he continues, "This is such a big step in international cooperation. I'm sure you're all wondering how things are going to work. Mayor Baldwin Kole is going to explain the process to getting a visitation pass and how to navigate the border crossing."

Baldwin holds up some official-looking, shiny, yellow papers. "Hello, my fellow country men and women!" The audience applauds again. "This is an exciting day for the entire country of Layland, and I want the volunteer crew from the City of Tifton to know how much I personally appreciate how much time and sacrifice they have given to make this border entry possible. I have watched you day in and day out. I have worked alongside you. This definitely couldn't have happened without you." I see Mick stand up and clap. I'm pretty sure everyone cheers just as loudly for Baldwin as they did for President Penn.

Baldwin continues, "We have daily visitation passes ready to give to people who have filled out the required paperwork and if they return within the designated amount of time, they will earn the right to get a weekly visitation pass next month." Everyone in the audience leans forward in their seats to get a look at the visitation passes. Baldwin continues, "If the week-long visitations passes are honored correctly, then the next month we will offer month-long visitation passes." The crowd erupts into cheers again.

Baldwin waits for everyone to calm down. "I know everyone wants to be the first to use this entry point, but we are trying to be cautious, on this grand opening day, so I have 20 visitation passes to hand out today, and there will be double that tomorrow and so forth as we learn what kinks need worked out of our system. If visitors disappear into the United Cities and don't come back, we will have to cut back on the amount of visitation passes granted, and possibly require yellow bracelets in order to track those who leave. I don't want that to happen, and I'm sure the rest of you don't want that to happen, so let's all commit to acting responsibly with our passes." I clap loudly with Mom and Maggie and other people around me. Baldwin steps aside for President Penn.

The President clears his throat. "Thank you, Mayor Kole. I have been pleasantly surprised at how smoothly this project as progressed with the help of the President of the United Cities. President Hamble is sending 20 visitors with visitation passes to this side as well, today. Please show these visitors every courtesy. We want a positive beginning to country collaboration. Feel free to show the United Cities visitors the benefits of our country. They don't have GroComs or a Gaming District like we do, for example."

Baldwin looks down at his hands, clearly unsure if the Gaming District is what we want to share with the United Cities.

President Penn continues, "Who is curious about the 20 visitation passes I'm about to hand out?" The crowd cheers.

I applaud with everyone around me. I sit back in my chair happy that 20 lucky people will get to see what I have already seen. I should apply for a visitation pass today. I yawn as I pick the paint off my fingernails, still there after painting the trim on the check-in building at midnight last night. If I'm lucky, Ernestine or Shasta might come over here. I look to the right and see Mr. Yesterly barely keeping his emotions in check. He has family on the other side of that wall. I hope he gets a pass today.

Baldwin and President Penn walk to the check-in building to show us how this process will go. I sit on the edge of my seat, so I don't miss a word.

Baldwin's microphone sounds just as loud when he's inside the building. As he leans out the window, his loud voice proclaims, "If you have applied for a visitation pass for a specific day, you will arrive here by car or on foot to the window and show the worker your Layland ID card and your application. The worker will look through the application and if everything checks out and there are still passes left for the day, you will get your pass. You may be told that your application has been denied or delayed. A patrolman will then guide you back to Layland. At the beginning of this process, many of you will be delayed, but don't give up."

Baldwin walks out of the building and points to the return side of the building. He continues "This visitation pass needs to be returned to the worker on the opposite side of the building when you return. You must return by midnight of your assigned day."

President Penn guides Baldwin back to the podium. The president pauses as he holds up the small stack of yellow passes. I look at Mr. Yesterly and try to will one to him.

President Penn declares, "I have enjoyed working on this project with Mayor Kole, and I know I will be censured for this, but after looking at all the applications this morning and at the urging of President Hamble, I have decided to give the first nine passes to the people who inspired us to make this border entry in the first place, the United Nine."

The crowd around me gasps but applauds loudly.

I just sit there in shock.

Mom has to pull me out of my seat. "Come on, Dandra. Don't make a scene." Conrad, Gordon, Marcella, Ed, and Adamar follow my family to the podium. I take my visitation pass with trembling hands and look at Baldwin curiously. He mouths the words, "I filled it out for you."

President Penn addresses the crowd. "I know it seems crazy to let the people who broke the law to get out of the country be the first to leave legally, but I know this is the right choice. These nine people, these United Nine, have united our whole country. They have made this day possible. I had them watched to see if they broke any laws the last several months, but all that was reported back to me was their incredible work ethic. You nine deserve these first passes, and I thank you for uniting us, United Nine."

The crowd jumps to their feet. The applause is deafening.

I turn around to look at Jed who is smiling and clapping. I look back at my family and friends and see emotion in their faces. Conrad's eyes are glued to mine as he kisses his yellow visitation pass. Baldwin smiles at me with red eyes. Marcella is hugging Gordon and crying. Ed whoops out loud and starts marching to the check-in window. We all wipe our eyes and follow him.

My feet are wobbly as I follow my friends to the check-in window I helped build.

Baldwin stops us all before we reach the window. He turns to me and says, "Dandra, you deserve to be the first."

I shake my head. "No, we should do this together."

Conrad speaks up. "I agree with Baldwin. Your blood, sweat, and tears have gone into this project for months. More than the rest of us. You should be the first. Do you agree, Laurel?"

Mom smiles at me. "Yes. I agree."

My heart swells as a tear slides down my cheek. My eyes linger on my yellow pass for a few seconds, and then I wipe the tear away.

Baldwin declares, "It is a great pleasure to have the first one across be the person who has worked tirelessly, often without pay or appreciation to bring this entry point about. Dandra, please, go, my friend."

I inhale and exhale as my friends pat my back and push me forward. I walk in my pretty red shoes with my pass in hand past the patrolmen who are doing their new duties. I turn around for one last look as I walk through the border wall. A tear rolls down my cheek as I watch people I love and people I've learned to love clapping for me. I take a deep breath and take the first step as a free woman past the border wall of my country. I cry and laugh at the same time. This is so surreal.

The walk through 15 feet of no man's land and tall concrete walls, feels ominous in a way, but happy tears keep sliding down my cheeks anyway. When I walk through the second border wall, I see a clean beautiful city and a tall, skinny person I adore waiting for me. I sprint to her and give Shasta a hug that might leave bruises. Ernestine is right behind her, hugging us both from the side. "Welcome back, Dandra."

Our three-person hug quickly becomes a group hug as the rest of the United Nine, President Penn, and the Yesterlys burst through the entry point.

I've never shed so many happy tears.

Chapter 67

WELL, THE BAD NEWS IS, I'm out of a job again. The good news is, I'm glad this time.

The border wall entry point project is done and working like a dream. People are using their visitation passes responsibly—so far.

Conrad has sold thousands of GroComs to people from the United Cities, which has actually benefited me, since I can call and send messages to Shasta and Ernestine daily. I made sure to apologize to Conrad for not wanting to give GroComs a chance. They have become almost as life changing as the border wall entry point, and I'm happy to admit I was wrong about them.

Laylanders are seeing how beautiful a city can be with a bit of effort, and I'm seeing visible improvement every week as I walk the streets of Tifton.

The mayor of Chester has visited the United Cities many times and wants to make an entry point from his city as soon as possible. If he gets the funds, and asks for help, I'll probably do it. Why stop doing what you're good at? And I have the best partners who won't let me do it alone.

President Brock Hamble's sister, Elira Yesterly, had her twin baby boys, and they have a great-grand-uncle who loves them and is spoiling them every month like nobody's business.

Doctor Hamble has found a new cream for me to try on my cement-burned legs which is making the scars I thought I'd have for life disappear.

Ernestine is already writing an appeal to the government to make the visitation passes longer.

Shasta is still housing people in need for the Hamble Foundation. She offers me a place to stay every time I visit.

Basically, I have been on cloud nine since the border wall opened up. It's just as good as I knew it would be. The only thing that hasn't been as good about it is Jed. He doesn't want to visit for some reason, not even to check out engineering classes.

It takes a couple of months, but I finally convince Jed to get a visitation pass with me, so we can visit high level schools like Herrington University in the United Cities.

"Look at the metal parts dropping out the end of that machine, Jed. You could do this." Jed watches the engineering students in the lab through the window and shrugs. He is such a calm person, it's hard to tell how impressed or depressed he is about all the schools we visit.

"I'm hungry. Can we stop for a bite to eat before we go home?" Jed asks as we leave the third engineering school. "I want to go somewhere nice. It'll be my treat."

I inhale all the delicious smells of downtown Herrington and say, "Absolutely. Doctor Hamble recommended a place when I met with him to get another tube of cream for my legs." We stop at the recommended restaurant called "Olie's" before we head back home. I take a bite of my steak and almost faint with the incredible flavor. "Mmm! How is your food, Jed?"

He barely picks at his lobster tail. "It's good."

I narrow my eyes at him. "What's the matter?"

He sighs, "Nothing really." I give him a knowing look and he relents, "I feel like you like it better here than our own country, and I just don't feel the same way."

I bite my lip and ponder the discontent that is so rare for him. "I like both countries, and I can only visit here, so I'm perfectly happy going home to the country I was raised in."

Jed's tense face softens, and he starts eating his lobster. "That's a relief."

I grin at him and inquire, "Did you at least like the night classes we saw here?"

Jed nods. "Um, yeah. They're very impressive. I'm just worried I'm not smart enough."

I remember that he was the one who figured out how to make the border wall doors work correctly and smile. "Don't worry, I know an excellent tutor."

Jed touches the new silver bracelet on my wrist. "This is a big upgrade from your last bracelet. Mr. Bronson was nice to give it to you."

I touch the bracelet fondly and nod. "He is just as jolly as ever and wants me to use a month-long visitation pass to work for him during the Christmas holidays." I pause. "He also likes my mom."

Jed chuckles. "I don't know if he has a chance. Patrolman Mark doesn't stop when he knows what he wants."

I nod. "That competition could be fun to watch though." I look at Jed cautiously before saying, "Mr. Bronson tried to convince Conrad to work at Casswell's again, but Conrad insisted that he doesn't need that job anymore. He insisted that they could be partners selling GroComs instead."

Jed nods. "Good. That will keep him busy. Maybe I'll buy my GroCom at Casswell's instead of the Gaming District."

I shrug. "That's up to you."

Jed throws a piece of lobster in his mouth, wipes the butter off his fingers with his napkin, and asks, "How is Baldwin doing? He sure has a lot of responsibility on his shoulders."

I chuckle, "His not-so-secret admirer, Josie, was waiting for him when he walked through the border wall that first day. She wrestled her way through the crowd and gave him a kiss he, and I dare say I, will never forget."

Jed raises his eyebrows. "Wow. I bet President Penn liked that."

I laugh, "I'm betting international marriages will be on the agenda at the next international conference."

Jed throws his napkin on his empty plate, sits back contentedly in his chair, and asks, "Are you ready to go home?"

I stretch my full stomach and reply, "Yes. I'm ready to go home."

As we walk toward the border wall, enjoying the clean streets and pleasant smells of dinners cooking all around us, I think about how great my life is.

Jed sees me smiling and asks, "What are you smiling about?"

I take his hand and swing it as we walk. "I'm just happy."

He gives me a crooked smile and asks, "Why are you happy?"

I take in all the things I see, smell, hear, and feel in this moment and say, "Well, it's a beautiful day, I just ate a delicious steak, I have a handsome date, my enemies are behind bars, and everyone I care about is doing well on both sides of the border wall. What is there not to be happy about?"

He stops and picks a wildflower growing by the border wall. He sticks it in my hair and says as we walk through, "Nothing. Nothing at all."

About the Author

Heather Hayes loves a good story. She believes a good story will entertain you and leave you feeling like a better person for having read it. She loves living in Idaho with her husband and five daughters. If she isn't writing, she is probably teaching English, watching a volleyball game, cooking, skiing, reading, enjoying the mountains, or planning a trip to somewhere new.

A Message from Heather Hayes

If you liked immersing yourself in Dandra's world, please tell your friends about it and leave a review on Amazon or Goodreads. It helps me out so much, and I love hearing from my readers.

Find more dystopian books by Heather Hayes on Amazon and HeatherHayesAuthor.com.

THE COMPLEX TRILOGY	THE DUST TRILOGY
The Complex Life	Dust and Deceit
The Complex Law	Dust and Dazzle
The Complex Leader	Dust and Destiny

If you like a good story for younger readers, check out my other books:

Unexpected Magic

A Tale of Regrets

Rissy's Summer Son

The Fantastic Backyard of Imagination

Before the Store

www.ingramcontent.com/pod-product-compliance
Lightning Source LLC
Chambersburg PA
CBHW022241020726
47496CB00004B/1007